CANAL DREAMS

CANAL DREAMS

IAIN BANKS

DOUBLEDAY

NEW YORK   LONDON   TORONTO   SYDNEY   AUCKLAND

PUBLISHED BY DOUBLEDAY
a division of Bantam Doubleday Dell Publishing Group, Inc.
666 Fifth Avenue, New York, New York 10103

DOUBLEDAY and the portrayal of an anchor
with a dophin are trademarks of Doubleday,
a division of Bantam Doubleday Dell
Publishing Group, Inc.

Library of Congress Cataloging-in-Publication Data
Banks, Iain.
    Canal dreams / by Iain Banks. — 1st ed.
        p.   cm.
    I. Title.
PR6052.A485C36   1991   90-29107
823'.914—dc20   CIP

ISBN 0-385-41814-0
Copyright © 1991 by Iain Banks
ALL RIGHTS RESERVED
PRINTED IN THE UNITED STATES OF AMERICA
SEPTEMBER 1991
FIRST EDITION IN THE UNITED STATES OF AMERICA
1   3   5   7   9   10   8   6   4   2

For Ken Macleod

CONTENTS

DEMURRAGE

dèmŭ'rrage *n*. Rate or amount payable to shipowner by charterer for failure to load or discharge ship within time allowed; similar charge on railway trucks or goods; such detention, delay. [f. OF *demo(u)rage* (*demorer*, as DEMUR see -AGE)]

1: Fantasia del Mer

tic tic tic tic . . . Tiny noises of compression, sounding through her skull.

She'd been alarmed, the first time she'd heard them, over the noise of her breathing and the tinny wheezes of the scuba gear which sat on her back, wrapping its plastic limbs round her and jamming rubber and metal into her mouth. Now she just listened to the ticking noises, imagining they were the signature of some erratic internal metronome; the unsteady beats of a tiny, bony heart.

The noises were her skull's reaction to the increasing weight of water above her as she dived, descending from the unsteady mirror of the surface, through the warm waters of the lake, to the muddy floor and the stumps of the long-dead trees.

She had held a skull once, and seen the minute fissures marking its surface; tiny hairline cracks stretching from side to side and end to end, jagged valleys on an ivory planet. They were called sutures. Plates of bone grew and met while the baby was still in the womb. The bones jammed together and locked, but left one area free so that the infant's head could pass through its mother's pelvis, producing the spot on a baby's head which remained soft and vulnerable until the bones had clasped there too, and the brain was safe, locked in behind its wall.

When she'd first heard the noises in her head, she'd thought it was caused by those bone-plates in her skull pressing harder in against each other, and the noise travelling through those bones to her ears . . . but then Philippe had disillusioned her; it was the sinuses which produced the faint, irregular clicking sounds.

It came again, like some slow abacus. *tic tic tic* . . .

3

She pinched her nose and blew, equalising the pressure on either side of her eardrums.

Deeper; she followed Philippe down, keeping his slowly stroking flippers a couple of metres in front of her, conscious of her rhythm matching his, her legs moving through the water in time to Philippe's. His white legs looked like stocky, strangely graceful worms; she laughed into the mouthpiece. The mask pressed harder into her face as they continued down. *tic tic* . . .

Philippe began to level out. She could see the lake floor clearly now; a crumpled, grey landscape fading slowly away into the gloom. The old tree stumps poked up through the mud, flat eruptions of drowned life. Philippe looked round briefly at her, and she waved, then levelled out too, to follow him along the water-buried surface of the land, over the sliced trunks and the slow bursts of mud produced by his flippers. *tic.*

The pressures equalised, the column of water above her and the fluids and gases of her body achieving a temporary equilibrium. The warm water moved against her skin in silky folds, and her hair ruffled behind her in the slipstream of her body, stroking the nape of her neck.

Settled into the pace of swimming, balanced and lulled, flying slowly over the slow settlement of a near-century, following the just-tangible turbulence of the man's wake, she let her mind wander.

She felt – as she always did, down here – untied from the commonality of breath that was the air above. Here, however briefly, she was free. It was a freedom with its own many and precise rules – of times and depths, atmospheres and experience, maintained equipment and weights of air – and it was a freedom purchased through surrender to the technology that was strapped to her back (clicking and hissing and burbling) but it was freedom. The air in the mouthpiece tasted of it.

Under the waves, with the skull adjusted. Headlong through the warm waters, like an easy and continual birth. Swimming like flying; the one buoyant image of her fear she could accept.

This had been rainforest; the trees had grown in the wind and the sunlight, and trawled the air for clouds and mist. Now they were gone, long turned to planks and rafters and ribs and seats. Perhaps some of the great trees were pulped, and became

4

paper; perhaps some were turned into sleepers for the railways that helped the canal be built; perhaps some formed the buildings in the Zone, and perhaps some became small ships; boats that had plied the lakes. Sunk, their waterlogged timbers would nestle in these shaded depths, rejoined.

Maybe some became musical instruments; a cello, even! She laughed to herself again.

She listened for more *tic*s, but heard none.

She followed the man. In a few strokes and kicks, she knew, she could pass and out-distance him. She was stronger than he knew, perhaps she was even stronger than he was . . . but he was younger; he was a man, and proud. So she let him lead.

In a few minutes, hypnotically over the drowned forest, they came to what had once been a road. Philippe stopped briefly, treading water over the muddied track, raising clouds of soft grime beneath him while he studied the plastic-wrapped map. She drifted near by, watching his bubbles wobble their way to the surface. His breath.

He put the map back under his T-shirt, nodded down the road and set off. She kept pace. She knew the gesture he'd just made, and knew the sort of grunt that accompanied it; she imagined she'd heard it translated through the water. She followed him, thinking dreamily of whale songs.

Before they found the village, they heard the noise of an engine. She heard it first, and hardly thought about it, though some part of her was trying to analyse the noise, put a name and a key to it. She realised it was engine noise just as Philippe stopped in front of her, looking around and up, and holding his breath. He gestured to his ears, looking at her; she nodded. They stared up.

The shadow of the boat's hull went past, not overhead but a few tens of metres to their right; a long dark shape dragging a twisted thread of bubbles after it. The noise of its passing grew, peaked, then fell away. She looked at Philippe once the boat had passed, and he shrugged; he pointed down the road again. She hesitated, then nodded.

She followed Philippe, but the mood was different now. Something in her wanted to go back to the Gemini. The inflatable they'd set out from was moored a hundred metres away, in roughly the direction the boat had been heading. She had wondered if the noise of the boat would alter after they'd passed, telling her it had slowed and stopped at the Gemini – after all, it might look as though it had been abandoned – but the boat seemed to have continued on beyond that, heading for the middle of the lake and the ships anchored there.

She wanted to go back, to return to the Gemini and then to the ships; to find out what that boat was doing, and who was on it.

She didn't know why she felt so nervous, so suddenly full of a low, nagging dread. But the feeling was there. The war might be coming to touch them at last.

The drowned road dipped, and they followed it. *tic tic* she heard, diving deeper. *tic tic*, as they swam towards the ruins.

When Hisako Onoda was six her mother took her to a concert in Sapporo; the NHK Orchestra playing works by Haydn and Handel. Hisako Onoda was a restless, occasionally recalcitrant child and her weary mother suspected she'd have to remove the squirming, wriggling, and quietly but insistently complaining child before the end of the first piece, but she didn't. Hisako Onoda sat still, looked straight ahead at the stage, didn't rustle her bag of *taka rabukoro*, and – instead, incredibly – listened.

When the concert was over she didn't clap with everybody else, but started eating the deep-fried tofu in the bag instead. Meanwhile her mother stood up with everybody else, clapping brightly and happily with small, fast movements of her hands, blinking furiously and gesturing to Hisako to stand and applaud too. The child did not stand, but sat looking around at the politely enthusiastic adults towering everywhere about her with an expression somewhere between mystification and annoyance. When the applause faded at last, Hisako Onoda pointed to the stage and told her mother, 'I would like one, please.'

Her mother thought – for one confused moment – that her seemingly gifted but undeniably troublesome and disobedient daughter wanted a Western symphony orchestra of her own. It was some time before she was able, through patient questioning, to discover that what the child wanted was a cello.

*　　*　　*

The drowned village was wrapped in weeds and mud, like tendrils of some solid, cloying mist. The roofs had all collapsed, caved in on their timbers, tiles lying scattered and ruffled-looking under the wrapping of grey mud. She thought the houses looked small and pathetic. Floating over a broken street, she was reminded of a row of rotten teeth.

The church was the largest building. Its roof seemed to have been removed; there was no wreckage inside the shell. Philippe swam down into it, and trod water above the flat stone table that had been the altar, raising lazy clouds of dust about him like slow smoke. She swam through a narrow window and rubbed one of the walls, wondering if there were any paintings under the film of mud. The wall was dull white, though, unmarked.

She watched Philippe investigate the niches in the wall behind the altar, and tried to imagine the church full of people. The sunlight must have shone on its roof and through the windows, and the people in their Sunday best must have trooped in here, and sung, and listened to the priest, and filed out again, and the place must have been cool in the summer heat, and white and clean. But it was difficult to imagine. The thickness of the underwater light, the monotonous ubiquity of the grey mud, the enfolding quietness of the place, somehow denied the past that had brought the village and the church into existence; it was as though it had always been like this, was always meant to be like this, and the chatter and light of the village – when only the wind had flowed down these streets and around these walls – had been a dream; a brief, breezy, immature little life, before the burying permanence of the water extinguished it.

The noise of an engine drilled through her thoughts. The sound was far away, just audible, and soon faded. She imagined the faint grumble echoing off the muddy walls of the drowned church's shell, the only vestige of music left to the place.

Philippe swam over to her and gestured at his watch; they both struck up for the surface, flippers waving down at the wrecked church beneath them, as though saying goodbye.

The Gemini bounced across Gatún Lake beneath a bright overcast sky, heading for the moored ships. She sat in the bows, slowly drying her hair, watching the three vessels coming closer.

'Perhaps it was the National Guard.' She turned round to look at Philippe. 'But it sounded bigger than a Gemini.'

'Perhaps.' Philippe nodded slowly. 'But it did not come from the direction of Gatún. Frijoles, perhaps.'

'The *Fantasia*?' She smiled back at him, watching his brown tanned face, looking at the small lines around his eyes which made him look older than he was.

A frown crossed the man's face. 'I think it is not to come until tomorrow.' He shrugged.

She smiled again. 'We'll know soon, when we get to the ships.'

He nodded, but the frown resurfaced briefly. He was gazing past her, watching their course. There were old logs floating in the lake, almost waterlogged, that could turn a Gemini over or break its outboard prop. Hisako Onoda studied the man's face for a while, and found herself thinking she ought to write again to her mother; perhaps that evening. Maybe she would mention Philippe this time, but maybe not. She felt a little warmth rise to her face, and then felt foolish.

I am forty-four years old, she told herself, *and still I feel embarrassed to tell my mother I have a lover. Dear Mother, Here I am in Panama in the middle of the war. I dive, we have parties, we see artillery battles and missile streaks, and planes scream over us sometimes. Food good, weather warm mostly. Love, Hisako. P.S. I have a boyfriend.*

A French boyfriend. A married French boyfriend who was younger than she was. Ah well.

She looked at her fingertips, crinkled from the water as though after a long bath. Maybe I should have flown, she thought, rubbing at the corrugated flesh.

'Hisako, Hisako, it's only a few hours!'

'To Europe?'

Mr Moriya looked exasperated. He waved his pudgy fingers around. 'Not much more. What am I? An airport information place?' He heaved himself out of his chair and went over to the window, where a repairman was kneeling, fixing the office air-conditioning unit. Moriya wiped his brow with a white handkerchief, and stood watching the young engineer as he stripped the faulty unit and laid the pieces on a white sheet spread over the fawn carpet.

Hisako folded her hands on her lap and said nothing.

'It will mean weeks at sea.'

'Yes,' she said. She used the word '*Hai*', which was almost like saying, 'Yes, sir!'

Mr Moriya shook his head, stuffed the sweaty handkerchief away in the breast pocket of his short-sleeved jacket. 'Your cello!' He looked suddenly pleased with himself.

'Yes?'

'Won't it . . . warp, or something? All that sea air; the salt.'

'Moriya-*san*, I did not mean to go . . . "steerage".'

'What?'

'I think the ship will have ventilation; air-conditioning.'

'Air-conditioning breaks down!' Mr Moriya said victoriously, pointing at the dismantled unit spread out on the white sheet like some dead machine being prepared for interment. The young engineer glanced up for a moment.

Hisako looked dutifully at the defunct unit. She could see the glittering towers of downtown Tokyo through the gap under the window where the unit normally sat. She shrugged.

'Don't they?' Mr Moriya was talking to the engineer now. He had to repeat his question before the young man realised he was being addressed. When he did he jumped up.

'*Hai*?'

'Air-conditioning machines break down, don't they?' Mr Moriya asked him. Hisako thought it would be a tricky question to answer in the negative, given that the young man was standing surrounded by bits of a machine that had done just that.

'Yes, sir, sometimes.' The engineer was practically standing at attention, gaze fixed at a point over Mr Moriya's head.

'Thank you,' Mr Moriya said, nodding. 'What can I do?' he said loudly, gesturing widely with his arms and walking past the engineer to look out of the window. The young man's gaze followed him; he seemed to be uncertain whether this was a rhetorical question or not. 'Eh?' Mr Moriya said. He tapped the young man on the shoulder, then pointed at Hisako. 'What would you do? This lady is one of the finest cellists in the world. The world! Finally, after years . . . decades almost of invitations,

9

she decides to go to Europe; do concerts, give classes . . . but she won't fly.'

The young engineer was looking embarrassed, smiling.

'Planes crash,' Hisako said.

'Ships sink,' retorted Mr Moriya.

'They have lifeboats.'

'Well, planes have parachutes!' Moriya spluttered.

'I don't think so, Moriya-*san*.'

Mr Moriya turned to the engineer. 'I'm sorry; forgive me; go back to your work.'

The young man looked grateful, and knelt down again.

'Perhaps the situation in Russia will change,' Mr Moriya said, shaking his head. 'They might open up the railway again.' He wiped his neck with the handkerchief.

'Perhaps.'

'Soviets, ha!' Mr Moriya said, angrily, shaking his head at the Tokyo cityscape.

Hisako raised one hand to her brow, traced the line of a bead of perspiration. She put her hands back on her lap.

'There will be storms around the Cape!' Mr Moriya said, trying to sound knowledgeable.

'There is a canal through Panama, I believe,' Hisako said, tiring of the argument.

'Is that still working?'

'It is.'

'There's a war there!'

'Not officially.'

'What? *Officially?* What is to be official about in a war?' Mr Moriya sounded incredulous.

'It has not been declared,' she told him. 'It is a local dispute; bandits in the hills. A police operation.'

'And all those American Marines at . . . at . . . last year, at— '

'Limón.'

Mr Moriya looked confused. 'I thought it was Cosa . . . Costal . . . '

'Costa Rica,' Hisako told him. She pronounced the 'r' sound in the *gaijin* manner, even exaggerated it a little.

'That was police?'

'No, a rescue mission.' Hisako smiled faintly. The air conditioning

10

engineer was scratching the back of his head. He sucked air through his clenched teeth and looked up at Mr Moriya, who wasn't noticing him.

'Hisako; if it looks like a war, sounds like a war— '

'The Americans will keep the canal safe.'

'Like this Rimón place?'

'Moriya-*san*,' Hisako said, looking up at him. 'I would like to fly, but I cannot. I go by ship or I do not go. I could go to California and then by train to New York and another ship, or through Suez, which I would also like to see, but I would prefer to come back that way.'

Mr Moriya sighed and sat down heavily in his seat, behind his desk, 'Couldn't you do what I do?' he suggested. 'Get very drunk the night before the flight – beer, sake, whisky and young Australian red wine always works, I find – so that you have such a bad hangover you feel death would come as a welcome release?'

'No.'

'Yes?' Mr Moriya said to the young engineer.

'Sir; may I use your phone? I will order a replacement unit.'

'Yes, yes, of course.' Mr Moriya waved the man to the phone. 'Hisako . . . ' He leant his smooth, bulky forearms on the desktop. The engineer chattered down the phone to his office. 'Couldn't you try? Take some sedatives . . . ?'

'I did, Moriya-*san*. I went out to Narita last week with a friend whose brother is a senior pilot for JAL, but I could not even sit on the plane with the doors closed.' She shook her head. 'It must be by ship.' She tried to look reassuring.

Mr Moriya sat back disconsolately in his seat and gently slapped his forehead with one palm. 'I give in,' he sighed.

'It will only be a few weeks,' she told him. 'Then I will be in Europe, in London, Paris, Berlin, Rome, Madrid, Stockholm; all the places we have agreed.'

'And Prague, and Edinburgh,' Mr Moriya said, sounding sad but looking a little more hopeful.

'It will be worth the time. I will practise on the journey.'

'And Florence and Venice.'

'I need a break from so many recitals and classes, anyway.'

'Not to mention Barcelona, and I think Bern want you, too.'

11

Mr Moriya watched the young engineer, who was still talking to his office. 'And Athens, and Amsterdam.'

'I'll arrive refreshed. So much sea air; it will be good for me.'

'It must be your choice,' Mr Moriya said, glancing at his watch. 'I'm just your agent; I just want to see you use your talent to the full. You don't have to listen to me.'

'I always do, Moriya-*san*. But I cannot fly. A few weeks; that's all it will take.'

Mr Moriya looked glum again. The young engineer put the phone down and said a new unit was on its way. He packed his tools away and then started wrapping up the pieces of the broken air-conditioner in the large white sheet.

Now it was more than two months later, and half those dates had been cancelled or postponed; her visits to those magically named cities – cities she had never seen before, and only ever dreamed about – had become casualties of an undeclared war, the list of their names growing every few days, like a slow accretion of the dead.

'*Là*,' Philippe said. 'The *Fantasia*.'

She followed his gaze, and just beyond the stem of the ship they were heading for – Philippe's ship, the tanker *Le Cercle* – she could see the small white shape of the *Fantasia del Mer*, heading for Gatún Port, pushing away from the three ships anchored in the centre of the lake.

'So it was her,' she said. 'Must have gone to Frijoles first, then.' She looked back to him. 'Perhaps we'll get some mail now.'

'Some real beer, even.' Philippe grinned.

'You be rucky,' she laughed, putting on a thick Japanese accent. He laughed too, and she felt, as she always did at such moments, about a third of her real age.

The warm, humid air blew about her as she turned to face the bows again, still trying to dry her hair.

The line of hills on the far side of the broad lake, beyond the trapped ships, looked like a towering dark wave somehow frozen against the steel-grey sky.

* * *

'Calvados! Rémy Martin! Fresh bananas! And two sides of meat! And Metaxa seven star!' Lekkas, the cook on *Le Cercle*, shouted down to Hisako and Philippe as they moored the Gemini to the small pontoon at the foot of the companionway and started up the steps, scuba gear hoisted over their shoulders. The *Fantasia del Mer* had delivered the first supplies for two weeks. 'I have olives!' Lekkas shouted, waving his arms about in circles. 'Flour for pitta! Bulgar! Feta! Tonight I make you meze! We'll have Greek meal! Much garlic!' He reached down and took Hisako's cylinders from her as she reached deck level. 'Ms Onoda; sounds good, yes?'

'Yes,' she said. 'Any mail?'

'No mail,' Lekkas said.

'Any news, George?' Philippe asked.

'Nothing on the radio, sir. Two editions of *Colón News* come with the supplies; Channel 8 . . . well, is just as usual.'

Philippe glanced at his watch. 'News in a few minutes anyway.' He clapped the cook on the shoulder. 'Greek tonight, eh?'

The three of them started walking along the deck; Hisako went to take her own gear, but Lekkas lifted it as he nodded to Philippe. 'And I have a bottle of ouzo and some of retsina I been saving. We have one good meal.'

They put the scuba gear in a storeroom on the main deck level; Lekkas went to the galley while Hisako and Philippe went up to the officers' quarters, aft of the bridge. Philippe's cabin was a smaller version of the captain's, across the corridor; a modest stateroom, a double-bed cabin with three portholes facing astern, a closet and a shower room. Philippe switched the TV on as soon as they got in. Hisako decided to take a shower. She could hear some game show on the TV over the noise of the water.

When she came out, Philipppe was lying naked on a towel on the bed, watching Channel 8 news. A uniformed woman of the US Southern Command read out the latest releases from the Pentagon, Cuba, Panama City, San José, Bogotá and Managua, then detailed guerrilla and government losses in Costa Rica, western and eastern Panama, and Columbia.

Hisako lay down on the bed beside him, stroking one hand through the black hair on his chest. Philippe took her hand and held it, still watching the screen.

13

' . . . for the peace conference in Salinas, Ecuador next week. Representative Buckman, spokesman for the congressional group, said they hoped to overfly Gatún Lake, in the Panama Canal, where three ships are at present trapped by the conflict.

'South Africa; and the increasingly beleaguered white régime in Johannesburg has again threatened to use— ' Philippe clicked the set to standby and rolled over to take her in his arms.

'So we can wave to the *yanquis* when they fly over us, eh? We should be grateful, yes?'

She smiled and said nothing, but put one fingertip on the end of his nose, wiggling it, feeling the cartilage under the skin. He moved his head up, softly biting her finger. He kissed her, moved against her, then looked at his watch again. He took it off.

'Ah, we have enough time then,' she said, conspiratorially. She knew he was due to talk over the radio to the shipping line's agent in Caracas soon.

'Just about; they'll wait.'

'What if they replace you?' she whispered, sliding one arm under his body. 'What would I do then?'

Philippe shrugged. 'If they can replace me, they can get you out too.'

It wasn't what she meant, and she wondered if he knew that. But he moved his arms down her spine – making her shiver – to the small of her back, and she didn't feel inclined to pursue the point.

She walked down the muddy highway. She wondered where all the traffic had gone. The highway looked broad enough for enormous trucks and vehicles, like the scrapers you saw constructing new roads, or the huge dump trucks in open-cast mines. She looked behind her, shivering, but saw nothing. The sky was dark but the ground was bright; corn swept back and forth on either side of her, like weeds in a stream. The corn was grey, like the sky and the ground and the road. Her feet raised slow clouds of dust from the road, and the clouds floated in the sky behind her. The road wound round the sides of low grey hills, twisting this way and that through the silent landscape. Away in the distance, through the slow-swaying weeds, men fought, swinging sparkling swords at each other. She had to jump up

14

and down to see the faraway figures; the weeds were crowding in around her.

Once, when she jumped up to see the warriors, she couldn't see them at all but instead, over the field of swaying grey crops, glimpsed another landscape entirely, far below and far away, with a great dark stretch of water lying among mountains; but when she jumped after that all she saw were the samurai again, swords striking sparks off each other, while the sky beyond boiled blackly, like smoke.

The track entered a dark forest where the bright leaves fluttered against the starless sky. Finally the path became twisty and narrow and she had to force her way through the wet foliage to the city.

The city was deserted, and she was surprised and angry that her footsteps made no sound; they ought to echo off the tall sides of the great buildings. Her boots were clean now, but when she looked back she saw that she was leaving a line of silvery footprints along the street; they glittered and wobbled where they lay on the paving stones, as though they were alive. It was growing darker in the town, and the alley had no lights; she was frightened of tripping on something. At last she came to the temple.

The temple was long and thin and tall; buttresses and the ribs of its roof made lines against the dull, orange-black sky. She heard something at last; metal ringing, and raised voices, so she started looking for a way into the temple. She couldn't find any doors, and began to hit the stone walls, then she noticed a great window, set low down in the wall, with no glass in it. She climbed through.

Inside it was like a factory, but the machines sat on the grass. At the far end of the building, on a stage raised a little off the grass, the samurai were fighting. She went up to tell them to stop, and saw that the two warriors weren't fighting each other; they were both fighting Philippe. She cried out to him, and he heard, and stopped to wave, putting his sword down.

One of the samurai pulled his sword arm back behind him, and then swung forward and down; the thin, slightly curved sword bit into Philippe's white dress uniform at the neck, and cut him in half, coming out at his waist. Philippe looked surprised; she tried to scream but no sound came out. The samurai bowed slowly, and put his sword back carefully into its scabbard; his left arm jutted out like a triangle from his side, and his thumb slid up the blunt side of the sword as it went back into its sheath; she saw a little bead of blood wiped off the edge of metal; it collected on the warrior's thumb.

Then the sword burst out of the scabbard again and started jumping about the altar like a firecracker, jumping and unravelling and making a noise like a flexible metal tape measure as it leapt and expanded and unfolded over Philippe's white and red body.

Philippe was weeping and so was the warrior, and so was she.

Philippe woke her, pulling her to his side. Her jerking legs had kicked him, and he'd heard her breathing oddly. She wasn't crying when she woke up, but she sighed deeply when she realised none of it had been real.

She buried her face in his shoulder and clung to him like some terrified monkey to its mother, while he gently stroked her hair and she fell gradually back to sleep again, and relaxed once more, breath slackening and slowing and shallowing.

2: Bridge of the World

She was promised a cello for her birthday, but she was impatient, so she made her own. Pocket money bought an old violin from a junk shop, and she discovered a large nail on a building site. She glued the nail on to the bottom of the violin to make the spike. 'Don't ever forget it's not a violin,' her mother told her, amused. 'You'll stab yourself in the neck!' She made a bow from a piece of wood salvaged from a broken screen an aunt in Tomakomai was throwing out, and some elastic bought in a Sapporo market.

The stretched elastic broke the wooden bow before she even had a chance to play the violin/cello, so she made another from a branch she found in the woods. She thought you were supposed to put chalk on the bow, so the violin/cello ended up covered in white each time she played it, as did her hands. She shook the chalk dust out of the holes in the instrument afterwards. Hisako and her mother lived in a tiny flat in the Susukino district, and the sound Hisako made was so terrible her mother raided her savings and bought the child a real cello in October, three months before Hisako's birthday.

Hisako had to wrestle with the huge instrument (and, much to her consternation, throw away a great deal of assiduously ground-up chalk begged from school), but finally succeeded in producing tunes her mother could recognise, and by her birthday the following January was clamouring for lessons. Mrs Onoda discovered – only a little to her dismay – that there was a gentleman in Sapporo able and willing to give cello lessons; a lecturer in the university music department who championed Western music in general and the string quartet in particular. Mrs Onoda made another resigned trip

17

to the bank and paid for a six-month course of lessons with Mr Kawamitsu.

Panamá – Puente del Monde said the taxi's number plate.

'Bridge of the world!' Mr Mandamus translated, though Hisako had guessed what it meant. This was one of the names they called the country. The other was 'The Heart of the Universe'.

'Ah,' she said, politely.

It was eight o'clock in the evening on Pier 18 in Balboa on the day the *Nakado* had docked after its Pacific crossing. They were taking a taxi into Panama City, which was lighting up the overcast sky beyond the orange-necklaced dark bulk of Balboa Heights.

'Oh, get in here, Mandamus, I'm hungry,' Broekman said from inside the cab. It had taken them longer than they'd expected to clear Customs.

'Puente del Monde!' Mandamus said, and with a clumsy flourish opened the passenger's door for Hisako, narrowly avoided jamming her ankle in the door as he closed it again, and got into the back seat beside Broekman.

'Panama City, *por favor!*' Mandamus shouted at the driver, a young man in a vest.

'Panama,' the driver said, shaking his head. 'Yeah, OK. Any particular bit?'

'Via Brasil,' Mandamus told him.

Hisako laughed, covering her mouth with her hand.

'Via Brasil,' the driver nodded. He stuffed the copy of *Newsweek* he'd been reading between the dash and the windscreen and put the auto into drive. The cab bumped over the rail tracks sunk into the rough concrete of the dock.

There was a brightly lit checkpoint where they left the Canal Area at the junction of Avenida A and Avenida de los Martires. The driver cursed and spat out of the window as they approached the short line of cars and light trucks, though they were soon waved through by the US and Panamanian troops. The queue of vehicles waiting on the far side of the barrier was much longer.

They drove through the city, through the stink of traffic fumes and sudden oases of flower-scent. 'Frangipani,' Mr Mandamus said, sniffing deeply, and nodding.

Hisako rolled her window down, letting the hairdryer-hot

moist air spill round her as they sped and lurched their way down the crowded avenues. The city was just waking up; it was bright and busy and full of cars with their windows down and their music turned up. Even the troop-filled jeeps they encountered usually had a ghetto-blaster perched on the rear or taped to the T-bar, beside the machine-gun. The population made the biggest impression, though. The streets swarmed with riotously different people; every colour and race she thought she'd ever heard of.

She had gone ashore in Honolulu for a day, while changing ships, and been surprised at how odd it felt to be surrounded by so many *gaijin* (though the Hawaiian natives hadn't looked all that unusual to her). Then, on the *Nakodo*, due to take her from Honolulu to Rotterdam via Panama and New Orleans, she'd been surrounded mostly by foreigners; the Korean crew; Broekman, the second engineer; and Mr Mandamus, the one other passenger. Only the three senior officers on the ship, and the steward, were Japanese. So she thought she'd adjusted, but the extravagance of the racial mix, and the sheer numbers of people in Panama, amazed her.

She wondered how Broekman felt. A South African, he professed, and seemed, to despise the white state, but he'd been brought up in it, and she thought Panama must still come as something of a shock to the system.

They drove to the Juji, on the Via Brasil. It was a Japanese restaurant; Mr Mandamus's idea of a surprise. She had wanted to eat local cuisine, but didn't let her disappointment show. The restaurant had a Japanese chef, a skiing fan from Niigata who knew Sapporo well, and they talked for a while ('Only water skiing in Panama!'). The *shabu-shabu* was good, and the *tempura*. Broekman grumbled about steaks, but seemed content enough after that. Mr Mandamus, having checked with Hisako that slurping was still quite in order, proceeded enthusiastically to slurp his way through every dish presented, even the dry ones, half-gargling with Kirin beer. On the other side of a screen a noisy group of Japanese bankers easily outdid Mandamus in volume and spent most of the time making elaborate toasts to each other and ordering more sake. She felt she might almost as well be at home.

When they left, the city was still waking up; the nightclubs and casinos opening for trade. They went to a couple of bars on Avenue Roberto Duran; Mr Mandamus didn't like the look of the first one because most of the men were GIs. 'I have nothing against our American cousins,' he explained to Hisako as they walked away. She thought he wasn't going to say anything else, but then he leant close and hissed, 'Danger of bombs!' and ducked into another bar. Broekman shook his head.

In the Marriott Casino they gambled, strolling among the green-felt tables and the stunning local women and the men in their white tuxedos. She felt small and dowdy in comparison, like a raggedly dressed child, but with a child's delight at the glitter and buzz of the place, too. The roulette wheels clicked, dice clattered across the baize, cards flicked from manicured hands. Guards the size of sumo wrestlers tried to lumber inconspicuously between the white jackets and long dresses, or stood impassively against the walls, hands behind their backs, displaying tailored bulges under their jackets, only their eyes moving.

Mr Mandamus lost little and often on the *tranganiquel*, stuffing quarters into the flashing machines and claiming he had an infallible system. Broekman won two hundred dollars at *vingt-et-un* and ordered champagne for Hisako, who gambled without much enthusiasm or luck at *dado*.

They took a taxi back into the centre and walked along the Avenue Balboa, by the side of the bay, where the Pacific broke whitely and patrol boats grumbled in the distance, then finished up in Bacchus II, where Mandamus found ('Ah! Surprise!') the *karaoke* room and spent an embarrassingly long time singing along with the Japanese backing tracks, trying to get Hisako to join in, and making noisy friends with the same group of bankers they'd encountered in the Juji.

She was falling asleep in the taxi back to Pier 18.

' . . . virgins at the shrine would take mouthfuls of rice, and chew it to a pulp and then spit it into the casks, and— '

'You're making this up, you crazy man!'

'No, no, really; that is how the fermentation was started. An ensign in their saliva— '

'A what?'

'An ensign in their saliva; their spit.'

'I know— ' Broekman broke off. Hisako jerked her chin

off her chest. She yawned. Her head hurt. 'Did you hear that?' Broekman said.

'What?' Mandamus said. 'Hear what?'

'Explosion.'

The driver – fat, silver-haired, watching a tiny colour Watchman stuck to the dash when he wasn't overtaking – turned and said something in Spanish. Hisako wondered if Broekman had really said 'explosion'.

She wasn't exactly sure how long afterwards the taxi stopped somewhere on Balboa Heights, the Puente de las Americas to their left, straddling the canal entrance and ablaze with lights. Mandamus helped her from the car, and the three of them and the driver stood at the roadside and looked back down into the bay-cupping city, where a huge fire near the centre was surrounded by a hundred flashing blue and red lights, and a thick column of smoke, like a black cauliflower, climbed towards the orange-smudged clouds.

The crackling of small-arms fire sounded like logs sparking in a grate.

Shaped like an S lying on its side, it was the only place on earth where the sun could rise over the Pacific and set over the Atlantic. One day in 1513 a Spaniard from the province of Extremadura called Vasco Nunéz de Balboa – who'd started out as a stowaway on somebody else's expedition, then taken over in a mutiny – climbed a hill in Darien and saw what no European had ever seen before; the Pacific.

Then, they called it the Southern Ocean.

Balboa made friends with the people who already lived in that stretch of land, and an enemy of the man who governed most of the isthmus, which the Spanish called the Castilla del Oro. The governor took his anger out on Balboa's own isthmus; he had him beheaded. The fact that Balboa had become his son-in-law did not stay the blade.

The governor, called Pedrarias the Cruel by history, founded a town on the Pacific coast, near a little fishing village called Panamá. In the local language, *panamá* meant 'lots of fish'. The Spanish called the trail between it and the Caribbean the Camino Real; the Royal Road. Down that road the looted wealth of the

Inca empire went by slave and donkey. The slaves were brought in from Africa to replace the locals, who'd been slaughtered. The donkeys were better treated, and so the slaves escaped into the jungle whenever they could. They were called *cimarrones*. They formed their own settlements and raised their own armed forces, and sometimes went in league with the English, French and Dutch pirates attracted to the area by the intense concentration of vast wealth; looting the looters.

In 1573 Francis Drake and his gang of licensed pirates attacked the Spanish gold galleons and the town called Nombre de Dios. They captured the town of Cruces and burned it to the ground. Ninety-eight years later, the Welshman Henry Morgan captured Panamá itself; he set fire to it. The treasure required 195 mules. The Spanish rebuilt the city along the coast with bigger walls. Fifty-eight years after that, when Britain and Spain were at war, Admiral Vernon captured Portobelo on the Caribbean coast, plus the fort of San Lorenzo.

A few years later, in 1746, the Spanish gave up and started sailing their treasure ships round Cape Horn instead. Panama was neglected, though not allowed to trade freely with the rest of Europe. In 1821 the Panamanians declared themselves independent . . . and joined Bolívar's Greater Columbia.

Which neglected them. There were revolutions.

Before the Spanish came to Panama there were over sixty native tribes living in the area. Afterwards, three.

Then somebody found more gold. Far to the north this time, in California. The plains of North America, still under invasion, were far more dangerous than a sea trip from New York or New Orleans to the Río Chagres, a short paddle and a quick mule ride to the Pacific and another voyage from there to San Francisco: Panama was back in business. The short paddle and quick mule ride was so much fun the forty-niners called it the Road to Hell. They died in droves, mostly from disease.

Some already rich Americans formed the Panama Railroad Company. Somehow persuaded of their righteousness, the Columbian government granted them a monopoly. It made money.

The track ran from Colón to Panamá, over one of the old Spanish gold trails. Then a golden spike was driven into its heart, thousands of miles to the north-west, in the United States of America: the first rail route from sea to shining sea was in operation.

So people began to neglect Panama again.

Ferdinand, Vicomte de Lesseps, builder of the fabulous sea-level, distance-reducing, desert crossing, Empire-linking, all-singing, all-operatic Suez Canal, a cousin of the French Empress, winner of the Grand Cross of the Legion of Honour, recipient of an English Knighthood, member of the Academy, began work on his world-stunning scheme to build a sea-level canal through the isthmus of Panama in 1881.

Gauguin worked on it, artist among the artisans.

Twenty-two thousand people died on it.

And in 1893 it was over; the company – La Compagnie Universelle du Canal Interocéanique, shunned by governments and banks, worshipped by the small investor, disseminator of bribes to press and politicians – crashed, and five directors were condemned. Eiffel, constructor of the soaring Tower, was laid low. De Lesseps was sentenced to five years in prison.

He died next year, heart excavated.

The United States of America was the major regional power now. It was determined to have a canal. First choice became the route through Nicaragua, but the manager of what remained of the French company sent all members of Congress a Nicaraguan postage stamp showing a volcanic eruption. He also made the point that Panama was outside the volcano belt; it didn't have earthquakes. Was there not an arch still standing (the famous Arco Chato, or Flat Arch, part of the church of San Domingo) which had stood intact for three centuries, in Panama City?

Congress was convinced. The word went out that it would be a good idea if Columbia let La Compagnie Universelle sell all its rights to the US. The Columbian Congress disagreed, and wouldn't ratify, no matter what President Roosevelt wanted. Incredibly, an uprising in Panama City played right into the US's hands, and when Columbian troops were sent to squash it, Congress sent a gunboat. Washington recognised the independent republic almost before it was proclaimed. It was 1903.

The new government of independent Panama thought it was a neat idea to cede partial sovereignty over a strip eight kilometres wide on either side of the canal route to the United States 'in perpetuity' for ten million dollars down and a quarter million a year (the latter eventually raised to close on two mill, when it got embarrassing).

The diseases were vanquished, despite everything. The problems of geography and topography were conquered by brains, brawn and lashings of cash. The temporary rail system built to help construct the canal was the greatest railway network in the world at the time. Mountains were moved, rivers dammed, forests drowned, islands created. The Zone became an island of clipped lawns in an ocean of jungle.

In August 1914, while the Great War in Europe was still beginning, the first ship passed through the new canal.

In 1921 the US paid $25 million to Columbia, to compensate for the loss of the isthmus called Panama. Cut to:

1978: Jimmy Carter agreed a new treaty. In 2000, it would all be given back to the locals.

(The Panamanians never had liked that 'in perpetuity' clause.) The Zone became the Area, but most people still called it the Zone. Pineapple Face spoiled things a little, but not so you'd notice. Things went on. The second millennium crept closer. And that was as far as Hisako's guidebooks took her.

The rain was warm and the air smelled of the land's own heat; vegetable and intense, like something that had willed itself into being through a chemical spell, without the intercession of the sun. Six o'clock and it was already dark, and the rain fell steadily, glowing in the lights of the *Nakodo*, swinging about her mooring in the gentlest of evening breezes. The waters of the lake looked dull and flat and oily, covered with the ever-changing patterns of the big raindrops, ephemeral dots and dashes on the slowly moving surface. The air was so thick and humid it was hard to believe the rain could fall through it so fast.

'Ms Onoda! Hisako! You'll get soaked!'

She turned from the rail to see Mandamus waddle up, coming from his cabin on the main deck level. Hisako brushed a few droplets from her fringe of dark hair; the rain was falling almost straight down, and the deck above had sheltered her. But Mandamus liked to fuss.

Mr Mandamus, the Alexandrian, portly and effusive, with greyly olive skin and dyedly grey hair, a friend of mankind, peripatetic expert in multitudinous fields and reputedly holder of degrees from universities on three continents, took Hisako Onoda's hand in his and kissed it precisely. Hisako smiled as she always did, bowing a little.

Mr Mandamus offered his arm and she took it. They walked along the deck, heading forward.

'And where have you been today? I was a little late for lunch, but you ate in your cabin, I believe.'

'I was playing,' she told him. The deck was dry near the superstructure, spattered with dark drops near the rails.

'Ah, practising.'

Hisako studied the deck, wondering who'd decided the pattern of tiny diamond shapes on the metal was the best one for providing grip. 'I worry about becoming out of touch; rusty.'

'Rust is best left to the vessels, Ms Onoda,' Mandamus told her, gesturing. They arrived at the forward limit of the *Nakodo*'s superstructure, looking out over the rain-battered hatches – bright under the masthead lights – to the forecastle. To starboard, the lights of *Le Cercle* and the *Nadia* burned through the night and the warm rain, floating islands of light in the darkness. She wondered what Philippe was doing.

When they'd made love the evening before, after the swim through the ruins, before the nightmare, Philippe had held her shoulders, his arms through her armpits, clutching at her shoulders from underneath, arching her. She'd had the dizzying sensation of still wearing the scuba gear, the straps pressing into her skin. She'd remembered the silky warmth of the water, and the sight of his long, tanned body sliding through it, wave lights rippling from the surface like grid lines across the sweet geography of his back and legs.

' . . . Hisako? Are you all right?'

'Oh!' She laughed, and let go of Mandamus's arm, which she'd been gripping too hard. She clasped her hands at the small of her back and walked quickly on, desperately trying to recall what Mandamus's last words had been. 'I'm sorry,' she said. *I am acting like a schoolgirl*, she told herself. Mr Mandamus caught her up, offering his arm again as they walked, so that it stuck out between them like a podgy guardrail. It had been something about rain and mud (how romantic!). 'Yes, yes it's terrible. But they are fixing this, no?'

'Too late, I fear,' Mandamus said, dropping his arm. They turned the corner, walked towards the stern. The companionway leading up to the level of the dining room lay straight ahead. The deck was quite dry. 'So many trees have been cut down, so much topsoil washed into the lake, the situation was quite serious even before the war. The canal has been deteriorating for years, Gatún Lake itself – ' Mr Mandamus gestured around them, ' – is shallower and smaller than it used to be, as are the dams feeding it. Before too long you and that dashing French *officier* will be able to go paddling rather than diving!'

They ascended the stairs. Hisako took another look back at the lights of *Le Cercle*, a kilometre or so distant across the lake, before being ushered through the doorway into the cool brilliance of the superstructure.

She had settled into shipboard life very quickly. The *Gassam Maru* carried her to Honolulu, over the empty blue Pacific. She watched the contrails of jets, eleven kilometres above, with a smile, and no regret. Within a couple of days of leaving Yokohama she felt comfortable and at home. Her place in the hierarchy of the ballasted tanker was that of honoured guest, with the privileges of an officer without the responsibilities; in rank she seemed to be just beneath the captain, equal with the first officer and the chief engineer.

The crew ignored her with extreme politeness, turning back down stairs if she appeared at the top, to let her descend (but averting their eyes), and looking confused if she thanked them. The junior officers were only a little more assertive, while the senior ones treated her as one of their own, apparently according her the respect they felt she was due as an expert in her field, which they regarded as no less complex and worthy than their own. Captain Ishizawa was cold and formal towards her, but then he was cold and formal with his officers too, so she did not feel his lack of warmth as an insult.

26

After the frenetic bustle of the last month she'd spent in Tokyo – finishing courses, making final arrangements for other people to continue her tutorials and classes, having several send-off parties, visiting various friends, trying to calm Mr Moriya, going to be hypnotised at his begging, being dragged out to Narita to board a plane, and still getting panicky and weak the moment she boarded, and almost hysterical (much to her shame) when they were about to close the door – life aboard ship seemed simple and easy. The set structure, the regular watches and rhythms, the adhered-to rules and definite lines of command, all appealed to the orderly side of her nature. There was the ship, and the rest of the world. All nice and definite and unarguable. The ship ploughed the ocean, affected by tides and wind, in touch via radio signals and satellites, but it was basically a unit, separated by its mobility.

The wide sea, the vast skies, the soothing consistency of the view – reliable in its simple outline, but ever various within its elemental parameters – made the voyage an escape, an experience of freedom of a type and duration she'd never encountered before; something sublime, like a raked garden or a perfectly proportioned room, like Fuji on a clear day, rising beyond Tokyo like a great tent being drawn up towards heaven.

And the Stradivari violoncello, circa 1730, rebridged and reend-pointed Beijing 1890, survived. She had taken a device which recorded temperature and humidity in her cabin, and a back-up air-conditioning machine which could work off the ship's electricity supply or use its own batteries for up to forty-eight hours. All this seemed a little excessive to her, but it kept Mr Moriya if not quiet, then at an acceptable volume of terrified hysteria.

She practised in her cabin, sheets taped (folded neatly) over one blank wall to get the acoustics right. Practised for hours, eyes closed, hugging the warm wood of the instrument, lost in it, so that sometimes she would start playing in the afternoon and when she opened her eyes it would be dark outside the cabin portholes, and she would sit there in the darkness, blinking and feeling foolish, back and arms sore with that rewarding ache of something worthwhile bought at the expense of effort. The steward must have mentioned the sheets taped to the wall, because the deck officer told her they had found some cork tiles in a store;

could they fix those to the offending bulkhead? Uncertain whether they would be insulted if she said no, she let them. It was done in a day; she asked them not to varnish the cork. The cello sounded better indeed, the last harshness of the cabin gone. She tried to listen to herself in a way she hadn't since her earliest days, with Mr Kawamitsu, and recorded her practice sessions on her old DAT Walkman, and thought – though she would never have admitted it to anybody – that she had never played better.

She was sad to leave the *Gassam Maru*, but had made no special friends, so would not miss anybody particularly. The voyage had been enjoyable in itself, and its ending was as much a part of it as any other, so the sadness was not deep, and almost satisfying. She boarded the *Nakodo*, another Yotsubashi Line vessel, though this time a car transporter chartered to carry Nissan limos destined for the North American market. She found the *Nakodo* busier, more cosmopolitan and more interesting than the *Gassam*; she settled in there quickly as well. Her cabin was larger and wood-lined, and the cello sounded good in its warmth.

She stood at the bows of the ship sometimes, a little self-conscious that they'd be watching her from the bridge, but she stood there all the same, like Garbo in *Queen Christina* but with her hair blowing in the right direction, and looked out into the creamy blue emptiness of the western Pacific, heading east-south-east for the isthmus of Panama, and smiled into the tropic wind.

Like Philippe's ship, the *Nakodo* was under the command of its mate. First Officer Endo sat at the head of the table, Hisako to his right, Mr Mandamus across from her. Broekman would sit beside the Egyptian, Second Officer Hoashi on Hisako's other side. Next to him was Steve Orrick, a student from Cal Tech who'd begged a lift on the *Nadia* in Panama City; he'd been trying to get out of the city for weeks and the *Nadia*'s American captain had taken pity on him, after radioing for permission from the ship's owners. When it became clear the ships were going to be staying in Gatún lake for some time, Orrick had offered to pay for his keep by helping out with whatever he could; at the moment he was on loan to the *Nakodo*, helping to paint her. He was tall, fair-haired, awkward, and built like an Olympic swimmer. Hisako found the young American a strain to talk to.

It was a Western cuisine night; knives and forks graced the brilliant white starched tablecloth. The predictable rotation of meals had become one of the most intense of the rituals practised on the three trapped ships; each vessel had its own rhythm, and each played host to the officers and guests of the other two ships on a regular basis, sometimes with the addition of people from Gatún; shipping agents, canal officials, occasionally somebody from the consulates in Rainbow City or Colón. Tomorrow night they would all troop over to the *Nadia* for a dance and a native feast, eating local for a change. Last night on *Le Cercle*, with Lekkas's Greek banquet, had been a break in the cycle, which she and Philippe had appreciated, but still the pattern of meals, drinks parties, dances and other social occasions helped to fill the time, while they waited for the war to run its course. Stagnant in the stalemate, only this ritualised consumption seemed to make much sense or offer a tangible link to the outside world. Hisako wondered if she still smelled of garlic.

The talk turned from the riots in Hong Kong to the US peace mission to Ecuador.

'Perhaps, we are free to go, before long,' said Endo, in carefully navigated English.

You be rucky, Hisako thought, toying with her heavy soup spoon.

'Well, yeah,' Orrick said, looking up and down the table. 'Could be. You get these guys talking and they can fix this thing up. Hell, all they got to do is get the Panamanians to let the Marines back into the Zone and get them F17s flying point and the old *venceristas*'ll have to head back into the hills. Park a battleship or two off PC; that'll get to them; practically fire shells right over the goddamn country.' He made a trajectoral motion over the white tablecloth with one broad, blond-haired hand.

'Our young friend is one of the old guard,' Mr Mandamus said to those at the end of the table.

Orrick shook his head, 'The old National Guard ain't gonna get rid of the reds; only way we're gonna get the ships out of here is get the Marines and GIs out of that Southern Command base and back into the rest of the Zone with the hand-helds and the microbursts.'

29

'Panamanians lose face to do that,' Endo shook his head.

'I guess they might, sir, but they lost the canal right now; heck, they're losing the whole country, and they can't even guarantee the safety of American citizens in their major cities. How much longer are we supposed to wait? These guys have had their chance.'

'Perhaps the congressmen will succeed in their mission,' Hisako said. 'We'll just have to— '

'Perhaps the reds'll see the light and join the Boy Scouts,' Orrick said to her.

'Perhaps I have an idea,' Mr Mandamus announced, holding up one finger. 'Why don't we open a book?'

They looked at him in puzzlement. Hisako wondered what Mr Mandamus could be talking about, then if he was showing signs of converting to some religion; opening the Bible at random for inspiration and guidance was popular with certain Christians, she'd heard, and Muslims did the same thing with the Koran. The steward – an old man near retirement called Sawai – came in with a tray full of soup bowls and a basket of bread.

'Wager,' Mr Mandamus explained. 'I shall be bookmaker; we can bet on what day the canal is finally reopened, or on what day the first ship completes its journey; whichever. What do you say?'

Officer Hoashi asked Hisako what the man was talking about. She translated, and thanked Sawai as he placed a bowl in front of her.

'I do not bet,' Endo said. 'But . . . ' He spread his hands.

'I'll bet that when they open the canal it'll be Yankees doing the opening,' Orrick said, and launched into his soup.

'I might be prepared to cover that wager,' Mandamus said, unenthusiastically.

'What are we betting on?' Broekman strode in and took his place at the table, nodding to Endo.

'When the ships are released,' Mandamus told him.

'Which decade? Which year?' Broekman snapped his napkin and twirled his spoon, waiting for Sawai to serve him. The engineer smelled of soap and cologne.

'A little sooner than that, we think,' Mandamus said, laughing heartily.

30

'Do you? Well, I won't be betting.'

'Mr Orrick want to send in Marines,' Endo said, slurping daintily at his soup and making a game attempt at the American's name.

'Standard US behaviour,' Broekman nodded.

'Yeah; it works.'

'Not in Beirut it didn't,' Broekman told the younger man. Orrick looked puzzled. Broekman waved one hand impatiently. 'Before your time, maybe.'

' "Send a gunship!" ' Mandamus said loudly, as though quoting.

'Well anyway, this isn't Beirut,' Orrick took a piece of bread from the basket, broke it in half and ate.

'Isn't Saigon, either, but so what?' Broekman looked suddenly annoyed, and scowled at the bowl the old steward put in front of him. 'Ach; it isn't up to us. It'll sort itself out one way or the other. We aren't even pawns in this.'

'The congressmen will see the ships though,' Hisako said. 'And we were mentioned on the news again last night.'

'Channel 8?' Broekman said. 'That's because we're local for them. And a lot these congressmen will see from seven miles up, anyway . . . *if* it's a clear day.'

Hisako looked down, sipped at her soup.

'We're a symbol, man,' Orrick told Broekman. 'We matter. That's why the reds haven't attacked us or blown away the dams.'

'They took out that lock at Gatún easily enough,' Broekman said.

'Yeah, but just one, like to prove they could do it.'

'And the tanker lying at the bottom of Limón Bay?'

'It was US registered, like you keep telling me, Mr Broekman,' Orrick said. 'And it hadn't gotten famous; it wasn't mentioned in the news till it was blown away. But the reds aren't gonna attack us. It's too public a situation; we mean something. That's why that plane's coming to look-see. We'll be centre-stage, numero uno.'

'You reckon,' Broekman said, dipping into his soup. 'Well, who am I to argue?'

'I will hazard,' Mandamus said, with slow deliberation and narrowed eyes, 'that if negotiations go well, the ships will be released before the end of the month.'

31

Broekman laughed, coughed into his soup, dabbed at his mouth with the napkin. Orrick nodded his young blond head slowly. 'Only if the guys come in. If the guys come in; then you'll see some action.'

'In what guise, though?' Mandamus said, as though to himself.

'Yeah; you wait,' Orrick said, tearing another piece of bread apart. 'You'll see.'

3: The Universal Company

'Hello? Hello? Hisako? Ms Onoda?'

'I am here.'

'Ah! How are you?'

'Well. Very well. And you?'

'Hisako, what are you doing? Why are you still on that ship? I've put the dates starting in Den Haag back by exactly one month except for Bern. Not always the same venues, but we can sort that out later. But you have to get out of there! . . . Are you listening? Hello?'

'It's not easy to get out, Mr Moriya. Helicopters are shot down, small boats are attacked . . . sometimes near the coast of the lake; Panama airport is closed— '

'They must have more than one!'

'—and because the . . . no, the city only has one civilian airport. Colón is shut down for— '

'I meant in the country!'

'And the Pan American is mined.'

'What? The airline? Mined?'

'No, the highway. Also, the rebels have taken hostages in Panama and Colón.'

'But you're Japanese, not American! I mean, why— '

'They've kidnapped . . . they've kidnapped Japanese, Americans, Europeans, Brazilians . . . many different people. One of the captains of the ships was taken hostage in Cristóbal; Captain Herval . . . I might get through, but I might not. At least here we are fairly safe.'

'Can't they get those ships out? Can't they move them?'

'The rebels have missiles. Also, they could blow up the

locks, or the Madden Dam, or the Mindi Dyke. The canal is . . . delicate, even though it is big.'

'Hisako, are these real names? No; never mind. Isn't there some way out? Somehow? There's more interest than ever because it's been on the news you're there, but the Europeans won't wait for ever, and you aren't – forgive me – but you aren't getting any younger, Hisako. Oh, I'm sorry. Say you forgive me; I'm not sleeping well, and I'm on the phone to Europe half the night, and I'm snapping at people and . . . I'm sorry I said that. Do say I'm excused . . . '

'That's all right. You are correct, of course. But I have talked to the consulate in Panama; they say it is safest to sit tight. They expect there will be peace soon, or that the Americans will take over the Zone again.'

'But *when*?'

'Who knows? Watch the news.'

'I watch the news! I can't take my eyes off the news! When I'm not running up a phone bill to Europe the size of the US national debt, I'm stuck to CNN Nippon! But watching the news does not get you to Europe to play the cello!'

'I'm sorry, Mr Moriya. But I can't think of anything I can do.'

'Oh . . . oh, me neither. But . . . but . . . oh, it's all just so frustrating! Ha! Why didn't I stay with the NHK like my mother said? Never mind! Are you practising? How is the instrument?'

'I am practising. The instrument and I are both fine. I didn't know you were in the NHK.'

'What? Yes; many years ago. Trumpet. I left because I was making more money doing bookings for other people. Also, playing it hurt my eardrums.'

'You are what they call "dark horse", Mr Moriya.'

'I am what they call broke agent, Hisako. And more broke the longer this call goes on. You keep practising.'

'*Hai*. Thank you for calling. Goodbye.'

'*Sayonara*, Hisako.'

The *Nakodo* stayed at Pier 18 for a week; there was a problem with the ship's propeller, which had stuck at one pitch. After two days of rioting and curfews the city had been declared safe again. Hisako went back in with Mandamus, Broekman, and first officer

34

Endo, while the divers tried to fix the prop. Captain Yashiro paced impatiently up and down the bridge watching a succession of ships sail under the Puente de las Americas, past Pier 18, and on towards the locks at Miraflores. Helicopters filled the skies, clattering between the Southern Command base at Fort Clayton and US aircraft carriers and troop ships stationed in the Gulf of Panama. The *venceristas* were said to be moving down from the Cordillera Central and the Serranía de San Blas. Cuba had warned the US not to intervene, and offered help to the Republic. The US reinforced its base at Guantánamo, on Cuba. The Soviet ambassador visited the White House to deliver a note to the President, the text of which was not released.

Mr Mandamus stirred his mint tea and looked out on to the Avenida Central, where the clogged traffic honked and hooted furiously, and outrageously decorated buses full of brightly dressed people contrasted with the matt camouflage of the Guards' jeeps and trucks.

They had started at the Santa Ana Plaza, where Mr Mandamus, guidebook in hand, led them down Calle 13 after having his shoes polished twice. Hisako, Mr Mandamus said, was the only Japanese person he'd ever encountered who didn't own – indeed had never owned – a camera. She agreed it was unusual. Officer Endo took photographs of everything, in a manner Mr Mandamus obviously considered a much more satisfyingly traditional Japanese fashion.

Hisako spent much time and money on Calle 13. The street was packed with shops and shoppers. She bought Kantule perfume from the San Blas archipelago, a *chaquira* necklace made by the Guaymí Indians, a ring with a small Columbian emerald set in it, a *chácara* bag, a circular *pollera* dress, a *montuna* shirt and several *molas*; a small pillow, a bedspread, and three blouses. Mandamus bought a hat. Broekman stocked up on Cuban cigars. Endo bought a *mola* for his wife and two extra diskettes for his camera. The men helped her carry all her shopping. Broekman thought some of the natives looked shifty, and said it was probably just as well they were all together, especially as Hisako had collected enough loot on her shopping expedition to make a *conquistadore* jealous.

They trooped down to the docks and through the fish market, then got lost in a maze of small, crowded, noisy streets. Mr Mandamus was delighted; the area was called 'Sal si puedes', which meant 'Get out if you can', and it was traditional to get lost in it.

'You mean you *knew* we'd get lost?' Broekman said, once they were lost. He waved away a variety of people trying to sell him things.

'Well, I thought we would,' Mandamus said thoughtfully.

'You *thought* we would, you crazy man?'

'Of course,' Mr Mandamus said, glowing with airy satisfaction, while a lottery ticket salesman and the owner of a Chinese restaurant studied the map of the city Mandamus had produced. (They were arguing.) 'They keep changing the street names, you see,' Mr Mandamus explained. 'The maps have the new names but the people call the streets after their old names. It's quite simple, really.'

'But what do you want to get us *lost* for?' Broekman said, almost shouting. 'This city's bandit country these days! We need to know what we're doing! We need to know where we are!'

'Don't worry,' Mandamus said, wiping his brow with a white handkerchief. He pointed to Endo, who was filming the arm movements of the two arguing Panamanians. 'Mr Endo is a navigating officer!'

Hisako looked round, clutching her shopping bags to her because Broekman had said she ought to, but – despite the heat, and the crowds, and the fact they were lost – feeling happy. Not because she'd bought so much, but because here she was, finally in a completely different place. It was dangerous, sometimes frightening, quite lawless compared to Japan, but just so different. She felt alive. She tried to think of what music it would be good to play now, what composition she could take this mood to, so that the notes would sing and speak and take on resonances she hadn't heard in them before.

They got out eventually. They continued walking, admiring the old Spanish villas, the cathedral, Plaza Bolívar, and the brilliantly white presidential palace with its flamingoes. 'I take it the anti-aircraft missiles on the roof are a recent addition,' Broekman said, looking over Mandamus's shoulder at the guidebook.

'So one would imagine.'

They went down to the sea, to the Plaza de Francia, and looked out from the old walls to the islands in the bay; the Pacific was green and blue and violet, shimmering under a cloudless sky. Seabirds wheeled in the baking air.

They strolled back up the Avenida Central until they came to a café called the International, run by a huge black man called MacPherson who spoke with an accent that combined Jamaican and English public school. They took tea. Mint for Mandamus, Chinese for the rest.

'Oh!' Mandamus said suddenly, still reading the guidebook. 'Listen: "The lower part of the ramparts, near the law courts, contains vaulted cells in which condemned prisoners were chained at low tide." ' Mandamus looked up, eyes bright. 'You see? And then, when the tide came in, the Pacific drowned them . . . the *moon* drowned them! We should go back and see these cells. What do you say?'

Her classmates made fun of her because she looked like a hairy Ainu. The Ainu were the natives of Japan; its abos, its Injuns. After the eighth century they'd been pushed further and further north by the Yamato Japanese moving in from the Asian mainland until they clung on only on Hokkaido, the most northern island. Stereotypically the Ainu were tall, thick-built and hairy, and Hisako – though of average build – had deep black hair, and bushy eyebrows which almost joined up with the hair at the side of her scalp. Her eyes were deep-set, which added to the Ainu look. So the children in her school taunted her and offered to tattoo her lips and wrists, the way real Ainu were marked.

In school she was poor at almost everything except English, and the other girls told her she'd never get to university – not even a two-year one – because she was stupid, and never get a husband because she was an ugly hairy Ainu, and she'd grow up a poor widowed office lady like her mother.

She ignored them, tried to read fairy stories in English, and practised her cello playing. Once, in the middle of winter, four girls caught her in a school cloakroom and held her hands down on a near-boiling-hot radiator; she cried, screamed, struggled, while her hands blazed with pain, and the girls laughed and imitated her cries. Finally, roaring with the agony and the unfairness of it all, she pulled her head free of their grip – leaving one of the girls with a handful of bloody, thick, black hair – and sank her

37

teeth in the wrist of the biggest girl. She bit as hard as she could, and heard the screams go on around her though her mouth was closed and her hands still burned.

She woke up on the floor. There was blood in her mouth and her head ached. Her hands were seared and red and tight, and she sat there, legs crossed, rocking back and forward with her hands in her lap, weeping quietly to herself and wishing that life was like a fairy story, so that her falling tears would heal her hands where the drops fell on the raw red skin.

Her mother seemed to accept her story about pulling an iron rod out of a bonfire on the way back from school. Mrs Onoda said nothing about the patch of missing hair, or the bruise on the side of her daughter's face, and Hisako thought her mother stupid and easily fooled for a while, until she heard the stifled sobs coming from her mother's room that night. Hisako let her hands be bandaged. She would lie in her mother's arms, being read to, or rest her English books in her lap, turning the pages with her nose, or just sit with her cello, looking at it and rubbing her cheek against it. Whenever she started to cry she buried her face in the crook of her elbow, in case her tears stained the cello's varnished surface.

Mr Kawamitsu had been delighted by the progress she'd made. She was exceptionally gifted, he told her mother (who sighed when she heard this, because it meant it would cost money). Mr Kawamitsu was very excited; he had written to the Tokyo Music Academy, and they had agreed to listen to the child, to see if she was as good as he said. If she was, she would be given a bursary. Of course, this meant travelling to Tokyo. . . . Mrs Onoda went to the bank.

It was too soon after her hands had been burned, but the date had been set and Mrs Onoda was terrified of upsetting the Academy. They were both sick on the ferry. She still felt terrible when she was taken into the room in the old building near Yoyogi Park, to sit in front of a dozen stern-looking men.

She played; they listened. They looked just as stern when she'd finished, and she knew she had played badly, that she had thrown away her chance and Mr Kawamitsu would be made to look stupid and her mother would weep behind the screen again.

She was right; she didn't get the bursary. They did offer her a place, but Mrs Onoda couldn't afford the money. Mr Kawamitsu looked sad rather than angry, and said she must still play, because she could do something very few people could do, and such a gift was not just hers, but belonged to everybody, and she owed it to everyone else to practise diligently. She found that difficult, and her playing became mechanical and without lustre.

The Academy sent for her again a month after their offer of a place had been rejected; another chance, for the last bursary place. But Mrs Onoda had little money left. Hisako thought about it, and came solemnly to her mother one evening, holding the cello like an offering at a shrine, suggesting they sell the instrument to raise the money for the fare; she could borrow one. If she had a chance to practise she might be able to adapt to a new cello . . . Her mother ruffled her hair, and went to the bank the next morning to take out a loan.

The ferry journey was smooth and for a long time she watched the wake the ship left stretching back to the dark island of her birth.

In the forbidding room in the old building near Yoyogi Park she played again; again the stern-looking men listened. Because her hands had healed, she could use them to tell the judges how much it had hurt when they were forced on to the rough metal of the radiator; how much she had been hurt; how much her mother had been hurt; how much everything hurt. They still looked stern, but they gave her the bursary.

She wore the *pollera* and one of the *mola* blouses to the party on the *Nadia*, the third ship stranded in the lake. The *Nadia* was a general cargo vessel, registered in Panama itself, but Japanese-owned. Like the *Nakodo*, it had been crossing from Pacific to Atlantic when the canal was closed.

The *Nadia*'s parties were held under an awning on an upper deck. It was a clear night for a change, and on the way over in the *Nakodo*'s launch, heading for the bright patch of light and the sound of Latin music, she watched the stars, fabulous and strewn, arching across the sky above the darkness of the lake.

Philippe was already there, looking tall and fine and tanned in his white dress uniform. She felt the way she always did when she saw him like this; afraid and embarrassed. Afraid that he would look at her one day and, instead of smiling (as he did now, coming forward, taking her hand, kissing it), scowling. She would know what that scowl meant; it would mean that he no longer wanted her, that he was wondering what he'd ever seen in her, what had possessed him to take this older woman, this small-breasted, unglamorous Japanese woman to his bed; that he was thinking how foolish, how blind he must have looked to everybody else, and how he could gracefully disengage from the association. So she searched his face for that look at almost every meeting, knowing the expression might be fleeting, knowing it might be almost invisibly brief, but sure she would recognise it when it came.

Her embarrassment was caused simply by the thought; what was *she* doing with this handsome young man?

'You are very ethnic tonight,' Philippe said to her, looking her up and down as they went to the drinks table.

She made a flouncing movement with the *pollera*. 'And you look most dashing.'

'But I expand,' he patted his jacket over his belly. 'Too much of this.' He nodded at the food and drink displayed on the tables under the awning.

She squeezed his hand. 'More exercise,' she told him, then said hello to the steward at the drinks table, and asked for a Pernod.

'Do you want to dive tomorrow?' Philippe asked her. 'We can dive at night, perhaps? The lights are ready.' Philippe had wanted to dive in the lake at night for weeks, but didn't have any underwater lights apart from a couple of small torches. Viglain, the engineer on *Le Cercle*, had agreed to make some lights for them.

She nodded. 'Yes, let's do that.' She raised her glass to his. '*Santé*.'

'*Santé*.'

Nobody had braved the journey from Frijoles, a few kilometres away down the canal towards the Pacific coast, or Gatún, about the same distance away in the direction of the Atlantic. Hisako spent a great deal of time dancing; the only other women there were the wife of Captain Bleveans – the *Nadia*'s skipper – and Marie Boulard, *Le Cercle*'s junior deck officer.

They sat down to eat; *ceviche de corvina*, *tamales*, *carimañolas*, lobsters and prawns. She passed on the *chicharrones*, small pieces of fried pork crackling.

She talked to Captain Bleveans; he'd been the only one of the people on the ships who'd known anything about her and her career before they met, though a few of the rest had at least heard of her. Bleveans had some of her more recent recordings, and she'd let him tape the two recitals she'd given since the ships were trapped.

On the other side of the table, Orrick and Broekman were arguing. Mandamus seemed to be reading Mrs Bleveans's hand. Philippe was talking to one of the *Nadia*'s engineers; Endo was doing his best to converse with his opposite number on the ship.

She tried not to keep looking at Philippe all the time.

They'd first met at a similar party on his ship, *Le Cercle*. It had been less than a week since the closure of the canal. Captain Herval, the *Nadia*'s captain, had suggested that the officers of the three ships have an informal gathering; passengers were invited too.

She'd been talking to Mrs Bleveans. The wife of the *Nadia*'s captain was a tall, thin woman who always dressed well and never appeared without subtle but obviously carefully applied make-up, but whose face, Hisako thought, looked faintly – if tastefully – dismayed, as though you were forever telling her something she really did not want to hear, but was not prepared to stoop to arguing about.

'Excuse me, Madame Bleveans.'

Hisako turned to see the tall, dark-haired Frenchman looking first at Mrs Bleveans, then at her, smiling slightly. They'd been introduced; his name was Philippe Ligny. He nodded to the American woman and to her. 'Mademoiselle Onoda?'

'Yes?' Hisako said.

'There is a radio call for you. It is from Tokyo. A Mr . . . Morieur?'

'Moriya,' she said, amused at his accent.

'He says it is urgent. He waits. I can take you to the radio, yes?'

'Yes, thank you,' she said. 'My agent,' she explained to Mrs Bleveans.

'Mr ten percent, huh? Well, give him hell, honey.'

Hisako followed the young Frenchman through the ship, admiring his back, imagining the feel of those shoulders under her hands, and telling herself she might have had too much wine. 'Ah, an elevator!' she said. Philippe motioned her to enter the small lift first.

'We are very . . . *décadent* on ships todays,' he told her, following her in and pressing the top button. She smiled at the 'todays', then told herself his English was ten times better than her French. They had to stand with arms touching. She felt awkward, standing so close to him. He smelled of an aftershave or cologne she could not identify. The lift hummed around them, sending vibrations up her legs. She cleared her throat, wanting something to say, but couldn't think of anything.

'The radio; is just like a *téléphone*.' He held out the handset for her while she sat in the chair just vacated by the radio operator. The wall ahead of her was packed with small screens, lights, dials and buttons; there were another couple of telephone-type handsets, plus two other microphones.

'Thank you.'

'I will be forward, on the bridge?' He pointed; she nodded. 'When you finish, you hang the . . . the piece here.'

She nodded again. She could already hear the squeaky voice of Mr Moriya coming from the receiver in her hand. Philippe Ligny closed the door behind him, and she sighed, wondering what Mr Moriya thought important enough to track her down here.

'Hisako?'

'Yes, Mr Moriya?'

'Look, I've had an idea; supposing I hired a helicopter . . .'

Mr Moriya retired defeated after about ten minutes, mollified by the information that the canal authorities hoped to have the canal operating within a few days. She left the radio room (it smelled of . . . *electronics*, she thought to herself) and went down a short corridor to the red-lit bridge, where more tiny lights winked.

The bridge was very long (or wide, she supposed), and full of even more complicated equipment than the radio room; multifarious surfaces, levers, buttons and screens glinted in the strange ruby glow coming from the overhead lamps. The bridge's sloped windows looked out over the dark lake to the lights of the *Nakodo*, a kilometre away, and beyond that she could make out what must be the lights of Gatún, normally obscured by the various small islands between the town and the buoy-field where the ships lay moored.

She went to the ship's wheel; it was small; about the size of a sport's car's. She touched it.

'Not bad news, no?'

She jumped a little (and thought at least her blush would go unnoticed in this ruby light), and turned to Ligny, who'd come from another red-lit room just off the bridge.

She shook her head. 'No. My agent is worried; I am due to play in Europe in two weeks, and— ' she spread her hands '—well, I will be late, I suppose.'

'Ah.' He nodded slowly, looking down at her. His face was smooth-looking and somehow theatrical under the red lights. She expected the usual questions – Why hadn't she flown? Would she be going to his country? – and so on, but he just looked slowly away. She noticed he was holding a clipboard. He glanced at it. 'Excuse me,' he said. 'I will call one of the men to take you back; I stay . . . it is my watch.'

'I can find my own way back,' she said.

'*Bien.*'

'I was just . . . ' she looked around, at the banks of controls and screens, ' . . . admiring all this machinery. So complicated.'

He shrugged. She watched his shoulders move. 'It is . . . more simple than it looks. The ship is . . . like an instrument. I think a *violoncelle* is more difficult perhaps.'

She found herself shrugging too, realising halfway through the action she was unconsciously imitating him. 'But there are only four strings on a *violoncelle*', she said. 'And one person can work it, not . . . twenty or thirty.'

'But . . . one person can work the ship,' he said. He motioned at the expanse of controls. 'We control the engine from here direct; this is the wheel; there is radar, echo sounder . . . the ah . . . machine for the anchor; we have computers and satellite location as well as paper charts . . . of course, in reality— ' (He said *réalité*; she decided she could listen to his accent for hours; days.) '—you need many more people . . . for maintenance . . . so on.'

43

She wanted to extend the moment, so moved along the edge of the controls sloped beneath the windows. 'But there's so much; so many controls.' She felt a little guilty at acting the ignorant female, but then although Officer Endo had shown her round the bridge of the *Nakodo*, she hadn't paid all that much attention. She ran her hand over one set of blank screens. 'What does this do, say?'

'Those are monitors; televisions. So that we can see the bows, stern, so on.'

'Ah. And these?' Was she being too obvious, running her fingers along the levers? This was silly, really. There was a very attractive young woman officer on this ship, much better looking than her. But what was wrong with flirting? She wasn't even really flirting, anyway. Probably he hadn't noticed; she was being over-sensitive.

'Pumps; to pump the cargo; the oil. And here . . . controls for fighting fire. Foam; water sprays.'

'Ah ha. So, you carry . . . crude oil?' She folded her arms.

'Yes. From Venezuela. We take it to Manzanillo, in Mexico . . . on the Pacific coast.'

'Ah yes. You were going in the other direction.'

He smiled. 'And so we meet.'

'Indeed,' she smiled back. He kept looking at her. She wondered how long she could keep up this eye contact.

'When I was young,' he said slowly.

'Yes?' She leant back a little, backside against the lip of the control deck.

'I was . . . I had to play the *violon* . . . violin. I tried the . . . how do you say *violoncelle*?'

'Cello.'

'Cello,' he said, smiling. 'I tried the cello, but I was not very good. I was just a little boy, you know?'

She tried to imagine him as a little boy.

'Your cello is Stradivari?' he said. He looked a little more boyish when he frowned. She nodded. *Just keep speaking, you beautiful man*, she thought. And : *What am I doing? This is absurd. What age am I supposed to be*?

'I thi – I thought he made *violons* only.'

'No, cellos too. Him, and his sons.'

'It is very good . . . cello, then.'

'Well, I like the sound it makes. That's the most important thing.' Inspiration! 'Would you like to . . . ' she gulped. 'Would you like to . . . to play it?'

He looked shocked. 'Oh no; I could not. I might hurt . . . I might damage it.'

She laughed. 'Oh, it's not so easily damaged. It looks delicate, but really . . . it's strong.'

'Ah.'

'If you would like to play it . . . if you can remember. Please do. I'd like you to. I could give you lessons, if you like.'

He looked almost bashful. She thought she could see him as a little boy, just perhaps. He looked down at the deck. 'I would be . . . is too kind of you.'

'No; I'm going to Europe to play, but also to teach. I must practise to teach as well as to play.'

He was still looking bashful. The tiny frown was there too. She wondered if she was being too obvious. 'Well . . .' he said. 'Perhaps . . . could I pay you?'

'No!' She laughed, and bent at the waist, bringing her head briefly near him. She shook her head quite hard, knowing it made her collar-length hair flare out. *What am I doing? Oh, please don't let me make a fool of myself.* 'I know,' she said. She looked down the length of the bridge. 'We'll trade. You could teach me how to work the ship.'

It was his turn to laugh. He waved the clipboard in the same direction she'd looked. 'Is . . . not really so much, not moored here. If you like, I show, you but . . .'

'Is there anything else you could teach me?' As soon as she'd said it she wanted to close her eyes and run away. She heard herself suck air in through her teeth.

'Have you ever . . . dived? With the . . . ah, aqualung?'

'Dived? No.'

'I could perhaps teach you that. I have a . . . a *système*, yes? And there is another, for the ship. I can ask *Capitaine* Herval; I think he would let you use that. Is a good trade?' His smile showed perfect teeth.

She nodded, put out her right hand, suddenly bold. 'Yes. A good trade.'

They shook on it. His hand was large and strong and cool, and he looked surprised when she met his grip with one just as firm and sure.

'That's complete crap.'

'Perhaps,' Mandamus agreed generously with Orrick. 'But it's an idea, if not a new one. Saying "that's complete crap" isn't even an idea. It's just an opinion. What is your idea?'

'I just can't believe you can be so pessimistic and . . . and still be alive. Jeez, if I felt that way I think I'd kill myself.'

'It's not pessimism,' Mandamus said. 'It's what I call the Bleak View, but it isn't pessimism. If it's right it's right. Truth is truth; I am old-fashioned in that regard. But I believe as I say; we are like a cancer. To be like a cancer in one way may be no bad thing; we live and grow. The question is how much we resemble cancer in any other way. If— '

'Just because we're smart? Is that what you're saying? Just being smart makes us bad? That's crazy.'

'You don't listen; the smartness— '

'I'm listening, I just don't believe what I'm hearing.'

'You must have heard of Gaia; the planet as organism. Well, we are the cancer in its body. Do you understand that? We were like an ordinary organ, once; part of the whole. We lived and died, we behaved ourselves like cells, existing and being replaced, just another species, preying on some species, preyed on by others . . . whether we lived or died as a species made little difference. Then; phut! Intelligence.' Mr Mandamus snapped his fingers. The younger man shook his head, drank from his beer bottle. The others were keeping quiet; even Broekman, who was sitting back in his chair looking tired and smoking a cigar, his collar undone.

Hisako glanced at Philippe, who winked at her.

'And with that,' Mandamus said, 'everything changes. We invent ways to blow up the world, but before that we start destroying other species; the other organs of the Gaia body. And we change her body. Oh, shake your head, Steven, but come with me to Alexandria; come to Venice. Alexandria becomes Venice, Venice Atlantis. The waters are rising; the ice is melting and the waters are rising. What we do means everything now. Whether we

46

survive or not matters not just to us but to all the other species we take down with us if we go under. Because we have the drives of any species; to live, to breed, to spread. But we have this extra thing, this consciousness nothing else has.'

'Yeah, what about whales?'

'Fah; if they were so smart they wouldn't let us kill them so easily. They'd post look-outs, they'd avoid all ships, or ships smaller than a certain size, or ships that turn towards them, or— '

'Maybe they are. Maybe some of them are but we just can't— '

'No; they can't hide from satellites,' Mandamus said quickly, and made a motion as though brushing this aside. 'But there we are; whales are intelligent, for animals; they are big, they are impressive and beautiful . . . but we kill them, we make them extinct because there is money in it, because we've made it easy; because we can. So we spread ourselves, and kill everything else. Only our intelligence lets us do this; it is what takes us beyond the "stop" message all other species have; they are limited by their specialisation, by the adaptation they have made to fit their niche. We take our niche with us; even into space. Thus we threaten to metastasise.'

'So we're just doing what we're supposed to do', Orrik said. 'And if we kill off other species maybe they should have been smarter. It's the smart survive; it isn't our fault if we're too smart for anybody else.'

Mandamus made a spluttering noise, and drained the rum he'd been drinking, shaking his head and wiping his mouth. 'Young man— '

'Christ,' said Broekman.

They looked at him. He came tipping forward on his seat, its front legs thudding into the deck. Those on that side of the table were following his gaze. Hisako turned with the others.

The sky to the west was flickering with silent blue-white bursts of light. Silhouetted against the unsteady flarings were the hills on the west side of the lake. The underbellies of the clouds snapped in and out of view with the fierce strobing of the light, like folds of cloth hung in some vast hall. Half the horizon glittered and danced. Gatún Lake reflected it all, a distorted mirror held up to the edge of the sky gone

47

crazy. The outline of *Le Cercle* sat upon the livid image like a toy.

'What the *fuck* is that?' Orrick breathed.

'L – language,' Mr Mandamus said, absently but shakily. 'Is it just . . . lightning?'

Points of flame appeared beneath the clouds; they blossomed and spread like vast slow fireworks, rubbing an unnatural sunlight on to the sagging undersurfaces of the clouds, then falling in a thousand curved yellow streaks towards the ground. Arcing coruscations flicked to and fro across the sky, winking out or disappearing in the clouds like red and silver sparks.

The first cracks and rumbles broke over them.

'That isn't lightning,' Broekman said.

The noises increased in volume and became more various, scattering into bizarre whizzes and screams against a background of sharp bangs and muffled crumping sounds.

Captain Bleveans stood up. 'I guess we better get inside. Mr Janney,' he turned to one of the *Nadia*'s junior officers, 'see what we're getting over the radio. Get Harrison to try the low-tech military bands; even if we can't unscramble it we can get an idea of the traffic. Ladies, gentlemen . . . ?'

'I think I go back to my ship,' Philippe said, rising with the rest. People began to follow Janney, who'd almost run through the nearest door into the ship.

'I too,' Endo said. He looked at Mandamus, Orrick and Hisako. 'You may be best to stay here.'

'I— ' Hisako began. She didn't know what to do; stay, go back to the *Nakodo*, go with Philippe?

'Inside, first, please,' Bleveans said. They were ushered into the ship.

The horizon was a billowed cliff of light and darkness split with fissures of fire.

It stopped after a few minutes. A dull glow was left in a few places, as the rumbles faded away from distant hills. The officers had waited a few minutes to find out what could be heard on the *Nadia*'s radio. It was silent. Whatever had happened, whatever sort of action or bombardment had taken place, it had done so without the accompaniment of any signals the ship's civilian communications gear was capable of picking up.

They used the VHF to contact a sleepy policeman in the office at Frijoles; he'd thought it was thunder. At Gatún the guards officer they talked to said he'd seen and heard it but didn't know what it was; they were awaiting orders from Panama and would probably send out a patrol in the morning.

They gave it a half-hour or so, crowding into the officers' mess and drinking some more. Hisako listened to them all, and to herself, and heard the sounds people make when they don't know whether to be frightened or not. The talk was light, jittery, inconsequential. Mandamus and Orrick did not return to their argument.

'Hisako-*chan*, you are not afraid?' Philippe asked her.

'No.' She held his hand. She'd stood in a corner, watching the rest. Standing close, he almost blotted out the rest of the crowded room for her.

'And now we must go.'

'Can I come back with you?'

That tiny frown, drawing in his black eyebrows. 'I think it isn't so good idea. We are closer to the *combat* and also . . . a tanker.' He squeezed her hand. 'I have to worry for the ship. To worry for you too . . . '

'That's all right.' She stood on tip-toes and kissed him. 'Take care.'

They went down to the water, down the long ladder at the side of the ship. The sky was milky in places, coming and going like some soft aurora. The boat hadn't arrived, but they could hear it coming through the fogbank.

She knelt down at the edge of the pontoon and looked at the water. The people behind her were still. She couldn't see their faces.

Whatever was wrong with the water? It was slopping and splashing very oddly and slowly; it looked wrong.

She drew back the arm of the kimono, reached down.

The water was warm and thick. The trees on the nearby islands looked very green. They floated above the creamy fog. The black prow of the first boat was appearing through the swirling mist.

49

The water felt slippy and too hot. She could smell it now; something of iron . . . for a moment she thought she couldn't withdraw her hand, but it did come out, though it seemed to resist, sucking at her hand, wrist, forearm. Her fingers were stuck together.

The sun came out, flooding everything in light. She looked at the blood dripping from her hand, wondering how she'd cut herself.

The blood dribbled down her arm to her elbow, and dripped from there and from her blood-glued fingers, falling in slow, ruby droplets down to the lake. But it was blood too. The whole lake. She lifted her gaze, from the red lapping tide at her feet, out across the calm, smooth surface, to the islands and the black boats. In the distance, a woman came up through the red surface, making a strange, plaintive hooting noise, and holding something tiny but bright between thumb and forefinger of one hand. Hisako felt her vision zooming in: the pearl was the colour of the fog and cloud.

The stench of blood overpowered her, and she fell.

Into her pillow. She dragged her face out, breathing heavily, looked round the cabin.

A chink of brightness where the curtain over one porthole let in light. The soft red glow of her old alarm clock on the cabinet, numerals refracted and reflected in the tumbler of water alongside.

She got up on one elbow, feeling her heart thud, and sipped at the water. It had become warm and tasted thick and stale. She fumbled her way out of the bed, to go to the bathroom and get some more.

On the way back she pulled aside the curtain over a porthole. The lit stretch of deck she could see looked the same as it ever did. She was looking in the direction of whatever had happened in the hills to the west, but if there was still any glow left in the sky, it was quite drowned by the *Nakodo*'s own lights.

4: Water Business

She hadn't thought it would be so beautiful. The rugged, lumpy little hills around the canal were covered in trees displaying a hundred different shades of green, broken here and there by clumps of bushes and stretches of grass smothered with bright blossoms. She had imagined low wastes of monotonous jungle, but here was a landscape of such variety of texture and shade, and such delicacy of proportion, she could almost imagine it was Japanese. The canal itself was impressive enough, but – save when the ship had entered the gloomy depths at the bottom of one of the massive locks – its scale was not as oppressive as she'd expected. As the ship slowly rose past the enclosing walls, floating on a raft of swirling water, the manicured grasslands and neat buildings surrounding each great double set of locks came gradually into view.

At the same time, she thought, something of the smoothness and massiveness of the operation, the sensation of inevitability and contained power involved in the raising of the ship in such a stately, nearly majestic fashion, somehow transferred itself to her and to the others on the ship; she thought they all became calmer and less fraught as each set of locks was negotiated, and not just because with each step along and up that ribbon of concrete and water they were closer to their goal, of release from Panama and a clear run through the Caribbean and the Gulf of Mexico.

The repairs to the prop had been completed. In that week of waiting the situation had become worse, with the *venceristas* mounting attacks on the towns of David and Penonomé and a brief raid on Escobal, which lay on the western shore of Gatún Lake itself. Worst of all, rockets had been fired at two tankers between

51

Gamboa and Barro Colorado, inside the canal. The rocket fired at the first ship had missed; another launched at the second tanker had glanced off the vessel's deck. The canal authorities had told a tanker making its way through from the Caribbean coast to moor in Gatún while the situation was assessed.

Canal traffic had dropped off sharply. Dozens of ships were tied up against the docks of Panama City and Balboa, moored in the bay, or swinging at anchor further out in the Gulf of Panama, awaiting instructions or advice from owners, charterers, insurance companies, embassies and consulates. The *Nakodo* was already late; the permission to proceed came through from Tokyo as soon as she was ready to sail.

And it all seemed so calm, so orderly and assured. The precise lines of the great locks; the tidiness of the expanses of grass, bordered by the concrete at the side of the locks like inlay edging a lacquer cabinet; the quaint-looking but powerful electric locomotives that pulled the ship through the locks; the deeply eaved, oddly temple-like buildings set at the side of the artificial canyons of the locks, or perched on the thin concrete island dividing one set from the other; the feeling of procession as the ship made its way up towards the level of the lake, as though it was a novice being gently guided, prepared and anointed and clothed for some fabulous and arcane rite in the heart of a great basilica . . . everything made the war seem distant and irrelevant, and the fuss about threats against the canal and the ships that plied it somehow undignified and paltry.

Miraflores locks, where the gush of fresh water descending from the lock above washed the Pacific's salt from the *Nakodo*'s keel; Pedro Miguel, where the buildings around the locks sat in disciplined rows like solemn spectators, and where a bulk carrier passed them, sinking in her lock as the *Nakodo* rose in hers (the crews waved to each other).

Her ascent completed, the *Nakodo* cruised quietly on, through the echoing depths of Gaillard Cut and on into the ruffled emerald landscape beyond, where the canal swung gradually towards the lake, and a train moved, outdistancing them, to their right.

They'd seen a few *Guardia Nacional*, wandering about the edges of the locks or draped over jeeps and trucks parked on the various roads, or sitting smoking in the shade of the canal buildings . . . but they'd looked nonchalant, unconcerned, and waved back as the ship passed.

Hisako had been allowed on to the bridge after making great entreaties; Captain Yashiro was worried that if the ship was attacked, any sensible guerrilla would aim at the bridge. However he had finally compromised by agreeing she could stay on the bridge until they approached Gamboa. But it was all so tranquil, so patently normal, that she was pleased but not at all surprised when Gamboa slipped by to starboard, and she was not asked to leave the bridge and go below.

The Panama Canal Commission pilot was chatting in English to Officer Endo. Gamboa, and the mouth of the upper reaches of the Chagres River, moved slowly astern; the train which had overtaken them earlier left the town and passed them again, carriages rocking and wheels singing, only a few hundred metres away. The morning sun slanted over them, between small clouds which speckled shadows over the forested slopes. Only in a few places could she see the naked hillsides where the trees had been cut down and gullies and ravines had formed, scarring the smooth green land. The Commission pilot had said something about problems in the hills; trees cut down, topsoil washed away, dams silting up and so decreasing the available water the canal required to keep functioning. She hadn't thought of that; of course, the canal could not operate without water at its head; water was its currency.

Gatún Lake. They moved under a slightly hazy sun, through the vague shafts of cloud shadows, with the land starting to shimmer on each side and the V of the ship's bow-wave breaking against the shores further and further away.

They cleared Barro Colorado, leaving the island nature reserve behind to port. There must have been a little tension on the bridge after all, because she noticed that people talked a little more now they were past the section the two tankers had been attacked in.

They were in the main part of the lake now. Ahead of them, across the sparkling waters of the lake, its lines sharp and definite against the jumbled greenery of the lake's scattered islands, lay the lone tanker the authorities had told to remain there while the current emergency existed.

It was French, registered in Marseille, and called *Le Cercle*.

They didn't hear or see the explosion at Gatún, but the VHF call came through just as they were passing the moored tanker, and the masts of another ship – the *Nadia* – were appearing over the trees of Barro Colorado island, behind them.

They'd told her, her mother had told her, Mr Kawamitsu had told her, but she hadn't thought they were serious; she had to leave her mother and go to live in Tokyo to attend the Academy. For months, whole seasons, at a time. She was twelve. She didn't think it was allowed to desert somebody who was just little, but everybody seemed to think it was for the best, even her mother, and Hisako didn't even hear her weep the night after the confirmed offer of the bursary and place came through. Hisako looked at the palms of her hands that night – it was so dark she wasn't sure whether she could see them or not – and thought, *So this is the way the world works, is it?*

She felt oddly remote from her mother over the next few months, and really didn't seem to feel very much when she was taken to Sapporo station to board the train. She was looking forward to the ferry journey; that was about it. Her mother was embarrassingly emotional, and hugged her and kissed her in public. As the train pulled out, Hisako stayed at the carriage door, face expressionless, waving goodbye, more because she felt it was expected of her than because she wanted to.

At the Academy everybody seemed cleverer and wealthier than she, and the cello lessons very basic. They were taken to hear the NHK; she preferred it when there wasn't a cello work on the bill, because when there was she couldn't help listening to learn, rather than just to enjoy. On Sundays the hostel children were usually taken round an art gallery or museum, or into the countryside; Hakone, Izu, and the Fuji Five Lakes, which was much more fun. She got to climb things and go on ferries.

To her dismay, the Academy teachers were just as scathing about her academic performance as the teachers in Sapporo had been. She remained convinced she had actually learned vast amounts throughout her life, and they were just asking the wrong questions. She came top in English, about average in her cello class, close to bottom in everything else.

Hokkaido was clean and clear and empty after Tokyo, on her first vacation, and fairly deserted and unspoiled even compared to the countryside west of Tokyo. Her mother took her walking in the woods, like in the old days. Once, the two of them sat beneath some pine trees overlooking a broad valley, watching the warm wind stroke slow patterns across wide fields of golden grain beneath them, and the tiny dots of cattle moving on the green swell of a hill on the far side. Her mother told her how she'd cried the night Hisako had left for Tokyo, but that really, she was sure, they were tears of happiness. Hisako felt ashamed. She hugged her mother, and put her head in her lap, though she did not cry.

She coped with Tokyo, she mourned for Hokkaido. Sundays were still her favourite days. Sometimes a group of them was allowed to go out without a teacher. They said they were going to museums but they really went to Harajuku to watch the boys. They strolled down Omote-Sando Boulevard, trying to look mature and sophisticated. Hisako's command of English began to be admired. She still came top in that, and her other grades were improving (not that that would have been difficult, as all the teachers pointed out), and she won a prize in the Academy's cello competition. She'd never won a prize in anything before, and enjoyed the experience. She wanted to use the small amount of money involved to buy some new clothes, but her mother's last letter had talked about a part-time job in a bar, so she sent the money home instead.

Another year; another too brief visit home to Hokkaido. The pace of Tokyo life, the urge to do as well in exams as any other child but to be a musical prodigy as well, even the regularity of the seasons; cold, mild, hot, stormy, warm; Fuji invisible for weeks then suddenly there, floating on a sea of cloud, a flurry of cherry blossom lasting hardly longer than a pink snowstorm . . . all seemed to conspire to sweep her life away from under her. Her grades went on improving, but the teachers seemed to make a special effort to remind her how important they were. She read novels in English; book in one hand, dictionary in another. She won all the Academy's cello prizes. She spent some on clothes, sent the rest home. She was getting used to the remarks about having a cello between her legs.

The Academy offered her a bursary for another three years; somehow she'd expected they would, but she didn't know whether to take it or not. Her mother said she must; Mr Kawamitsu said she must; the Academy said she must. So she supposed she had to.

Philippe had hoped there might be fish in the lake that would be attracted to their lights, as well as simply desiring the novelty of diving at night. So far, in their day-time dives, they had seen hardly any fish. The aquatic life in Gatún Lake had suffered twice over. First there had been a series of algae blooms caused by fertilisers washed down from the distant hills around Madden Lake and the far western shores of Gatún itself; then the fish and plants had been affected recently by deforestation chemicals used in the early stages of the war. The scientific station on Barro Colorado said the lake was safe to swim in again, but the plant community and fish stocks were recovering very slowly.

Philippe's blue flippers waved back at her. The lake felt warmer than it did during the day, which surprised her. Perhaps it wasn't really any warmer; perhaps it just seemed so because she expected the dark depths to be cold.

The sense of placelessness, of being contained and cut off yet somehow free as well, was intensified by the darkness. With the day's silvery surface removed, the limit of visibility became what their lights could illuminate, and the lake felt both tinier and greater than it had before; tinier because at any moment they could see only a short distance around them, and so could have been swimming in some small pool, but greater because there was no immediate way of telling the surface was not far above, and the floor not far beneath.

Using the lights, the lake waters became like some swirling and disturbed version of space; in the white beams of their lamps a galaxy of minute particles was revealed, each mote glowing against the darkness like a swiftly passed star. Colours were more vivid, too, though there was little enough to see; just the blue of Philippe's stroking flippers and the bright orange of the line he was paying out behind them, to lead them back to the Gemini. She pointed her lights straight down, and saw the floor of the lake gliding greyly by, smooth and ghostly and quiet.

*　　*　　*

The National Guard reported there had been a *venceristas* bombardment of Escobal and Cuipo, followed by a retaliatory strike by Panamanian Air Force jets. This was the official explanation for the fireworks on the night of the *Nadia*'s party. The incident made the Channel 8 news, briefly. Reading between the lines, it appeared as though whatever had first happened hadn't warranted the pyrotechnics they'd seen unleashed.

'Bullshit,' Broekman said, leaning against the *Nakodo*'s rail. He had come up from the engine room for a cigar, and met Hisako sitting near the stern on a deck chair, reading. She joined him at the rail, looking out to the heat-wavering line of green hills; the bombardment had taken place somewhere behind them.

'You don't believe that?' she said.

Broekman spat the stub of the cigar down to the waters of the lake, and watched it drift slowly under the stern. 'Ah, it all sounds very plausible . . . more plausible than what we saw, perhaps . . . but it wasn't what we saw. It all started at once, and I didn't hear any jets. The PAF wouldn't get everything that coordinated anyway; God help us, they'd probably have bombed us if they had been around.'

'I thought that was why we keep all our lights on.'

'Yes, good theory, isn't it?' Broekman laughed, clasped his hands over the rail. 'Never convinced me.' He spat into the water, as if aiming for the cigar stub. 'First time any terrs take to the water at night, and the Guard call up air support . . . we'll get clobbered. You watch. Excitable bastards; just as well the Yanks don't let them fly at night.'

The last two days had been peaceful. The only unusual activity they'd noticed had been a couple of National Guard patrol boats, venturing out from Gatún and Frijoles to disturb the peace with their droning outboards. Broekman had watched the inflatables with binoculars, claiming he half-expected them to be towing water-skiers.

Hisako had ventured out on deck after lunch. Her cello practice took up about two hours each day, but that was what she thought of as her 'tick-over' rate; it would take the prospect of a proper master class or a concert in the near future for her to summon up the enthusiasm to practise more thoroughly. She did some keep-fit in her cabin; her own mixture of Canadian Air

Force exercises and aikido movements. But that could only hold her interest for about an hour, so she still had a lot of time left to fill each day, and got bored watching television in the passengers' lounge or the officers' mess. Mr Mandamus's appetite for interminable games of chess and gin rummy seemed undiminished, but she could only take so much. That was why she'd been teaching him *go*. To her surprise, there wasn't a *go* set on any of the ships, so she'd made one, drawing the grid on the back of an outdated chart and scrounging three hundred washers from the ship's stores; half brass, half steel.

Philippe had radioed again that morning; they could go diving tonight, if there were no further excitements. She'd agreed.

'Well,' she said. 'It all seems peaceful enough.'

'Mmm.' Broekman sounded unconvinced.

'Though Panama seemed peaceful, until that explosion,' she admitted, trying to imagine what he was thinking. 'And the canal seemed peaceful, until they blew up the lock . . . and sank that ship in Limón Bay.' She shrugged. ' "Third time lucky",' she quoted. 'Don't they say that?'

Broekman nodded. 'They say that. But then there's the third light off the one match, too.' Broekman snorted. 'They also say look before you leap, and he who hesitates is lost . . . so take your pick.'

'Three is unlucky? I thought it was thirteen.'

'Three if you're lighting cigarettes. Thirteen for voyages.'

'In Japan, four is an unlucky number.'

'Hnn,' Broekman said. 'Just as well we don't have another ship here then.'

'I wonder if the Panamanians have an unlucky number,' she said, still watching the hills. 'I liked Panama. The city, I mean.'

'It was all right,' Broekman agreed. He inspected his thick, blunt fingernails. 'Very . . . cosmopolitan.' He was silent for a while longer, then added, 'We might have had something like that where I come from. Hnn.' He pushed himself away from the rail and clapped his hands together. 'Well; no rest for the wicked.' He winked at her enquiring expression. 'They say that, too.'

She went back to her book.

*   *   *

She'd taught him the rudiments of cello playing. He took to it quickly, though he would never be very good, she thought, even if he wanted to be; his hands were the wrong shape and probably not supple enough (but she got to touch those hands). He began teaching her to dive. He was experienced, qualified to tutor others in diving, which made it all even more correct and proper, and pleased her. They swam and dived, and she was adolescently, roguishly delighted by the slim, muscled body he revealed. They swam beneath the boats, inspected the buoys they were moored to, investigated the floor of the lake, with its felled, drowned forests and traces of roads and trails, and swam round some of the islets near by, circling the summits of the mostly drowned hills under the quicksilver carpet of waves.

He talked, in a self-mocking but still fascinated way, about how some day he'd like to dive in the harbour of Portobelo, on the Atlantic coast of Panama; the body of the English sailor Francis Drake had been buried there in a lead coffin. Imagine finding that!

She thought that it must happen, then that it never would. She went through brief storms of despair and elation, never trusting herself to believe fully that she really wanted it to happen, never able entirely to stop thinking about him. She discovered he was married; depression. But they were unofficially separated, both thinking about it; elation. She found that Marie Boulard, the junior officer on *Le Cercle*, didn't interest him, even annoyed him a little; elation. But then that they had had a brief liaison; depression (and dismay that she was depressed and a little jealous). She started to wonder if really he was gay; depression. Then she told herself it was good to have a friend, and if he was gay it would probably just make them even more relaxed together and they might become close friends; pretended joy, faked resignation.

He likes me because he spends so much time with me. He only pretends because there's nothing else to do. He's humouring me; I'm old and pathetic and he won't even have thought about it and if I made a move he'd be revolted, feel it was like his mother making a pass at him. No, he really does like me and he doesn't want to say or do anything because he feels he'll lose me as a friend, and I ought to flirt more obviously to encourage him.

But if I do he might think me ridiculous; I might be ashamed, and this is a small community; not Tokyo, not Sapporo, not a university . . . more like the size of an orchestra. An orchestra on tour, living in the same hotels; that was probably closest. Settle for a friend, then . . .

And so she went round in circles, on the trapped ship.

She moved his fingers over the neck of the cello, bending her head and neck near him. She stood behind him; he sat on a chair in her cabin. Another lesson. More delicious frustration.

'Hmm; that perfume?'

'Kantule,' she told him, frowning as she tried to form his fingers into the right shape. 'I bought it in Panama, remember?'

'Ah yes.' He paused, and they both watched her place his fingers just so on the neck of the instrument, trapping the strings at the appropriate points. 'When I was in Japan,' he said, 'few women wear the perfume.'

She smiled, finally satisfied with the shape of his hand. She shifted, taking up his hand holding the bow. 'Oh, we wear it, though perhaps not very much,' she said. 'But then I'm very Westernised.'

She smiled, turned to look at him.

Very close. She felt the smile falter.

'Kantule,' he nodded, shaping the word just as she had. 'It is very nice I think.' She found herself watching his mouth. He sniffed, frowned minutely. 'No, it is gone again.'

Her heart thudded. He was looking into her eyes. Her heart! He must hear it, must feel it, through her breast, her blouse, his shirt and shoulder; he must!

She leant forward a little over his shoulder, so that she looked down the length of the cello. She raised her hand – the hand that had held his fingers to the cello neck – to her own neck. She moved her hair aside to reveal her ear, then with one finger flexed it forward slightly. '*Ici*,' she said, quietly.

They found the wrecked boat when the line was almost fully paid out. Philippe had been swinging his lights from side to side and, at the extremity of one sweep, they both saw something white flash against the darkness, on the lake floor. When the beam returned, it showed a straight white line; an edge of some sort. It looked artificial, something shaped by humanity. Philippe pointed, looking back. She nodded. The orange line made a perfect curve as they swooped towards the white triangle.

The boat was six or seven metres long; open, with no sign of a mast or rigging. It was fibreglass, and it lay, without any obvious sign of damage, flat upon the floor of the lake. There was a layer of mud inside it, perhaps a quarter of a metre deep. She wondered how long ago it had foundered, and how accurately you could date its sinking from the depth of mud inside. It had, probably, been a fishing boat; a few pieces of string or line moved like tendrils in the mud within its bows, and some netting protruded from its centre-line, waving in the water like odd, graphed weeds. Philippe moved to the boat's stern, and found its outboard motor, missed initially because it was black and comparatively small. He pointed enthusiastically.

Then, like the sound of a ghost, she heard an outboard.

She stiffened, felt her eyes go wide. A brief panic seized her and she struggled for breath. She breathed, listened. Philippe still didn't seem to have noticed; he was inspecting the drowned engine.

Whirr; a shrill, distinctive noise, burbling in her ears. She shook her head but it was still there. It was a relief when she saw Philippe look up, his face behind the mask looking surprised, even shocked. She nodded and pointed from her ear to the surface, then at the outboard he still held.

The noise came closer. She thought she could hear not one high-revving propeller, but several. Philippe gestured hurriedly at her, fiddled with his lights, gesticulating at them. They blinked out. She realised immediately, and switched hers off.

The darkness was absolute. The moon was only a sliver, and the clouds had moved over in late afternoon, blanketing the skies above the lake. The ships were a kilometre or more away. She was blind. The water moved round her limbs, the lights felt weightless in her hand. She let go of them, just to feel the slight tug on her wrist as the lanyard tightened, gently trying to pull her to the surface. Then she pulled the lamps back again. The prop noise swelled, like something angry and vindictive; a drowning whine.

A dark force seemed to gather in her throat, as though a sea

61

snake had wrapped itself round her neck. She fought it, struggling to breathe again, trying to concentrate on the high, gargling sound of the approaching boats, but the feeling increased, blocking her air passage, making her gorge rise. She brought her hands up to her mask, to her neck. Nothing there; nothing round her neck.

Hisako went limp, relaxing, giving in to whatever it was.

She hung there, arms limp, one hand hanging at her side, the other hand raised over her head by the slightly positive buoyancy of the lights, her legs dangling and her head down, on her chest, her eyes closed.

Slowly, the asphyxia started to loosen its hold on her.

She wondered if she was sinking or rising.

tic tic tic.

Ah.

The noise of the boats peaked and passed. Her flippers met the soft mud of the lake bottom, and she kept on going down, her legs buckling slowly, knees folding. She felt the cool mud waft up around her thighs. She stopped like that, in equilibrium.

There. She tested herself, taking a few deep breaths. No problem. Hisako opened her eyes, looked around at nothing but darkness. She brought her watch up, to make sure she could still see as well as to check the time. The luminous face glowed dimly at her. They'd only been down ten minutes; lots of air left.

The sound of the outboards cut suddenly. She brought her lights down so that she could grasp them again.

She tried to remember which way the foundered boat might be. Perhaps she ought to search for it, try to find Philippe. But she might get it wrong; head off in the wrong direction. She could try going in ever-increasing circles, until she found the line that led back to the boat . . . if she didn't swim under or above it.

She could kick to the surface; it was calm and she would be able to orient herself by the moored ships and find the Gemini. But whoever was in the boats that had gone overhead and then stopped might see her.

She would wait here for a while; for ten minutes. Or until she saw Philippe's lights again, or heard the boats move off. She undid the pop-fastener on the big diver's knife hanging at her hip, as much to reassure herself she was doing everything she could do in the circumstances as to ready herself for a fight.

She knelt in the soft mud, submerged in darkness, breathing slowly, looking around every now and again.

The high whine came again after seven minutes; one outboard, then two . . . perhaps one more. She turned her head in the direction the noises seemed to come from. She'd wait till they disappeared entirely, then give it another minute before turning on her lights.

A light! It was far away, twinkling like a tiny drowned star, but it was real; blanked out by her hand, and disappearing when she blinked. She kicked once out of the mud, then again to free herself from its slack grip. She swam towards the light. It disappeared, wobbling and dimming then extinguishing, but she kept towards it. It reappeared, a little stronger this time, and started to resolve into two lights, not one. It dimmed, all but disappeared. And then came back; definitely two lights. She swam on, brought her own lamps in front of her.

She was about to put them on when she thought, *What if it isn't him?* She hesitated, kicking less powerfully, though still heading for the twinned, distant glow. Finally she brought the knife out of its sheath and held it alongside the lights in front of her.

She switched them on.

The lights in the distance started to dim again, then jerked back, wobbled up and down. She did the same. It had to be Philippe. She kept the knife where it was.

Philippe turned the lights on his own face when she was about three metres away. Flooded with the relief, she copied that too.

She swam straight into him, ramming him, hugging him, lights floating, knife clenched awkwardly in her fist, trying to keep it away from his back and his air hoses.

'I don't know,' he said, when they'd kicked to the surface. She could just make out the white smudge of his face. 'But they had no . . . navigation lights? I think military. I . . .' she thought he was going to say something more, but he didn't.

They bobbed in the water, directly above where they'd met. She sheathed her knife, looked towards the trio of distant ships.

63

She listened for the noise of outboard engines, but couldn't hear anything.

'Where were you? Where did you go?' she asked.

'I swam up; towards them,' he told her. 'I heard them talking, but it was . . . *espagnol*.'

'What now?' She spat some water out, looked round for their Gemini.

'Back to the ship.' He looked round too.

'I lost the line,' he said. He nodded in the direction she was looking. 'You think that way to the Gemini?'

'I think so.'

'Me too.'

They set off, keeping the ships to their right. She was waiting for an explosion; a sudden flare of light, a livid mushroom cloud from *Le Cercle*, or a burst of gunfire, the water leaping around them, a sudden sledge-hammer blow to the exposed back of her skull . . . but they swam on, the noise of their own progress through the water the only sound.

A glint in the distance, a little to the left. She squinted. There; again. 'Philippe-*chan*,' she whispered. 'Over there.' She moved to him and pointed, lining his face up with her arm. The tiny glint again; perhaps the ships' lights reflecting on the glistening hull of the inflatable.

'*Magnifique*. And I thought all *japonais* are wearing . . . *les lunettes*, no?' She saw him make circles in front of his eyes with his fingers.

She giggled in spite of herself.

They climbed into the Gemini, sat breathing hard for a while. Philippe shook his head. 'Should have brought a radio.' He looked at the outboard. 'Well, sometime we have to start it.'

They both kept down as they headed back to the ships. The Gemini bumped against the pontoon; he left her to moor the boat while he sprinted up to the deck.

She met him there a few minutes later, as she arrived at the top of the steps carrying both sets of scuba gear. He laughed when he saw her, took both of them from her. 'Hisako; I'm sorry. You did not have to lift mine too.'

'It's all right,' she panted. 'Everything all right?'

'Certainly,' he nodded, looking briefly at the gauge on his

64

air tank, then stopping, frowning at it. 'Everything is all right,' he continued. 'I radioed; no one has seen any boats.'

'Something wrong?' she tried to look at the air gauge too.

'Is stuck. I go down to engineering; you have shower.'

She went up to his cabin, showered and dressed, then wondered why she had dressed, and considered whether she ought to undress again. She was looking out of one of the portholes, wondering if she'd heard a motor, when he came back. 'I try with new cylinder; the . . . point thing . . . ' he gestured, frowning.

She smiled. ' "Point thing?" '

'*Oui. Sur le cadran.*' He mimed a circle with a pointer inside it.

'The needle,' she said, laughing at his clumsy miming.

'Yes; the needle is stuck, is all. I fix tomorrow.' He skinned off his damp T-shirt. The intercom buzzer sounded. '*Merde*,' he breathed, lifting the phone. '*Oui?*' He listened. '*Moment.*' He hung up, grabbed a dry towel from the rail in the shower room and wriggled out of his pants, moving to the wardrobe. 'Is Endo, over on launch. Wants to talk.'

She watched him dry himself roughly and haul on trousers and a shirt. He flicked his hair into a semblance of order, dragged a comb through it once. She lay on the bed, still watching him, smiling to herself. He went to the door, looked back at her. 'Why you dress?' he asked, looking surprised.

She shrugged slowly. 'Forgot.' She rolled over and undid a button at the wrist of her blouse. 'Don't be too long.'

So she did undress, and slid between the crisp white sheets, and cuddled herself for a moment, a thrill running through her, and she moved herself in the tightly made bed, just to feel the cool sheets on her skin. She put the main cabin light out, leaving the bedside lamp on.

The intercom buzzed, making her jump. She left it. It sounded again, twice, and she got up out of the bed. '*Merde*,' she muttered.

'Hisako,' Philippe said.

'Philippe. Yes?'

'Please come to the officers' mess.' He hung up.

There was no dialling tone; the handset was dead in her hand. She looked at it, slowly hung it up.

She didn't put on her jeans and blouse; she went to the closet and took out a *yukata*, a kind of light kimono, and – dressed in that – went down to the officers' mess, suddenly nervous.

When she started in through the door she was caught by one arm and dragged to one side. The room was full; she looked quickly round, saw what looked like the entire crew there; Lekkas, Marie, Viglain. . . . It was only when she saw Philippe, standing grimly at the end of the mess-room table, that she realised the hand holding her wrist wasn't his; she'd just assumed that nobody else would touch her like that.

She looked into the unknown face of the man who was holding her. He wore dark National Guard battle-fatigues; he was blacked up, but sweating through it. His beret wasn't National Guard issue; there was a little red-star badge on the front. His voice sounded vaguely Latin as he turned to Philippe and said, 'That is all, Captain?'

'I am not captain,' Philippe said dully. 'That is all.' He nodded. 'There are no more.' Endo sat at Philippe's side. There were three other battle-fatigued men standing against the same wall as her, levelling guns at Philippe and the rest.

Hisako twisted her wrist to free it from the man's grasp, and started to feel angry and think about forcing the issue. Then she looked down, and saw the man was holding a small gun with a long, curved magazine, a stubby nightsight and a short barrel, which was pointing into her kidneys.

She thought the better of trying to apply the way of gentleness.

The man looked at her and smiled; white teeth in the blackened face. 'Welcome to the party, Señora. We are from the People's Liberation Front of Panamá, and you have just been liberated.'

CASUS BELLI

casus belli (kas*us* bĕ′li *or* kahz*us* bĕ′lĭ) *n.* Act or situation justifying or precipitating war. [L]

5: Concentration

They had gone to the *Nakodo* first. The men in the first
boat were wearing National Guard uniforms, but anyway weren't
spotted until they were on board; nobody had heard the muffled
outboards on their Gemini. They went straight to the bridge and
radio room, taking both over without a fight; they had silenced
pistols and boxy-looking Uzi sub-machine-guns, and nobody had
been foolish enough to argue with them. Another Gemini had
whispered out of the darkness and unloaded more – and more
heavily armed – men, while the first boat made for the *Nadia*,
taking Endo with them to further reassure the *Nadia*'s crew if
they were challenged. They were seen approaching, and met
when they came on deck. Endo asked to see Bleveans. The
captain was having dinner with the other officers and his wife;
they put a gun to Mrs Bleveans's head, and told her husband
to summon the radio operator. Officer Janney was on the bridge
when the *venceristas* went to take it over. He tried to fight, and
was pistol-whipped. That was the end of any resistance on the
Nadia. The second inflatable off-loaded *venceristas* on to the ship
while the Gemini of fake National Guards took Endo over to *Le
Cercle*. By the time Philippe had made his radio calls to the other
two ships, they had already been taken over, guns pointing at the
heads of the radio operators as they told Philippe everything was
just fine.

'I am Comrade Major Sucre,' the man who'd caught her arm
said; he waved her to a seat. 'We have taken over your ships for
a little while. Please be patient. You do not try to hurt us, we
won't hurt you. OK?' He looked round the mess at the silent
people. The officers and Hisako sat at one end of the table, the

crew – some French, most Moroccan and Algerian – either sat at the other end, or on the floor.

'OK?' the Comrade Major repeated sharply.

Finally, Philippe said, 'Yes.' He looked at some of the Moroccan seamen sitting near by. 'Can I say what you just said in French? These men do not understand English.'

Sucre smiled. 'OK.' He hefted his assault rifle. 'But you remember we have the guns.'

Philippe spoke to the others. The men nodded; a few grinned at the *venceristas*, gave a thumbs-up sign.

'Good,' said Sucre. 'You sit here now; I come back soon.' He put one finger to his lips. '*Y, silencio, huh?*' Sucre left the mess, taking two of the other armed men with him. The two *venceristas* who were left stood at either side of the door. They had come off the second Gemini; they wore black fatigues and black berets with red-star badges like the one Sucre had worn. They cradled nightsighted assault rifles with long, curved magazines; they had automatic pistols stuffed into their belts, extra assault-rifle magazines webbed to their belts, and two small round grenades attached to their combat jackets near their shoulders. One of them slowly wiped his forehead and cheeks with a cloth, rubbing off most of the black night-camouflage.

Hisako looked at Philippe, sitting expressionless at the head of the table, hands flat on the surface. He looked at her after a moment. She smiled. He gave a small twitch of his lips, seemed as though he was about to nod, then looked up at their two guards, and fixed his eyes on the area of table between his hands.

Sucre came back in, alone, clipping what looked like a small radio to his belt. He put his hands on his hips, looked round at them all. 'You behave yourself? Good. Gonna take you on a boat trip; you're going to the other ship, OK? The *Nadia*.' He turned to one of the other *venceristas* to say something, then saw Philippe standing up slowly at the far end of the room.

Sucre turned back. 'Yes, Captain?'

'You mean, we all go?'

'Yeah; everybody.'

'I cannot; I have to stay. This ship is my . . .' He seemed to be searching for the right word. Sucre took the automatic pistol from his belt and aimed it at Philippe. Philippe swallowed, went

70

silent. Hisako tensed; Sucre was a metre away. She looked from Sucre to Philippe, who glanced at her.

When she looked back at Sucre, he was still looking at Philippe, but the gun was pointing straight at her. She felt her eyes widen. The automatic's muzzle looked very big and dark. She could see the rifling at the end of the barrel, producing a hole that reminded her of a gearwheel from an old-fashioned watch. A thin film of oil glistened on the gun's steel.

'Yes?' grinned Sucre. 'You come too, Captain?'

'I'm not the captain,' she heard Philippe say. 'Yes, I come too.'

Sucre stayed just as he was for a moment, then turned to look at Hisako, smiled broadly, and turned the gun round so it was in profile for her. 'Safety on, see?' he said. She nodded. He stuffed it back into his belt.

'Captain; how many people your launch hold?'

'Twelve,' Philippe sighed. Hisako took her eyes off the gun sticking out of the comrade major's belt. How dry her mouth had gone, she thought.

Sucre nodded, looked slowly round the room, lips moving soundlessly. 'OK; we take you over . . . ten each.' He pointed at her. '*Uno, dos, tres* . . .' he pointed at nine of the crewmen. '. . . *diez*. You go now. Captain, you tell them.'

Philippe told the men what was happening. Hisako stood with the rest. They were taken down to the Gemini, and with one *vencerista* sitting watching them from the bows, and a second operating the outboard with one hand while pointing his gun at them with the other, they were taken over the calm black waters of the lake to the brightly lit shape of the *Nadia*.

He was her bow; so she thought of him. The English pun amused her, though it was too obscure to try and explain. Nevertheless, it felt true; she could hold him to her, one hand at his neck and the other on the small of his back, and she was the instrument he played upon, she was the shape he pressed against and made sound, the four-folded string he touched.

She had not had very many lovers. She was sure she had not had enough to estimate the general range of male sexuality, to know how many emotional and physical octaves they could encompass, so she could not tell if she had just been a little unlucky in the past, or exceptionally fortunate now. Her bow; as matched. And sometimes as close, as complete and as one as if she was the case and he the cello, fitted and nested and secure and embraced at every point and part. They spent days and nights in her cabin, forever touching and looking at each other, and being amazed that each touch and sensation still felt so new and good, that each gaze was returned, and that each succulent act seemed only to increase the desire for more, sating and kindling at once.

It was an open secret, and she thought no one wished them ill, but they kept up the appearance of friendship only, and she didn't come to *Le Cercle* to lie with him there. That was where he had to go to work, always leaving looking regretful and tired, and so big but vulnerable she wanted to hug him for ever. And so their partings, like their couplings, were always full of touches and small caresses . . . before he was borne off by the launch that she watched all the way across, and she was left to curl up and sleep in the narrow empty bed, exhausted and slightly sore, but almost immediately aroused by just smelling his dark male scent off the sheets and pillows, already wanting him again.

Still, they found time to dive, which she enjoyed, and enjoyed even more knowing that he loved it so much and that it meant more to him having somebody else to dive with him, someone with whom he could share the joy he obviously felt, and to whom he could teach the skills he was so proud of. He kept on with his cello lessons – though she suspected he was somehow humouring her – and did indeed school her in the basics of operating an oil tanker. That she found interesting too, appreciating the ship – as he'd said – as a kind of instrument, and one which had to be maintained and kept in tune if it was to deliver all it was capable of.

Only the immobility of it all frustrated her; she could play with the satellite location system and mess around with the radar set, but the satellite read-out always displayed the same numbers, and the view on the radar only altered according to which direction the wind had swung the ship in. Still, it was fun to discover the vessel's many systems; how you could pump oil from tank to tank to keep the load as even as possible; how, from the bridge, you could monitor even something as obscure as the amount and type of metallic fragments suspended in a gearbox's

72

oil, and so determine how each gear was wearing. Keeping the terms of their trade equal, she tried to improve his English in return.

Then Captain Herval left to return to France. The shipping line had decided they would run the ship down to a skeleton crew.

She was terrified Philippe would be the next to go. The embassies and consulates advised staying put because the *venceristas* had begun a new campaign of urban terrorism which included kidnapping foreigners, but everyone thought the diplomats were being excessively cautious. A few of the *Nadia*'s crew, and Captain Yashiro of the *Nakodo*, also left for home or new ships. Captain Herval travelled to Colón to pick up another ship, but never made it; he disappeared, pulled out of his taxi by gunmen half a kilometre from the docks. The shipping line decided the crew should stay on the ship. Hisako tried not to feel glad Herval had been taken.

Philippe was in command of the *Le Cercle* now; he changed with the responsibility, but not very much. And now at least she felt comfortable with the idea of sometimes staying overnight on his ship, in his double bed.

The war went on around them, the parties did the rounds from ship to ship, the *Fantasia del Mer* made occasional trips from Gatún with supplies and mail, and some of the nearer islands in the lake were visited on picnics. On a couple of nights they saw distant flashes in the sky, and heard the dull, thudding noise of bombs and shells exploding. One afternoon a flight of PAF jets blasted overhead, a trio of glittering arrowheads trailing a brown wake of shattered air and an airport scent of used kerosene.

The *Nadia* had a large lounge; that was where they were taken. It was strange to see everybody together and yet so quiet and powerless, she thought; a little like seeing actors out of costume and away from the theatre. The people from the three ships – even those from the *Nadia* – looked just as naked and placeless, wrenched from their customary setting.

They were herded into the lounge by the *venceristas*. There were two outside the door and another inside the room, sitting on a high stool behind the bar, heavy machine-gun resting on a beer pump. The man behind the bar had told them – in broken English – that they had to keep the blinds and curtains drawn, and no, they couldn't get a drink from the bar. They were free to talk and walk about, as long as they didn't try to cross the semi-circle of small stools set a couple of metres out from the bar itself. There were two toilets at that same end of the room; they could use them so long as they went one at a time and didn't stay long.

Hisako saw the people from the *Nakodo* and went over to them, hugging Mandamus (a slobbery kiss on the cheek), Broekman (an encouraging pat on the back) and even Endo (rigid fluttering surprise).

'Dear lady, are you all right?' Mandamus enquired.

'Fine,' she told him. She felt a little foolish in her light kimono, like the one person at the party wearing fancy dress. 'What's happening?' she asked Broekman, still wearing his engineer's overalls. 'Do you know? Why are they here?'

They all sat down together on the carpet. 'Could be part of a general push,' Broekman said. 'More likely it's an ambush of some sort; I bet they're expecting the National Guard out here; something like that.' Broekman hesitated, looked around. 'Have you seen the Americans?'

'What?' She looked around, peering over the tops of chairs and couches.

'Captain and Mrs Bleveans,' Broekman said softly. 'We know they clobbered Janney, but where are the Bleveans? And Orrick?'

'I think Orrick was up in the bow, smoking, when they came aboard,' Mandamus said. He wore his usual baggy, creamy white suit.

'You didn't say that,' Broekman said, obviously surprised.

Mandamus shrugged massively. 'I just remembered. He goes there to smoke the *kif*. I have smelled it. I never wanted before to mention it.'

'Well, either they've got him but haven't brought him here like everybody else, or he's hiding . . . or escaped,' Broekman said. 'Whatever. It did occur to me the Americans might be singled out; shot, maybe. Hostages perhaps.'

'They've kept the radio operators separate, too,' Mandamus pointed out.

'I think Bleveans help Mr Janney,' Endo said. He was

obviously letting himself go; Hisako spotted his loosened tie and an undone top button.

'Could be,' Broekman agreed.

'But what should we do? This is the question.' Mandamus looked laden with the responsibility of it all.

'You mean,' Broekman said, 'should we try to escape?'

'Dig a tunnel?' Hisako couldn't resist it. They looked at her. 'Sorry.'

'Well, that *isn't* one of our options,' Broekman grinned. 'But ought we to think about trying to get away?'

'Depends on their intentions,' Mandamus said, glancing at the man behind the bar.

'They no kill us yet,' Endo said, smiling.

' . . . with us split up,' Mandamus was saying. 'They haven't *said* they will kill others if one tries to escape, but I think one has to assume this is implied. We live in an age where the etiquette of sieges and hostage-taking has become – as one might say – public domain. They assume that we know the rules. I think we have to test these assumptions before we make any hasty moves.'

'The etiquette of *hostage-taking*?' Broekman almost choked. 'What are you talking about, some avant-garde theatre show or something? These bastards are threatening to turn us into hamburger meat and you're talking about *etiquette*?'

'A turn of phrase, Mr Broekman.'

She stopped listening to them talk. She stood up and looked to the door as it opened. More of *Le Cercle*'s crew; Marie Boulard came to her and they embraced. The small Frenchwoman's hair smelled of roses; her skin of . . . some allotrope of normal human sweat; fear perhaps. Hisako looked anxiously at the door, but it closed again. Marie kissed her cheek, then sat beside Mandamus, who patted her hand. *Le Cercle*'s chief engineer, Viglain, stood before Hisako, tall and vaguely cadaverous and smelling of Gitanes. He took her solemnly by the shoulders and announced, '*Il viendra*,' in his surprisingly deep voice.

She nodded. '*Je comprends*.' (But thought, *How does he* know *he will come*?)

Viglain sat down with Marie Boulard.

She watched Broekman share a cigarette with one of the *Nakodo*'s Korean crew, and wished that she smoked.

It was another twenty minutes by her watch before they brought Philippe and the rest of the crew in. She ran to him, threw her arms round him. They were hustled further into the lounge by the armed men.

They reassured each other they were both all right, and sat with the others. Philippe and Broekman started talking about what might be going on. She half-listened, but really only wanted to sit there, holding Philippe's hand, or with her head on his shoulder. His deep voice lulled her.

She was shaken awake gently. Philippe's face looked very large and warm. He was holding her left wrist oddly. 'Hisako-*chan*, they want our watches.' He stroked her wrist with his thumb. She had to ask him to repeat what he'd said. It was still night, the lounge was warm. Comrade Major Sucre stood in front of her, assault rifle strapped over one shoulder. He was holding a black plastic bag. Philippe took off his big diver's watch and dropped it into the throat of the bag as Sucre held it out to him. She looked at her watch; she'd snoozed for less than fifteen minutes. She fumbled with the strap on the little Casio, wondering fuzzily where she'd left her own diver's watch. Probably in Philippe's cabin.

'Don't worry, lady,' Sucre said. 'You get it back when we're finished here.'

'Why do you want our watches?' she said, feeling her mouth stumble over the words. The strap resisted her. She tutted, leant forward, then Philippe held her hand, helped her.

'Hey,' Sucre said. 'You that violinist?'

She looked up, blinking, as the watch came free. 'Cellist,' she said, dropping the watch into the bag with the others. 'I play the cello.' She only realised then that she hadn't thought of the instrument; of course, it might be at risk. She formed a question to enquire after its safety, then thought the better of it.

'I heard of you,' Sucre said. 'I bet I heard your discs.'

She smiled. Sucre had wiped most of the blacking off his face. He looked young beneath it; a lean Hispanic face.

'Comrade Major,' Broekman said, putting his watch into the

bag, 'I don't suppose you're going to tell us what you're doing, are you?'

'Huh?'

'Why are you doing this? Why are you occupying the ships?'

'Is Free Panamanian Navy,' Sucre laughed. He moved off to take watches from other people. He stopped, looked back at Broekman. 'Where you from?'

'South Africa,' Broekman said.

Sucre sauntered back. 'You fascist?' he asked. Hisako felt her palms start to sweat.

Broekman shook his head. 'When I was there they called me a communist.'

'You like blacks?'

Broekman hesitated. Hisako could see him composing his reply. 'I don't like anyone automatically, Comrade Major; black or white.'

Sucre thought about this, nodding absently. 'OK,' he said, and moved off again. Hisako breathed out.

She bought a new cello with one lot of prize money. She took her old cello back to Hokkaido for the winter holiday, leaving the new one in the Academy, not knowing quite why she did this. Hisako had a decision to make. She might stay on at the Academy, or she might go to *Todai* – Tokyo University – every Japanese kid's bright shining wept-for goal. She'd known people who had broken their hearts when they could not get into Tokyo. You heard all the time of people killing themselves because they didn't get good enough grades, or because they'd failed when they got there and found the work too hard.

Did she want to do this? English at *Todai*. It would have seemed absurd just a few years ago, but her grades had improved that much; she honestly had no idea why. She thought she probably could do it; she had become a good student, and she had the enthusiasm in the subject she thought necessary to carry her through.

But was she ready for the pressure? Did she really want to be a diplomat or civil servant, or a teacher or translator? Or somebody's highly qualified wife? None of those things attracted her. She didn't particularly want to travel, for one thing, which closed off diplomacy, or marriage to a diplomat; she always felt slightly queasy at the thought of getting on a plane. And she wanted to read and speak English because she enjoyed it, not because it was her job.

But she didn't know if she wanted to play the cello for a living either. She loved that too, and thought she might be good enough to join an orchestra, but the same problem applied; anything she loved that much might be spoiled if it became her work.

As though to take her mind off it, she had become very athletic, spending more time in the Academy's gym than her cello tutors thought proper. She lost herself in the developing abilities of her body.

The ferry journey north that winter was a wild, rough affair, but she sat outside part of the time, hugging her old cello case to her, her teeth chattering, her hands raw and red in her mittens, the salt spray a taste on her lips and a cold and grainy sweat on her face, while the ship pitched and rolled and the white waves tumbled and slid, battering the ferry like one sumo wrestler slapping another out of the ring.

Her mother looked suddenly aged. Hisako sat with old friends in Sapporo cafés, and found she had little to say to them. She went to the ice festival, but found it preposterous. She did some skiing but sprained her ankle early on in the holiday and spent the rest of it either in bed or hobbling around.

She went to see Mr Kawamitsu. It was too long since she'd visited him, always finding excuses. She had called once before and, finding him out, realised she was relieved he wasn't there. But now she went in hope, and he answered the door.

Mr Kawamitsu was pleased to see her. His apartment smelled of *yuzu* and new tatami mats. Mrs Kawamitsu made tea for them.

They talked about Jacqueline du Pré. Mr Kawamitsu thought Hisako could be an oriental du Pré. Hisako laughed nervously, hand over her mouth.

'Oh . . . judo, karate, kendo . . . you have become *ninja*, Hisako,' Mr Kawamitsu said when she told him of her new-found interests.

She bowed her head, smiling.

'But this is not very feminine for a young woman,' he told her. 'So . . . aggressive. Won't you frighten off all the boys?'

'Perhaps,' she agreed, still staring at the floor. She fiddled with the cotton edging of the tatami mat.

'But perhaps that is not so bad, if you want to be a great cellist?' She bit her lip.

'Do you want to be a great cellist, Hisako?' Mr Kawamitsu asked, in a formal manner, as though it were part of a temple ceremony.

'I don't know,' she said, looking up at him, and suddenly feeling very young and somehow clear, and seeing how Mr Kawamitsu too had aged. She felt glowing and pure.

Mr Kawamitsu nodded slowly, and poured more tea.

On the ferry back she sat outside again, watching the pitching, ragged sea, and the dark veils of distant squalls. Once more, she clutched the old cello case to her, looking across the empty deck and out over the cold turbulence of sea, resting her chin on the shoulder of the cheap but – to her – precious old case, and shivering every few seconds.

After a while she stood up, crossed unsteadily to the rail on the shifting deck, lifted the cello and its case up over her head, and threw it into the water. It fell flat to the waves and hit with a thud she thought she heard. It floated off, falling astern, tossed and blown across the cold grey sea like some strange up-ended boat.

She got into trouble; somebody saw the case in the water and was sure it was a body. The ferry slowed and turned, heeling over alarmingly as it turned broadside to the storm, and headed back. She hardly noticed at the time, locked in a toilet, sobbing.

The ferry was way behind schedule anyway, but lost another couple of hours retracing its course to look for the 'body'. Incredibly in that furious sea, they found the old case, bobbing mostly underwater, just the head showing. They got a rope round it and hauled it aboard. Hisako's name was inside the case. The Academy was informed. She was punished with extra duties in the hostel, and additional lessons on a Sunday.

The old cello was ruined, of course, but she kept it, and then one Sunday in the spring, after her punishment had ceased, and while the cherry blossom painted the Tokyo parks pink, she took the water-warped cello and its salt-stained case on the train to Kofu, climbed to the bald summit of a hill to the north of the Fuji Five Lakes, and in a clearing – using several cans of lighter fluid – cremated the instrument in its battered, twisted coffin.

The cello groaned and creaked and popped as it died, and the strings snapped like whips. The flames and smoke looked pale and insubstantial against the budding trees and the bright sky, but the heated fumes, rising through the clear fresh air of spring, made Fuji itself tremble.

The warriors moved amongst the people trapped in the great room. She sat with Philippe. The room was like a vast ballroom, with a complicated ceiling. Metal beams soared overhead, painted yellow and grey but – when she looked harder – she was not sure if they supported panes of glass or not. In the huge room there were pools of water and clumps of trees and little hills covered in shrubs and flowers, and naked women moved slowly in the distance, carrying towels. Mists rose from the warm waters of the pools, curling around red ceremonial arches, which stood in the choppy waves like letters in a foreign alphabet. On a black shore, by the side of a gently steaming pool, smiling people all lying in a line were being slowly covered with dark sand.

Out in the pool, its surface half-obscured by the rising folds of vapour, a woman surfaced, wearing a black bathing cap on her head, a pair of rubber goggles over her eyes, and nose-clips on her nose. She bobbed in the water, making a sad whistling noise. In her hand, between thumb and forefinger, she held something small and lustrous and white.

She looked away from the woman. On the beach they were still being covered by the black sand; yellow-uniformed attendants with plastic shovels heaped the dark stuff over the smiling, chatting people, slowly burying them. She looked up at the clock, high up in the dome, but it was half-melted, like a painting, and stuck at 8:15. She looked at her own watch, but it showed the same time.

The warriors came closer, collecting bits of people.

On a hill outside the great glass room she could see the castle. It was warm in the ballroom, but outside there was snow. The massive dark stones of the castle were edged in white, and on each level of soaring roofs – like the wings of some great black crow, frozen in flight – snow lay, blending the castle's tall shape into the milky sky.

80

The warriors came to her and Philippe. They wore long stiff skirts of brown and grey, and their faces were obscured by long mesh masks; they held long cane rods in both hands. They brought the rods down on people, turning the parts they hit to gold. They touched them on the hand or the foot or the leg or the arm, or touched their torso, or their head. Wherever they touched somebody, they would name the part they touched. That part would turn to gold, leaving the rest unharmed. The unharmed bits lay inert and dry on the tiles, or only twitched slightly. Warriors following behind the cane-swordsmen collected the golden body-pieces in a big sack, apologising.

The swimming boy had a leg removed, the fat pharaoh his head (he sat, headless, a smooth pink stump where his neck had been, impatiently tapping his fingers on the tiles at the side of the pool), the little brother his arms, the black man his torso (his limbs kept trying to reassemble themselves in the right pattern, as though his body was still there, but each time it seemed they were about to succeed, one arm or leg would twitch a little and spoil the whole effect, and an expression of annoyance would pass across the face on the be-torsoed head).

The warriors bowed to them, touched Philippe's feet, and then her hands. Her hands glinted gold in the light, and fell into her lap. One of the men with the sack lifted them and dropped them into its dark depths with a dull clunk. She looked down at her wrists, all rosy and new-looking; the stumps smelled like a baby's skin. Her watch had fallen off and now lay on the tiled floor. It still said 8:15. She kicked it into the steaming pool, over the monkeys crowding round its rim. The watch flew a long way and disappeared into the mists. She heard a plop.

The line of smiling people on the black sand had been covered from toes to neck. They chattered like birds, though she could not hear what they were saying. The yellow-uniformed attendants looked tired and glum. Philippe stroked her back, making her arch it a little.

Through the clouds of steam on the far side of the room, she saw a golden, bearded Buddha standing on a small hill, surrounded by trees. One of the diving women rose up out of the water, covered in a black suit and holding a face mask and a wooden bucket. The woman came up to her and picked

81

something out of the bucket; it was her watch. The woman made a soft hooting noise. She thanked the woman and tried to put the watch on, but couldn't. It was still stuck at 8:15, though she could hear it ticking. She needed hands to adjust it.

She ran after the warriors, took the sack from one of them, and started rummaging around inside it, looking for her hands. There were so many it was difficult, but she found them eventually; they were the slightly melted ones. They fitted perfectly. A warrior came up to hit her, but she took the stick from him and struck him over the head. He fell into the water. All the warriors fell into the water, taking the sack with them; it sank quickly.

A terrible screaming noise came from behind her, and she turned, still holding the bloody sword. All the people she had left behind were writhing on the floor, their blood smearing the yellow tiles as it gushed from their mutilated limbs.

The line of people on the beach was completely buried; just a long line in the black sand.

The sky beyond the grey metal beams of the dome had gone black.

When she turned back, the water in the pools had turned red and thick, and she couldn't feel her hands, or her arms. The sword dropped from her and clanged on the tiles. A great red fountain burst suddenly out of the turgid surface of the pool. A terrible wailing noise filled the air. She smelled iron.

Philippe stroked her back, speaking her name, and she woke on a couch in the lounge of the ship. It was darker than it had been, and quiet; nobody talking. The brightest light was at the bar, where it reflected off the bottles and glasses and the barrel of the guard's machine-gun. She didn't remember going to sleep on the couch. She must have twisted while she slept; her arms were trapped beneath her, cutting off the blood. She struggled to turn round again, while Philippe asked her if she was all right; she'd been making strange noises. Her useless arms tingled and pulsed as the blood returned, burning in the veins as though it was acid.

6: Sal Si Puedes

The *aguacero* came in the middle of the day; a rapid darkening of the lightly clouded sky, the sound of the wind around the ship, quickly increasing. Then the storm itself, spattering rain against the windows, howling around the superstructure, and the ship starting to roll a little; heeling one way then the other, without rhythm, as the wind swirled and switched direction and gusts pushed the vessel across the lake, swinging it around its mooring, stem to its buoy and tied there like a nose-ringed bull to a post.

They had all slept during the night; most, fitfully. It was warm and stuffy and uncomfortable. The ship's air-conditioning was working, but struggling with the heat produced by the sheer density of bodies crammed into the lounge. The atmosphere was kept constantly smoky by the cigarettes of the Moroccans and Algerians; the smokers had gravitated together in what looked like a form of racial segregation, sitting furthest from the bar. Still, their smoke drifted throughout the lounge. Broekman went down to sit with them a few times, at first to smoke the two cigars he happened to have on him when he was taken off the *Nakodo*, and later to bum cigarettes.

Hisako had the privilege of sleeping on a couch, as did Marie Boulard. Some of the others had cushions from seats and couches. The *venceristas* had brought a few blankets and sheets and pillows down from the cabins, so that most people had something to cover themselves with if they wanted to. In the heat of the lounge most people went without.

Late in the night, the gunmen took one of the larger Algerians

83

away. The people still awake waited to see if he'd come back. He did, holding the rear end of Gordon Janney's stretcher; Captain Bleveans carried the front. Mrs Bleveans led the party in, followed by two *venceristas*. Janney waved from the stretcher and told people he was OK really. His head was bandaged; the right side of his face was bruised from chin to eyebrow. They suspended the stretcher between two seats, and made up a bed on a couch for Mrs Bleveans.

The *Nadia*'s captain made sure his wife was settled, then joined Philippe and Endo. Hisako sat beside Philippe; she hadn't been able to get back to sleep after her nightmare. Broekman was curled up under a sheet near by, looking oddly childlike. Mr Mandamus lay on his back under another sheet, for all the world like a thin man pinned to the floor by a large sack. Philippe and Endo – with Hisako's help – told Bleveans what had happened on their ships.

'So, no other casualties?' Bleveans asked.

'No, Captain,' Philippe said. They sat under a window near one corner of the lounge, level with and about five metres from the bar, where one of the *venceristas* sat, machine-gun resting on the polished surface, drinking a Coke.

Endo sat forward, a little closer to Bleveans. 'Mr Orrick . . . not with us.' He rocked back again.

Bleveans looked at Philippe and Hisako. 'They took him away?'

'They didn't get him at all, we think,' Hisako said.

'Hmm.' Bleveans rubbed the back of his neck tiredly, looking down at the carpet. Hisako hadn't noticed he was going bald before.

'And the radio operators,' Philippe said. 'They are not here.'

'Yeah, they've got all three of them together, in our radio room,' Bleveans said. 'Pretending everything's normal, you know; like they're all on their own ships.'

'How is Mr Janney?' Hisako whispered.

Bleveans shrugged. 'I think he's concussed. I'd get him to hospital, normally.'

'Men tell you,' Endo said, 'why this?'

'No,' Bleveans frowned. 'But . . . they seemed, ah . . . annoyed . . . unsettled over something they heard on the news.' He rubbed the back of his neck again. 'We were in my cabin with the door open . . . and we could hear they had CNN . . . maybe Channel 8, on in the bridge; that's their command centre, far as I can make out. Logical, I guess. Anyway; sounded like the news, and about halfway through . . . it was like being in a bar and the local team gets shut out, you know?' Endo looked blank; Philippe frowned. Hisako translated for Endo while Bleveans rephrased for Philippe. 'Like they got some bad news,' Bleveans went on. 'And something else . . .' he stretched back, flexing his shoulders but at the same time getting to glance back at the guard behind the bar. 'They're talking to somebody else. They're using their own radios to talk to each other . . . there's some of them on the *Nakodo*, I guess, but . . . you reckon they all came off *Le Cercle*?' Bleveans looked at Philippe, who nodded.

'I count them when they were together; and also two of my crew see them in the boat, and there were six. All the six come over with us to the *Nadia*.'

'So that's two groups . . . and their high command, or next military level; on shore, I guess. They seem to talk different to them.'

'In what way different?' Philippe said.

'I don't know; slower, I guess.'

'Perhaps the *venceristas* have suffered a defeat,' Hisako said, not looking at them.

'What's that, ma'am?' Bleveans said.

'Oh. When they sounded upset hearing the news. Maybe the *venceristas* lost a battle, or somebody high up was captured or killed.'

'Could be,' Bleveans agreed.

'What of . . . congressmen?' Endo said, struggling with the word a little.

'How's tha— ' Bleveans had sat forward to hear Endo better, then stopped, and just nodded. 'Hmm.'

'Yes,' Hisako said, looking at Philippe. 'They were to fly over tomorrow.' She looked at her watch, to see if it was past midnight, but of course they'd taken her watch. At least that had not been a dream. 'Today, if it's past midnight.' She looked round the others. 'Is it?'

'Yes,' Philippe nodded. 'Near four and a half in the morning; I think they change guards on four-hour watches, and the last change was not long ago.'

'So it's today,' Bleveans said, tapping the carpet with one finger. 'The plane's meant to fly over today.' He looked at Philippe and Endo. 'What d'you think, guys; SAMs?'

'*Pardon?*'

'*Wakarimasen.*'

Hisako translated Surface to Air Missiles for Endo; Bleveans used the words rather than their acronym for Philippe. Both nodded and looked worried.

'I no see any . . . *samus*,' Endo told Bleveans.

'No,' Philippe agreed. 'Their weapons I see are . . . guns; grenades.'

'Same here,' Bleveans said. He glanced at Hisako. 'Just a thought. But if that is what they're up to I guess they would keep the heavy weaponry away, out of our sight.'

'On the *Nakodo*?' Hisako ventured.

'Mm-hmm,' Bleveans yawned, nodding. 'Yeah, the *Nakodo* rather than the *Le Cercle*. Safer loosing off rockets from that than a tanker full of fuel.'

'You think they shoot plane?' Endo said quietly.

'Maybe,' Bleveans said.

'Is very dangerous, I think,' Philippe said, frowning.

'Might just start World War Three, Mr Ligny,' Bleveans said, nodding in agreement. 'Yeah, I'd call that dangerous. If that's what they intend doing.' He rubbed his eyes, sniffed. 'Anybody thought of any escape plans yet?'

'No,' Philippe said.

'Hmm. I guess they got this bit thought out fairly well.' He stretched again, looking back for a moment. 'Leaving us free is a kindness; gives us something to lose. Keeping those stools in front of the bar is gonna make rushing the guy next to impossible . . . unless we want to take serious casualties. We could try a diversion, but . . . I have a feeling that's always looked a lot more easy in the movies than it really is.'

'Doesn't everything?' Hisako blurted, then put her hand to her mouth.

'I guess so, ma'am.' He started to get up. 'They letting us use the heads?'

'Yes,' Hisako said, when the two men looked blank.

Philippe understood. He shook his head. 'I check in there, Captain; I do not think is way out there.'

Bleveans smiled as he got to his feet. 'I guessed that much, Philippe; I just want to take a leak before I crash, you know? Excuse me.' He nodded to them and walked off, swinging his arms slowly, holding each shoulder alternately. He gave a sort of half-salute to the *vencerista* behind the bar, who waved the Coke bottle in return.

Todai is not to be taken lightly; it is The Place, the Harvard, the Oxbridge of Japan; virtual guarantor of a job in the diplomatic service, the government or the fast track of a *zaibatsu*. In a country more obsessed with education than any other in history, Tokyo University is the very summit. Still, she sailed through it. She had grown; shot up in height at the last moment, becoming briefly gangly, her aboriginal, Ainu heritage catching up with her again. Still smaller than most *gaijin*, she became used to looking down on the average Japanese man. She swam, she hiked, she went gliding a few times and sailing occasionally. She kept up her Japanese sports too; the way of gentleness; the open hand; archery; kendo. These activities were financed with the money she got from the string quartet she helped form; they were popular, always raising their fees to keep demand down. She knew she didn't practise enough, and she scraped through numerous exams, because no matter how smart and how energetic you were there was still only so much time in each day. She still thought of it as sailing through, then and afterwards, and never lost a night's or even an hour's sleep over an exam, while her friends and the other people around her got far better grades and worried themselves sick.

She knew she didn't have to worry; she would float through everything, she'd be found regardless, and at her finale mountains would tremble. So she thought of it sometimes, in her wildest moments, when she'd had too much beer with her friends. She would survive; she would always survive. She was smart and strong after all, and with *gaijin* words or a *gaijin* music box, she'd get by.

For a while she had just three problems. Two were solved in one night. After a great deal of thought, having decided she didn't need love the way everybody else said they did, or thought

87

they did, at least not the sort that you couldn't get from a mother or a few close friends, or feel towards a piece of music, or your homeland, she decided to be seduced, and to let a *gaijin* do the seducing.

He was called Bertil and he was from Malmö in Sweden; two years older than her, spending a year at a language college in Tokyo. He was blond – which she loved – and oddly funny, once you got past a layer of half-hearted Scandinavian gloom. She was still plucking her eyebrows and shaving her legs and arms, thinking them hairy and horrible, but when they got to the Love Hotel in Senzoku, and he undressed her – she'd told him she was a virgin, she hoped he wouldn't be put off by the way she trembled – he stroked her pubic hair (so that suddenly she thought, *Oh no! The one place I didn't shave! And it's a forest down there!*) and said . . . well, she was too flustered to remember the exact words, but they were delighted, admiring words . . . and the one word she didn't forget, the one that a quarter of a century later she still could not hear without shivering; the word which had become almost synonymous with that feeling of a soft, sensual stroking, was the English word – how pleased he had sounded to think of it – *luxuriant* . . . .

Bertil had to go back to Sweden a week later; the parting was excitingly bitter-sweet. She threw her razor away.

Which left just one problem; she hated the idea of flying. She traipsed out to Narita sometimes, to watch the jets take off and land. She enjoyed that, it was no ordeal. But the idea of actually getting on to a plane filled her with horror.

She auditioned for the NHK, the same orchestra she'd heard in Sapporo when she'd been a little girl and decided she wanted a cello. That she *was* nervous about.

But her fate was unstoppable now. She scraped through her last exams at *Todai* just as she'd scraped through the rest, but it was still a pass, and she'd hardly finished celebrating when the letter came from the NHK.

The day before her mother was due to arrive from Sapporo, she went back to the bald summit of the hill north of the Fuji Five Lakes, and sat there cross-legged in her kagool, listening to the rain drip off the trees and spatter on her hood, and watched the clouds trail like skirts round the base of Fuji. She took the letter out a couple of times and re-read it. It still said yes; she had the place; it was hers. She kept thinking something was going to go wrong, and prayed her mother didn't change her mind at the last moment and in a fit of extravagance fly down to Tokyo.

'In the Caribbean,' Mr Mandamus said in the midst of the storm, pronouncing the name of the sea in the British manner, with the emphasis on the third syllable, 'if you are on a low-lying island or part of the coast, you must beware of the slow-timed waves. The normal timing of waves hitting a shore is seven or eight per minute, but if the frequency becomes four or five beats a minute, you must flee, or be prepared to meet your maker. First of all, the sky will be cloudless and brassy, and the wind dies, leaving a leaden heat. The sea goes strangely greasy-looking, becoming uniform and undisturbed except for the long, ponderous waves; all lesser movements are smothered. The breakers hit the beach with a slow monotony, regular and machine-like and mindless.

'Then, in the sky; streamers of high cloud like ragged rays of dark sunlight, seeming to imanate from one place over the horizon. They spread over the head, while in the distance, beneath them, clouds form, and the sun looks milky, and a halo the colour of ashes surrounds it, so that it begins to look like an eye.

'In time, the sun is put out by the clouds, and it begins to go gloomy; quick dark clouds fill the middle air while on the horizon a wall of cloud starts to engulf the sky. It is the colour of copper at first. As it comes closer and grows higher, it darkens, through brown to black, and half the sky is covered by it. It is like an impossibly tall wave of darkness, tall like the night; the winds around you are still slight and uncertain, but the surf is hammering the beach like thunder, slow and heavy, like the beat of a cruel god's mighty heart.

'The dark wave falls, the winds land like hammer blows; rain like an ocean falling from the sky; waves like walls.

'When you think – if you are still alive to think – it can grow no worse, the sea retreats, sucked back into the darkness, leaving the coast far below the lowest low tidemark draining away into a violent night. Then the ocean returns, in a wave that dwarfs all previous waves; a cliff; a black mountain spilling over the land like the end of the world.

'Perhaps you have seen satellite photographs of a hurricane; from space, the eye looks tiny and black in the centre of the white featheriness of the storm. It looks too small and too perfectly round and black to be natural; you think it is something lying on the film. The hurricanes look very like galaxies, which I hear also have black holes in their centres. The eye is maybe thirty kilometres across. The air pressure can be so low sailors have said blood comes to the mouth and the eardrums ache. The water at the bottom of the eye is sucked up three metres above the rest of the ocean. Seen from a ship which has survived the winds, it is like being in a cauldron; the walls of blackness swirl round about, but in the eye the air is calm, humid, and appallingly hot. The circling storm moans from all around. The waves on the water froth and jostle and leap up, coming crashing in from every direction, colliding and bursting their spray into the boiling calm air. More often than not, raggedy, exhausted birds fly aimlessly inside the eye, those not killed by it; confused and beaten, they fill up the moaning air with their cries. A circle of clear sky overhead looks like Earth seen from space; blue and far away and unreal; sun and stars shine as though through gauze, removed and unreal. Then the screaming winds and the blackness and the drowning rain starts again.'

'You ever *been* in a hurricane, Mandamus?' Broekman asked.

'Merciful heavens, no,' Mandamus shook his big head heavily. 'But I have read about it.'

Hisako listened to the sound of the *aguacero* howling outside, and thought Mr Mandamus was very likely the sort of person who talked about air crashes during a bumpy flight, attempting to reassure nervous passengers with the thought that they wouldn't feel a thing, possibly. She decided not to correct him on 'imanate'.

The storm passed quickly, as *aguaceros* always did. Behind the drawn curtains of the stuffy lounge, it looked like a pleasant day.

Gordon Janney had slept badly, and his speech was slurred. Mrs Bleveans was changing the dressing on his head. Her husband was still sound asleep on the floor. There were two and sometimes three *venceristas* behind the bar at any particular moment. One was reading a Spanish-language Superman comic.

90

Then the *venceristas* took one of the cooks away; some time later he returned with a trolley of burgers, potatoes and salad. The gunmen watched them eat and passed out bottles of water and Coke.

Mrs Bleveans persuaded Sucre she should be allowed to collect some toothpaste, a few toothbrushes and a bottle of antiseptic. Before she went she checked with Marie and Hisako, to find out if either of them needed any sanitary protection; neither did.

'Christ, I suppose that could be it,' Broekman said, rubbing his lips with one hand. Philippe, Endo and Hisako had told him of the theory that the *venceristas* had come to shoot down the plane. The noise of Mr Mandamus snoring as he slept off his meal covered any sounds short of a shout they were likely to make.

'Is just a thought,' Philippe said.

'Flight today,' Endo confirmed.

'Crazy bastards; what're they trying to do?'

'Maybe we're being paranoid,' Hisako said. 'We'll know soon anyway.'

'If the flight *is* today,' Broekman said. 'On the news yesterday there was talk of some last-minute hitch; might be a delay.'

'There was?' Hisako looked at Philippe and Endo. Nobody else had heard this.

'On the World Service, just before our friends arrived.'

Philippe looked worried. 'Captain Bleveans; he said the *venceristas* became . . . upset? Upset, when they hear something on the radio. Last evening.'

'Shit,' Broekman said. 'Sounds uncomfortably neat, doesn't it?' He rubbed one bristly cheek. 'I didn't think the *venceristas* were that crazy.'

'I think we must get to the radio,' Philippe said.

'How do we do that?' Broekman said, patting his overalls pockets for cigars that weren't there. 'Rushing the guy at the bar would be suicide, and all we get's a gun or two and a couple of grenades, plus we alert the others. If we had the time and a screwdriver maybe we could unscrew the windows,' he nodded slightly towards the curtains, 'if they aren't rusted up. But we'd have to distract them for ten minutes or more. There's no outside access from the toilets; no access anywhere. The alternative is, one of us can try to get out on some sort of excuse and aim to overpower whoever they send with us. That's probably our best bet. And they probably know that.'

Philippe shrugged. 'What excuse, you think?'

'Try pretending we have to do something to one of the ships; tell them we have to turn on the bilge pumps or we'll sink, or transfer fuel to the generator or we'll lose power; something like that.'

'You think they believe us?'

'No.' Broekman shook his head.

'So is not much hope?'

Broekman shook his head. 'Doesn't mean it isn't worth a try. Perhaps we'll be lucky. They've been very casual so far; maybe they're not as confident and professional as they look; maybe they're just sloppy.' Broekman ran one hand through his hair, looked round at where the *Nadia*'s captain lay, one arm raised over his head to keep the light out of his eyes. 'We'd better get Bleveans in on this; it's his ship we might break if it goes wrong. Do we wake him now or leave him to get up in his own time?'

Hisako confirmed Endo had understood. 'Leave him,' Endo said.

Philippe pursed his lips. 'I don't know . . . if this plane— '

The lounge door opened. Sucre stood there, pointing the gun at Hisako with one hand. '*Señora* Onoda,' he called. Bleveans stirred a little at the noise. Mandamus snored loudly and muttered something under his breath in Arabic. Hisako stood up into a layer of smoke, smelling Gitanes.

'Yes?' She was aware that everybody was looking at her.

Sucre waved the gun. 'You come with me.' He stood away from the door. There was another armed man in the corridor behind him.

Philippe started to get up too; she put a hand on his shoulder. 'Philippe-*chan*; it's all right.'

He squeezed her hand. 'Hisako, don't— ' he began, but she was moving quickly away.

'Is just a phone call, *Señora* Onoda,' Sucre told her on the way up to the radio room. He was about the same height as she, though much more muscled. His skin was coppery-olive and his face held no trace of the blacking; it looked freshly shaved. He smelled of cologne. She suspected his black curly hair was trimmed and perhaps even curled to make him look Guevara-ish.

'Mr Moriya?'

'Sounds like,' Sucre agreed, shepherding her up a companion-way.

She wondered if she could escape; perhaps kick down, disabling Sucre, taking his gun. But it was better to wait until she was in the radio room. Her mouth was dry again, but at the same time it was as though there was some strange electric charge running through her teeth and gums, leaving a sharp, metallic taste. Her legs wobbled a little as they walked along the central corridor that led to the ship's bridge, senior officers' quarters, and radio room. A *vencerista* rested against the wall outside, between her and the bridge. She smelled more tobacco smoke; cigars or cigarillos.

Sucre took her elbow and stopped her, swung her round so that she bumped into the metal corridor wall. He pressed against her, the automatic pistol he'd pointed at her the evening before in his hand again. He put the gun up under her chin. She tipped her head back, looked into his dark eyes.

'*Señora*— ' he began.

'*Señorita*,' she told him, then wished she hadn't.

'Hey, you're cool,' Sucre grinned. He moved his thumb. There was a click which she both heard and felt through her neck and jaw. 'Hear that, *Señorita*?'

She nodded slowly.

'Now no safety catch. Safety catch off. You say anything on the radio, I blow your brains out. Then I give the other two women to my men; we been in the jungles long time, yeah? And then after that I take the *cojones* off your *francés*-man.' He put his free hand between her legs, patting her through the light material of the *yukata*. He smiled broadly. Her heart thudded. She felt as if she might lose control of her bowels. The gun was hard under her chin, half-choking her, making her want to gag. 'Understand?' Sucre said.

'Yes.'

'Yes; good. And you make it short.'

'He will want to speak Japanese,' she told him. Moriya would have used English to ask for her, but of course would expect to talk to her in Japanese.

Sucre looked surprised, then briefly angry. Finally he grinned. 'Tell him your *francés*-man want to listen too.'

She nodded carefully. 'All right.'

He took his hand away, backed off, waved her to the radio room.

The *Nadia*'s radio operator let her into the seat. Sucre sat to her right, facing her, the automatic against her right ear. 'OK,' he said quietly, not taking his eyes off her.

She picked up the handset, put it to her left ear. It was the wrong side; it felt strange. 'Hello,' she said, swallowing.

'Hisako, what takes these people so long? And where did you get to anyway? Never mind. Look, it's getting ridiculous— '

'Mr Moriya; Mr Moriya . . .'

'Yes?'

'Talk in English, please. I have a friend here who does not understand Japanese.'

'What . . . ?' Moriya said in Japanese, then switched to English. 'Oh . . . Hisako . . . have I to?'

'Please. For me.'

'Very well. Very well. Let me see. . . . Perhaps we have cancellings altogether. They still . . . they still . . . ah, want you appear some time, but – oh, I am sorry. I am impolite. How are you?'

'Fine. You?'

'Oh dear; you are being short with me. Always I know I say wrong thing when you are short with me. I am sorry.'

'I'm all right, Moriya-*san*,' she told him. 'I am well. How are you?'

'Are you well really? You sound different.'

Sucre rammed the gun into her ear, forcing her head over to the left. She closed her eyes. 'Mr Moriya,' she said, trying to sound calm. 'Please believe me; I'm all right. What did you call for? Please; I have to get back . . .' Hot tears came to her eyes.

'I just want know if anything . . . anything, umm happen out there. Umm; what gives? CNN say *venceristas* maybe to attack Panama city. This is true? You must to get out. Must to go away.'

The pressure on her ear had relaxed a little; she brought her head up, pushing against the gun, stealing one angry glance at Sucre, who was staring intently at her, unsmiling.

She blinked and sniffed the tears away, ashamed at having cried. 'Well, no,' she told Moriya. 'Not right now. Maybe later. Perhaps later. I can't get out now. Sorry.'

She had decided; she would say something. Not to warn, but to find out. She would say something about them waiting for the congressmen's plane to fly over. Her heart pounded in her chest, worse than when Sucre had had his gun at her throat. She started to phrase the sentence, to try to say something that would get Mr Moriya to respond and tell her if the plane was delayed or not. Something which would not get her brains blown out would be a good idea, too.

'You look,' Mr Moriya said, 'I call back when we talk together alone. Is too uneasy so, OK?'

'I . . . uh, yes,' she said, suddenly shaking, unable to think straight. The hand round the handset was aching; she realised she was gripping the receiver as though she was hanging from it over a cliff.

'Goodbye, Hisako,' Mr Moriya said.

'Ye – yes; goodbye . . . *sayonara* . . .' She could not control her trembling. Her eyes were closed. The line made clicking noises. Somebody took the handset from her, prising her fingers off; she loosened them as soon as she felt the other hand on hers. She opened her eyes as Sucre put the handset back on its hook.

'You did all right,' he told her. 'That was OK. Now we go back.'

Afterwards, her ears still ringing, she found it all a little difficult to piece together. It seemed as if things had happened in some strange, disordered, disjointed manner, as though such violent action happened in its own micro-climate of reality.

She was walking down the corridor, still a little shaky, with Sucre behind her. There was a hint of movement at the far, aft end of the corridor, where it led out of the superstructure to an outside deck. She took no notice, still thinking about what she might have said to Moriya, and feeling guilty at her relief that she hadn't had the chance to say anything and so endanger herself.

They were almost at the companionway leading back down to the lower decks. There was a muffled shout from that end of the corridor. She looked up. Then a shot; percussive and clanging. She froze. Sucre said something she didn't catch. Another shot. She was pushed from behind. The stairs were at her right.

Steve Orrick appeared, dressed in swimming trunks, holding a hand gun and an Uzi, from a cabin doorway right in front of her. She felt her jaw drop. His eyes went wide. He brought the gun up, pointing it over her shoulder. She was struck from behind, pushed against the rail at the top of the companionway, almost sending her over into the stairwell. She swung round and caught a glimpse of Orrick grimacing, clicking the trigger of the boxy-looking Uzi futilely. Sucre raised his own gun.

She kicked out with one foot, hitting Sucre's rifle. It blasted into the ceiling, filling the metal corridor with stunning noise. She had her balance back by then; she chopped Sucre across the neck, open handed, but he had started to move away. It was only the second time she'd ever hit somebody in anger. Sucre staggered, looking more surprised than anything else, and stumbled against the far wall. Orrick was fiddling with the small gun. Then he ducked, and fired between her and Sucre, down towards the bridge. Her ears were ringing. The Uzi made a noise like heavy cloth ripping, magnified a hundred times. Fire sounded down the corridor; Orrick leapt back, into the doorway he'd appeared from. Something tugged suddenly at the hem of the *yukata*. She turned, glanced down into the stairwell, to see one of the *venceristas* pointing a gun at her. She dived across the corridor, into the cabin where Orrick was.

It was dark, blinds closed. The acrid smell of powder smoke filled the place. There was a dead man in the bed. Firing sounded behind her, making her flinch; Orrick knelt at the door, peeping out and firing.

She recognised the dead man. It was one of the men who'd guarded them during the night. The one who'd waved the Coke bottle at Bleveans. He was missing most of the left side of his head, and there was a huge patch of glistening darkness staining the white sheets around his midriff. The noise of gunfire resounded through the cabin, filling her. She felt bad, and had to sit down on the floor between Orrick and the bed. Orrick's broad, water-spotted back filled most of the doorway. The trunks had a little belt on them; attached to it was a big sheathed knife. She recognised his trunks, remembered them from a day they'd all gone picnicking on—

She shook her head. Orrick was firing with the pistol, the Uzi lying at his knee. She looked around the cabin. The Uzi magazines lay on the small table, in a pile beside an open copy of *Hustler*. She grabbed them, clattered them down on the floor beside Orrick and nudged him. She stood up. The Uzi's ripping noise started again.

The side of the superstructure at this level was flush with the deck beneath, but she leant over the bed and opened the blinds and looked out of the porthole to make sure. She wondered if she might squeeze through, and started unscrewing the wing nut securing the glass.

'Grenade!' Orrick screamed, and fell back into the cabin. He tried to kick the door shut; half-succeeded. It burst open again in a cloud of smoke and a blast that seemed to reverberate through every atom of Hisako's body.

She'd fallen; she was lying on the warm stickiness of the dead man, blood soaking into the *yukata*. She struggled away from him, the cabin ringing like a bell about her. More firing behind as Orrick squatted once again at the door. She looked around, wild-eyed, saw the dead man's combat jacket. She took it, felt its heaviness and turned it round, searching. The grenades were there. She tore them from their velcro fastenings. Orrick was back at the door, apparently unharmed. She collapsed to her knees beside him, nudging him again and offering the grenades. He saw them, grabbed one, dropped the other, still firing with his other hand. He shouted something at her.

'—Out!— ' she heard. She felt as if she had road drills lodged in each ear. She shook her head. '—go first!— ' Orrick screamed at her. He looked at the grenade he held, took the ring in his teeth and pulled; it worked. He threw it down the corridor towards the bridge, picked up the other grenade from the deck, and a magazine. He emptied the Uzi down the corridor after the first grenade, then leapt out, disappearing aft, astonishing her; a sudden increase in light from that direction, then dark again and a metal door slamming. Instantly the grenade detonated, a blast and clattering screech from forward.

A noise like a waterfall filled her ears. She found herself sitting on the floor. Her head buzzed; everything was going grey and watery, reality dissolving in the reeking smoke and the obliterating noise.

She felt herself start to tip back and to the side, but her arm moved in slow motion, as though it moved through treacle, while the rest of her body moved through air. She hit the floor.

Blinked.

She knew she was going to die. Perhaps they all were. At least Sucre had probably been the first. The others might not know she'd hit him.

She could see Sucre's face; so smooth and shining; the neat black fatigues – not as though they'd been in the jungle (jungle?) for weeks at all – the pert little beret with its chic little red badge; those black curls. . . . His face seemed to swim in and out of focus above her. No beret, this time. Curls in disarray. He was looking down at her, mouth twisted.

He reached down, dragged her up. He was real, and alive.

That's it. I'm dead.

She was thrown out into the corridor, hit the far wall. Then she was pushed out into the sunlight. She stood blinking in the glare, blinded. The aft hatches of the *Nadia* lay below her; water sparkled beyond, holding the green shadow of an island. Sucre pushed her to the rail. Men were running along the aft deck, to the stern of the ship. They held guns.

At the rail, she looked down along the hull of the ship. A couple of men were leaning over the decks below, firing down into the water towards the stern. At the *Nadia*'s landing stage, midships, a black Gemini looked limp and low and crumpled in the water, stern down. She remembered the hunting knife on Orrick's trunks.

The men running to the stern stopped and looked over the rail every now and again, pointing their guns down, sometimes firing them.

Sucre held her arm painfully far up her back, forcing her on tip-toes, grunting with the pain. He shouted to the men at the stern of the ship. They shouldered their guns and reached for their grenades.

She bent over the rail, easing the pressure on her arm a little. Yes, she could still see the ripples. Orrick must have jumped. Swam – probably underwater as much as possible – to the stern, where the overhang would protect him from the guns. But not from the grenades.

She watched them splash into the waves around the rear of

the ship. She looked up into the blue, lightly clouded sky. No sign of any plane. What a nice day to die on, she thought. Sucre was still shouting behind her. Men and their noise.

Suddenly, in a dozen places around the stern of the ship, the water bulged and went white, like a series of giant watery bruises. The bruises burst; fluting and climbing, white stems exploding in the sunlight and falling back. There was hardly any noise. The ship rail under Hisako's sternum vibrated with each shock.

Sucre shouted again. Then there was silence. She felt the sunlight on her neck and forearms, could smell the distant land. An insect buzzed distantly, through the continual ringing in her ears.

Orrick's body floated out after a minute; pale and face down, spread like a parachutist in free fall. The *venceristas* cheered, and emptied their guns into the man's body, making it disappear in a tiny forest of white and red splashes, until Sucre's shouting made them stop.

He twisted her back round to face him. He looked uninjured, but shaken and dishevelled. He took the pistol out of its holster.

She ought to do something, but she couldn't. There was no fight left. *I won't close my eyes. I won't close my eyes.*

Sucre brought the pistol up to her face, up to her eye, pressed it forward. She closed her eyes. The gun's muzzle pressed on to her eyelid, forcing her head back. She could see a halo of light against the brown-black, like an image of the gun barrel and the twisted hole the bullet would travel.

The gun was taken away. A slap jerked her head one way, then another. Her head sang; another instrument in the orchestra of internal noise that was crowding into her skull.

She opened her eyes. Sucre was standing grinning in front of her.

'Yeah, you're pretty cool, *Señorita*,' he told her. He flourished the pistol; it glinted in the sunlight. 'You a man, I'd kill you.' He re-holstered the gun, glanced to the stern of the ship, took a deep breath and whistled. 'Woo; that was something, huh?'

She swallowed a little blood, and nodded.

Then the sound of rapid, automatic gunfire came through the open door behind them, from down inside the ship.

7: Salvages

She stood, confronting her fear at last. Everything had led up to this. It had been forever coming closer, like a distant storm, and now it had arrived and she was powerless and weak, wallowing without way in the face of the dread she'd tried and tried to confront but with which she had never been able to connect.

In school once, in a physics class, she'd tried to push two very strong magnets together, north against north and south against south, and sweated and gritted her teeth and braced her arms against the bench and watched her straining, quivering hands push the big U-shaped lumps of metal together, constantly trying to stop them glancing away, sliding to one side, struggling to twist out of her grasp, and felt her strength going and so finally putting everything into one last explosive burst of effort, and shouted out as she did so as if screaming the targeted part of the body in a kendo thrust. The magnets slid across each other, writhing in her hands like something alive, clunking one south pole against one north, the other ends of each U sticking out, so that she was left holding a solid, S-shaped piece of metal. It took an even greater effort than that she'd just made to stop herself throwing the magnet down to the floor, or just slamming it into the wooden bench top. But she put the gunmetal lump down quietly, and dropped her head a little, as though saluting a victorious opponent.

It had been the same with her fear. She had tried to force it to a confrontation, to pin it down, to wrestle with it . . . but it had always twisted away, wriggled mightily even as she tried to grapple with it, and sunk back into the usual shape of her life.

So now she stood in Narita airport, waiting with the rest of the NHK orchestra to board the JAL 747 bound for Los Angeles.

She'd sat in the departure lounge with some of the others, chatting nervously and drinking tea and watching the clock on the wall and glancing all the time at her wristwatch, stroking the new leather bag she'd bought for the trip, trying to make the cold tangle of cramp in her belly go away.

The others knew she hadn't flown before, and that she was afraid. They joked with her, tried to take her mind off it, but she could not stop thinking about the plane; the fragile aluminium tube of its body; the screaming engines, encasing fire; the wings that flexed, heavy with fuel; the wheels that . . . it was that moment, the visual instant when the spinning wheels left the ground and the aircraft tilted its nose to the sky and rose, that sank her. She could think no further. She had watched that moment on television and movies many times, and could see that there was indeed a slow-motion grace about it, and could quite happily admire the plane maker's and the pilot's skill, and know that the same manoeuvre was completed thousands of times each hour throughout the world . . . but the thought of being on one of those delicately huge contraptions as it lifted itself into the air still saturated her with terror. It made her bones ache.

The others talked to her. One of the younger men in the orchestra told her he'd been scared of flying at first, but then had looked into the statistics. Did she know, he said, that you were far more likely to die in a car crash than in a plane?

But not when you're in a plane! She wanted to scream at him.

Chizu and Yayoi, her flatmates, who were also in the orchestra string section, talked of a previous trip to the States, when they'd been students. How vast it was, and how beautiful; Yosemite, the Mohave, the Redwoods . . . a single state like a whole country, sprawling and empty and unmissable, even before the Rockies and the Grand Canyon, the fertile wasteland of the wheatfields from flat horizon to flat horizon, like an ocean of grain; the colours of a New England fall, and the dizzy verticals of Manhattan. Unmissable. Not to be missed. She must not miss it.

The hands of the clock swept on, impossibly thin wings.

The time came. She stood with the rest, clutching her new leather bag. They went to the tunnel. She lifted the bag up, cradling it tightly in her arms. It smelled luxurious and sweet and comforting. She saw the plane outside in the sunlight;

massive, secure, anchored-looking. It was linked to the terminal at nose and tail by the fitted collars of the access jetties, and fuel hoses looped under its wings from tanker trucks. At one side, a catering vehicle's raised body stood perched on an X of struts over the braced chassis, its platform extended to an open door in the aircraft's side; tall thin trolleys were being wheeled from truck to plane by two men in bright red overalls. A squat, flat truck sat under the 747's bulbous nose, fixed there with a thick yellow towbar. Various other vehicles scurried like toys about the poised bulk of the big plane, squires and armourers to the impassive warrior-king above them being readied to join battle with the oceanic air.

She moved towards the tunnel. Her legs felt as if somebody else was operating them. The leather bag smelled of animal death. She wished she'd taken the pills the doctor had prescribed. She wished she'd got drunk. She wished she'd told them at the start she wouldn't be able to go abroad with the orchestra. She wished she'd turned down the job. She wished she was somebody else, or somewhere else. She wished for a broken leg or a ruptured appendix; anything to stop her having to board the plane.

The tunnel finished her. The smell of fuel, the sound of an engine, the quiet flow of people in the windowless corridor, tipping towards the corner that led to the plane itself. She stopped, letting people go past her, staring ahead; Chizu and Yayoi stopped too, in front of her, talking to her (but she couldn't hear what they were saying). They touched her, guided her to the side of the corridor, where she stood shivering in a cold sweat, smelling that fuel smell and hearing the increasing whine of the engines and feeling the list in the floor tipping her towards the craft the people were filing into, and she could not think and could not believe this was happening to her.

So well. It had all gone so well. She'd fitted in, she'd made friends, she'd enjoyed the concerts and hadn't been very nervous apart from the very first one, and recording could be boring but you could switch off to some extent; nobody expected to do their most inspired work after thirty takes. . . . She had money, and a new cello, and her mother was proud of her; her life looked set and certain, and her future bright and exciting, and she'd wondered what could go wrong, because she was used to things balancing out, and this was it.

What was ironic was that the balancing disaster came from inside, where she was most vulnerable. She'd never needed to develop the spurious justifications and excuses, or the fragile ego-props and unlikely hopes so many other people had to construct to cope with their lives.

She'd lived with some inner certainty they hadn't had; safe inside, defences turned outwards, weapons trained beyond her immediate space . . . and now she was suffering for her hubris.

They did get her on to the plane eventually; Mr Yano, the orchestra's tour manager, and Mr Okamoto, the leader of the orchestra, came to talk to her, and gently guided her down the rubber slope, between the metal corrugations of the white walls, to the open door of the plane, where stewardesses waited and the plane was big and full of bright seats inside, and the thick door sat, a curved slab, against the bulge of the plane's skin. She was shaking. They took her inside.

She wanted to scream. Instead she moaned, went down on her haunches and curled up around her bag, as though trying to press herself inside it and hide, and crying into her folded elbows, her hands gripping the top of her head. She was being stupid. She had to act sensibly. She had to think of the others in the orchestra. What would her mother say? Her cello was already on board. There were three hundred passengers waiting on her; an entire plane. America; think of that! All those great cities, the thousands of people, waiting. Her ticket had been paid for, all her tickets paid for, hotel rooms reserved, programmes printed. It was unheard of to be so selfish, so self-obsessed.

She knew all this. All these things had convinced her – over the months since the tour had been announced and the various arrangements made – that when it came to it, she would find it simply unthinkable that she could turn round and not go. Of course it would be appalling, disgraceful, unutterably contemptuous of everybody else in the orchestra, irredeemably self-centred. She was grown up now and some things just had to be done; fears had to be conquered. Everybody was relying on her, expecting her to behave like everybody else, like any normal person; that wasn't much to ask.

She knew all that; it didn't help. It meant nothing – a set of

103

irrelevant symbols in a language that was not the reverberating note of her fear. Mere scrawls on a page pitched against the resonating physical chord of terror.

They tried to lift her, but she thought they were going to drag her to a seat and belt her in, join her to this hollow machine which smelled of jet fuel and hot food, and she cried then, dropping the leather bag and clutching at somebody and pleading with them. Please no. She was letting everybody down. Please don't. She was behaving like a child. I'm sorry I'm sorry I can't. A spoiled child, a spoiled foreign child. Please don't do this to me. A *gaijin* brat tantrumming for cookies. Please don't. She would be in disgrace. Please.

She was led out eventually, up the welcoming slope of the jetty, back to the lounge again, then to the restroom. A JAL ground staff lady comforted her.

The plane was delayed by half an hour. She would not leave the restroom until it had taken off.

Alternate feelings of relief and guilty dread flowed through her in the taxi back to the tiny apartment she shared with Chizu and Yayoi. It was over. The ordeal had finally ended.

But at such a cost. What shame she had brought upon herself and the others in the orchestra! She would be sacked. She ought to resign now. She would. Could she ever look any of them in the face again? She thought not.

She went home that night, setting off for the station and Hokkaido with the bag she'd bought for the trip and had almost left on the plane and then almost left in the restroom; a beautiful bag in soft, natural glove leather, still containing her virginal passport and a guide to the United States, and as she sat, red-eyed and miserable on the train heading north through the night (her friends, her workmates, would be somewhere over the North Pacific just then, she thought, crossing the date line, defying the sun and gaining a day while she lost her career), she looked down at the glowing, pale brown skin of the bag, and noticed the deep, dark dots marring its silky surface, and could not brush them off, and realised, with another twist in the deepening spiral of her self-inflicted dejection, that the marks were her own, produced by her tears.

*   *   *

104

Sucre looked wide-eyed at her for a second. She stared back. The firing deep inside the ship went on. Sucre grabbed her hand, spun her round in front of him and threw her through the door, back into the corridor he'd bundled her out of minutes earlier. 'Down!' he shouted, ramming the rifle into her back, making her run. She half-fell down the stairs, Sucre clattering behind her. The firing stopped beneath them as they went down the next companionway.

Grey smoke drifted from the doorway of the *Nadia*'s saloon into the corridor. She could hear crying and shouts. Sucre screamed at her to keep going; the gun hit her in the lower back again.

The saloon was thick with acrid, stinging smoke. Bodies lay amongst the plush chairs and couches like obscene scatter cushions. She was standing behind one of the *venceristas*; he was shouting, waving his gun around. Another *vencerista* stood behind the bar, heavy machine-gun poised, smoke curling from it.

She looked at the bodies. The ringing in her ears made it difficult to hear things, but she thought somebody was calling her name. The bodies covered much of the floor, almost from end to end of the room. A few of the dark-skinned men were still at the far end, standing there with their hands behind their heads, looking cowed and terrified.

'Hisako!' She heard her name, and raised her head. It was Philippe. She was shoved towards him anyway, pushed in the back so that she had no choice but to move, and so ran across the bloody carpet, stumbled over bodies to him. He hugged her, mumbled in French into her hair, but the ringing noise smothered all his words.

Sucre was shouting at the other two *venceristas*. Then he ran down the length of the saloon and screamed at the Moroccan and Algerian men standing there. He slapped one, punched another in the belly, and clubbed a third with his rifle, sending the man crumpling to the deck. More *venceristas* piled in through the door, waving their guns. Sucre kicked one of the Algerians in the leg, making the man hop about, trying to keep his balance while not moving his hands from the back of his head; Sucre kicked him in the other leg, making him fall over.

'Hisako, Hisako,' Philippe said. She leant her head on his shoulder, and looked through the room; at Sucre kicking the

105

curled up Algerian lying on the floor near the far wall; at Mandamus, squatting beneath an up-ended chair, bulging out from under it like a snail too big for its shell; at Broekman, lying on the floor, looking up now; at Janney and the Bleveans, Captain Bleveans holding his wife's head down near the floor at the side of the couch the motionless Janney lay upon; at Endo, sitting back against the wall, cross-legged, like a slim-line buddha.

'Hisako— '

'These men were very stupid!' Sucre shrieked at them, waving his gun at the Moroccans and Algerians. 'They died, see!' He kicked one of the bodies on the floor. They weren't all dead; Hisako could hear moans. 'This what you want?' Sucre shouted. 'This what you want? They died like that stupid gringo kid out there!' Hisako wondered if any one of the people Sucre was shouting at would realise he meant Orrick. 'You want this, do you? You want to die? Is that what you want, huh? Is it?'

He seemed really to want an answer. Bleveans said, 'No, sir,' in a calm, measured voice.

Sucre looked at him, took a deep breath. He nodded. 'Yeah, well. We been kind too long. You get tied up now.'

Bleveans and Philippe tried to argue, but it did no good. They were all made to sit down. Three *venceristas* covered them while Sucre disappeared for five minutes. He came back with a box full of plastic restrainers; loops of toothed nylon which fitted over their wrists and were pulled tight. Sucre and one of the other *venceristas* started with the remaining Algerians and Moroccans. Hisako watched; they had to put their hands behind their backs first before the restrainers were put on. Philippe tried to talk to her, but one of the *venceristas* hissed at him when he spoke, and shook his head. Philippe held Hisako's hand.

A third guerrilla was dragging the bodies away, taking them by feet or hands and hauling them out through the door. She was sure that even over the ringing in her ears she could hear moans as the Algerians and Moroccans were pulled out. The *vencerista* was away for few minutes each time. She wondered if they were just dumping the bodies over the side, but doubted it.

She sat on the lounge carpet, trying to assess how she felt. Jangly; as though her body was some assemblage of delicately balanced, highly stressed components which had been roughly shaken and left ringing with the after-effects of shock. Her face stung a little on both cheeks, where Sucre had slapped her. She tasted blood in her mouth, but not very much, and she couldn't find where it was coming from. The atmosphere in the saloon seemed thicker now; the air tasted of smoke and blood, and the place looked old and worn-out, already grubby after just one night. She felt herself shiver in the *yukata*, though she wasn't cold.

'Comrade Major,' Bleveans said to Sucre, after the *venceristas* had tied up the Koreans in the middle of the room and approached the others. 'Leave the women, huh?'

Sucre looked down at Bleveans, who gazed as calmly back. Sucre smiled faintly. Mrs Bleveans sat curled up between her husband and the couch where Janney lay, eyes open again and blinking confusedly up at the ceiling. Sucre had one of the nylon restrainers in his hand. He played with it, twisting it around his hand as though he was tossing a coin.

Bleveans put his hands out towards Sucre, wrists together. 'Will you?'

Sucre took hold of both Bleveans's hands in one of his, and pulled the American round, as though pirouetting a dance partner. When Sucre let go, Bleveans brought first one hand then the other round behind him; Sucre slipped a restrainer over his wrists and pulled it tight. He put his mouth near Bleveans's ear and said, 'Say *please*, Captain.'

'Please, Comrade Major,' Bleveans said evenly. Sucre turned away, expressionless. He looked down at Gordon Janney, lying with his eyes half-open under the bulky bandages, but moving – and his lips working – like somebody having a bad dream. Sucre used two of the restrainers to secure one of the man's ankles to the arm of the couch. He ignored Mrs Bleveans.

Philippe let himself be tied. Sucre looked at Hisako for a moment, rubbing the side of his neck where she'd hit him earlier. She wondered what he was going to do. Maybe he would tie her up after all.

Sucre grabbed her right ankle, pulled her towards him a half-metre or so across the carpet. 'Su – Comrade Major— ' Philippe began. Sucre took hold of his ankle too. He put one nylon loop round Philippe's leg and put a fully opened restrainer round Hisako's, then passed one through the other and tightened them, leaving her and Philippe hobbled to each other.

Broekman let himself be tied up without comment.

'Comrade Major, this really is unnecessary,' Mandamus said. He was sweating heavily, and a tic jigged at the side of his face. 'I am no threat to you. I am not of a shape or size to crawl through portholes or engage in other acts of derring-do, and while I may not agree with all the *venceristas*'s methods, I am broadly on your side. Please, let me ask you to— '

'Shut up or I tape your mouth too,' Sucre said. He secured Mandamus, then Endo, who was already sitting quietly with his hands behind his back. He left Marie Boulard with her hands free, too.

'This was stupid,' Sucre told them, when he'd finished. He put his boot under the last body left on the floor and turned it over. The *vencerista* taking the bodies out came back into the saloon; Sucre nodded to him, and he dragged that corpse away as well, adding another smear of blood to the patterned carpet.

Sucre looked at Hisako. 'I want to know who the blond kid was.' He glanced at Bleveans, but his gaze settled back on her.

She looked down at the 8-shaped nylon bands shackling her to Philippe. 'Steve Orrick,' she said.

She had to repeat the name. She explained who he'd been; the others confirmed what she said when Sucre asked. He seemed to believe them.

'OK,' he told them. 'This time we good to you, OK?' He looked round them, as though wanting to be contradicted. 'OK. You stay like that till we go.'

'Uh, what about using the heads, Comrade Major?' Bleveans asked.

Sucre looked amused. 'You just have to get help, Captain.'

'We weren't being allowed into the heads with anybody else,' Bleveans reminded him.

Sucre shrugged. 'Too bad.'

'How much longer you going to keep us here, Comrade Major?' Bleveans asked.

Sucre just smiled.

* * *

108

The *vencerista* behind the bar was counting used cartridges into a series of beer glasses. The chink chink noise formed a background like the sound of coins being dropped into a till. They were allowed to talk quietly. They'd been split into more distinct groups; the officers and passengers formed one, the remaining Moroccans and Algerians the smallest, and the Koreans the largest; the rest were lumped together into another. They could talk with people in their own group, but weren't allowed to communicate with another.

'As soon as they heard the shooting, they were talking, and some started to . . . rise, get up,' Philippe told her, when she asked what had happened. 'They must have planned for a time before, I think. It was as if they would go then, but they did not, and the man with the machine-gun shouted at them; at all of us, but then, when the firing stopped, that was when they jump up . . . and run towards the gun.' Philippe took a long breath, closed his eyes. She put her hand to his neck, stroked him. His eyes opened and he took her hand, smiling ruefully. 'Was not very nice. They fell.' He shook his head. 'Fall everywhere. Is big machine-gun,' he looked towards the bar. 'Big bullets, on . . . a chain. So he just shoots and shoots and shoots.'

His hand clenched, almost crushing hers. She tensed her own hand.

The saloon was quiet. It was late afternoon, the heat just waning. The thick atmosphere in the lounge sat like a weight on them all. The blood-matted carpet gave off a rich, iron smell. Some people were trying to sleep, propped up against seats and couches, or lying on the floor, shifting uncomfortably, trying to move their trapped arms and ease the ache in their shoulders. Mandamus's snores sounded vaguely plaintive.

'Maybe,' Philippe said, looking over at the bar, 'if we all had run *en masse* . . . Maybe we take the gun. But we did not . . . we did not run . . . together.' He turned to her, and Hisako had never seen him look like he did then; younger than he was; almost boyish, and somehow lost, adrift.

She had told him more details of what had happened after the call from Mr Moriya; the rest had been given only a brief account of Orrick's vain attempt to help them. Philippe had been admiring and chiding, impressed that she had dared lash out at Sucre, but

109

concerned for her safety; they were at the mercy of these people, after all.

She'd listened to the men talk. The feeling now was that there was nothing they could do; they would just have to wait and hope that whatever the *venceristas* had come here to do would soon be over with. The guerrillas had shown themselves quite able to deal with both the lone commando and the mass attack; to attempt anything now, when they were keyed up after these two incidents, would be suicidal. So they had convinced themselves, breathing the air of the *Nadia*'s lounge, with its scent of smoke and blood. Nobody talked about the planeload of congressmen, except to say that there was probably some other reason for the *venceristas* to want to take over the ships.

The disturbed siestas went on into the late afternoon; sunlight made bar-shapes through the blinds behind the curtains. Gordon Janney mumbled something in what might have been his sleep; it was becoming difficult to determine when he was awake and when not, as though his brain – confused into accepting any sort of stability – was trying to average out his awareness over the whole day and night, leaving the man aground on the same dozy level of semi-consciousness all the time.

The cartridges went chink chink chink.

Philippe was talking quietly to Bleveans and Broekman. Hisako sat against a chair, trying to recall each second between the time she'd first seen Orrick that morning, and her last view of him, floating face down, body jerked by bullets, the water white around him. They had heard the grenades in here, Philippe said.

'You OK?' Mrs Bleveans knelt in front of Hisako. Her face looked haggard, the last traces of make-up producing an effect worse than none at all.

Hisako nodded. 'Yes.' She thought more was expected of her, but she couldn't think what else to say. Her ears still weren't right.

'You sure?' The American woman said, frowning a little. Hisako thought Mrs Bleveans had never looked more human. She wanted to say that, but she couldn't.

Hisako nodded again. 'Really, yes.'

Mrs Bleveans patted her leg. 'You get some rest.' She moved back to her husband, then went over to Marie Boulard.

Hisako listened to the ringing in her ears and the chink chink chink noise coming from the bar, like a currency of death.

Her head nodded, jerked back up. The noises around her sounded far away and somehow hollow. She wanted to move her leg but she couldn't.

There was a stairway underneath the ship; they were led down through the vessel, past holds full of plants and gardens and huge rooms full of furniture, through another hold where hundreds of cars sat, engines droning, horns sounding, drivers leaning out of the windows and doors with big red faces, shouting and cursing and waving their fists in the air. Beneath that came a dark space full of rods and levers and strange, sickly smells. She couldn't make out who she was with, or who was leading them, but that was probably because the light was bad. She thought she was probably dreaming, but dreams were real too, and sometimes what wasn't a dream was too real; too much for reality to support, too much for her to cope with. A dream could actually be more real, and that was good enough for her.

Under the ship the air was stifling and humid; it was like walking into a thick blanket soaked in something thick and warm. The surface of the lake was red glass, and supported above the undulating dark floor of the lake by enormous, grotesquely gnarled red pillars; they looked like immense wax-smothered bottles, holders of a thousand gigantic candles each of which had burned down and left its solidified flow behind. One of the pillars supported the ship they were descending from.

The steps ended on the dark ash of the lake floor. It was difficult to walk in, and they were all struggling. She looked up through the glass – there was a hole there, burned as though the glass was plastic – and saw Steven Orrick painting the bows of the *Circle*, standing on a little wooden plank. He was working very slowly, as though in a trance, and didn't notice the people underneath him. Some of the people with her let little fluttering balloons go, releasing them like doves; they beat nervously up through the air, past the great red pillars, through the melted hole in the glass, and up towards the young man painting the hull around the *Nakodo*'s name.

The balloons got bigger as they rose, and when they got to

111

Orrick they were larger than he was; they spread their wings and wrapped themselves round him; he dropped the brush, dropped the paint tin, and was held there on the little wooden plank, gripped by first one, then two, then many of the expanded balloons, which nestled tighter and tighter in with their wings, and then – soundlessly – burst apart, blowing out in a scattering of white feathers that rained slowly down while Orrick's shrivelled body fell, cartwheeling lazily, from the bows, and crashed through the red lake surface. He fell in a hail of quick red glass and slow white feathers. Where the paint tin had fallen against the bow of the ship, it had left a long streak of red lead over one of the letters of the ship's name, so that the letters now spelled out *NAD A*.

She didn't see where Orrick landed. The air was full of white feathers. The lake surface healed up where he'd fallen through.

At the end of the lake, where the dam had been, the surface ended abruptly above them, while the lake floor continued out into the open air, down the course of a long dry river. She felt glad to be back, and to have left the other people behind. Above her, the milky clouds let through a diffuse glow of sunlight.

The clouds had a grid written on them; dark lines stretching north–south and east–west. She walked the dry, black dust, passing shattered and deserted buildings in the distance to each side, and watched the grid of the sky gradually fill up with huge circular shapes; they occupied the interstices of the grid; some were dark, like the ash beneath her feet, and some were milky, like the clouds themselves, and hardly visible; just giant halos of light in the sky. It became darker as more of the huge shapes floated down into place. DNA, said the shapes.

This must be going on everywhere, she thought. Like a giant game of *go*. Light and dark; everywhere. She wondered who would win. She wanted the light-coloured ones to win. They appeared to be winning. She walked on, noticing that the city around her seemed to be growing. The buildings were less wrecked and not as far apart as they had been. The sky was lightening again, as the milky shapes above surrounded and took over the dark ones. The city was crowding in now, buildings creaking upwards into the sky as she watched. There were people as well. They were small and still far away, but they moved about the grid of the city, beneath the towering, stretching buildings.

The sky was milky, the sky was clear. The sky-wide circles had taken over the sky. A terrific wind started up, and howled round the buildings as the sky became brighter and the sunlight slammed down. She kept walking but saw everybody else swept away and whirled into the air, fluttering whitely. The sun glinted through one of the great lenses in the sky, dimmed briefly, then flared, exploded, blinding her and wrapping a cloak of heat across her face.

When she opened her eyes the buildings had melted and stood as pillars over the grey ash beneath her feet, supporting a sky of cracked red glass, like something old and fused and smeared with blood.

The grey ash shuddered, sending a tremor up through her feet, shaking her. The sky called her name.

She woke to find Philippe shaking her shoulder. Sucre stood at her feet, kicking them, looking bored. In one hand he held a large knife, in the other her cello case. Her eyes widened; she sat up. Sucre put the knife in its sheath and hefted his assault rifle. The plastic restrainer joining Hisako to Philippe had been cut; she was free.

Sucre jerked his head towards the door. 'You come with me; we go to a concert.'

8: Conquistadores

They took her across to the *Nakodo* in *Le Cercle*'s Gemini; the one she and Philippe used on their dives. The sunlight was bright on the water through the patchy cloud, and she hugged her cello case to her, gaining some distant comfort from its leather smell. Sucre sat in the bows, facing her, mirror shades showing the cello case, her, and the *vencerista* at the outboard. There was a small thin smile on his face; he hadn't answered any of her questions about why they were heading for the *Nakodo* with the cello. He kept the Kalashnikov pointed at her the whole way across. She wondered what would happen if she threw the cello case at him. Would it stop the bullets? She didn't think so. He would probably puncture the Gemini if the gun went off on automatic; maybe he would even hit the *vencerista* at the stern, but her own chances of surviving would be small.

She imagined, nevertheless, throwing it at him, leaping after it; Sucre somehow missing it and her, her grabbing his gun, perhaps knocking him overboard (though how to do that without losing the gun, strapped round his shoulders?), or just knocking him unconscious, still getting the gun from him in time to turn and fire before the man in the stern could reach for and fire his own machine-gun . . . yes, and she could swim away from the probably sinking Gemini, using the cello case as a life raft, and rescue all the others or get word to the outside world, and everything would be just fine. She swallowed heavily, as though consuming the wildness of the idea. Her heart beat hard, thudding against the cello case.

She wondered how often people had been in such a situation; not knowing what was going to happen to them, but so full of

114

fearful hope and hopeless fear they went along with whatever their captors were arranging, praying it would end without bloodshed, lost in some pathetic human trust that no terrible harm was being prepared for them.

How many people had been woken by the hammering at the door in the small hours, and had gone – perhaps protesting, but otherwise meekly – to their deaths? Perhaps they went quietly to protect their family; perhaps because they could not believe that what was happening to them was anything – *could be* anything – other than a terrible mistake. Had they known their family too was doomed, had they known they were themselves already utterly condemned and without hope, destined inevitably for a bullet in the neck within hours, or for years – even decades – of toil and suffering in the camps before a cold and disregarded death, they might have resisted then, at the start, when they still had a chance, however futile their resistance might finally be. But few resisted, from what she knew. Hope was endemic, and sometimes reality implied despair.

How could you believe, even in the cattle trucks, that what had been the most civilised nation on earth was preparing to take you – all of you; the entire trainload – and strip you, remove and sort artificial limbs, glasses, clothes and wigs and jewellery, gas you by the hundreds in a production line of death, and then pull the gold teeth from your skull? How? It was the stuff of nightmares, not reality. It was too terrible to be true; even a people inured over the centuries to prejudice and persecution must have found it hard to believe it could really be happening in the West in the twentieth century.

And the doctor or engineer or politician or worker in Moscow or Kiev or Leningrad, roused from sleep by the fists on the door; without knowing he was already dead as far as the state was concerned, who could blame him for going quietly, hoping to impress with his co-operation, to save his wife and children (which, maybe, he did)? Nervously confident in his knowledge that he'd done nothing wrong and had always supported the party and the great leader, was it any surprise he quietly packed a small case and kissed his wife's tears away, promising to be back soon?

The Kampucheans had quit the city, seeing some warped logic in it at first, thinking it best to humour the men from the jungle. How could they have known – how could they have taken seriously the idea – the glasses on their noses would bring the iron rods down on them, smashing them to bits, consigning them to mud?

Even knowing what was going to happen, perhaps you still hoped, or just could not believe it was really going to happen to you, in (in their times) Chile, Argentina, Nicaragua, El Salvador . . . Panama.

She looked away from her reflections on Sucre's smiling face. The distant land was green and squashed. Perhaps help would come from there. Maybe Orrick had succeeded in a way; somebody ashore might have heard the shots and explosions as they killed him. The National Guard would come and the *venceristas* would flee, leaving their hostages alive; it would be absurd to kill any more, wouldn't it? International opinion; outcry; condemnation, retaliation.

She hugged the case closer, felt herself shiver. The rectangular bulk of the *Nakodo* filled the sky in front of her, blocking off the sun.

She followed Sucre up the steps from the landing pontoon, still holding the cello in its case in front of her. Another *vencerista* met them on the deck and led them into the ship. She was ushered into the officers' mess. The curtains were drawn; two lights shone from the far end of the mess-room table. She could just make out a figure sitting there. A chair was drawn up a metre or so from the end of the table nearest her. Sucre motioned her to sit there, then went to the vaguely seen figure sitting behind the lights. She screwed her eyes up, peering forward. The lights were Anglepoise lamps, sitting on the table, shining straight at her. The air-conditioned room made her shiver again, making her wish she wore something more substantial than just the *yukata*.

'Ms Onoda,' Sucre said, from behind the lights. She shielded her eyes. 'The *jefe* wants you to play for him.'

She stayed as she was. There was silence until she said, 'What does he want me to play?'

She saw Sucre bend to the other man, come upright again. 'Anything; what you want.'

She thought about it. Even asking whether she had a choice

116

seemed pointless. She could ask for her music and so delay things, but she could see no good reason for doing so. She would rather do this and get back as soon as she could to Philippe and the others. Wondering who the man behind the lights was, and why he wanted to keep his identity secret, seemed just as useless. She sighed, opened the case and took out the cello and bow, laying down the case.

'It will take a little while to tune it,' she said, adjusting the spike to the right height for the small seat, then drawing the cello to her, feeling it between her thighs and against her breasts and neck.

'Is OK,' Sucre told her, as she drew the bow across the strings. The A string was a little flat; she brought it into line with the others, closing her eyes and listening. She had always visualised tuning. In her mind the sound was a single vibrant line of colour; a column in the air, changing like oil on water but always coherent and somehow solid. If one shade jarred from an edge, like a badly printed colour photograph, it had to be refocused, brought back into line. The cello sang, hummed against her; the column of colour behind her eyes was bright and definite.

She checked, fingering through a few exercises, finding her knuckles and joints were less stiff than she'd feared.

She opened her eyes again. 'This is . . . Tung Loi's "Song of Leaving",' she told the lights.

No reaction. It wasn't a classical piece, and she wondered if perhaps her shy captor would object to a modern work, but the *jefe* behind the lights said nothing. Perhaps he didn't know enough to comment, or perhaps he knew the piece and approved; it was what had come to be known as New Classical, part of the melodic *fin de siècle* reaction against mathematical atonality.

She bent to the instrument, closing her eyes slowly with the first broad sweep of the bow that was the awakening of the woman and the dawning of the day the piece would sing about.

Technically it was a fairly undemanding piece, but the emotion it called for, to wring all that could be wrung from the music, made it difficult to perform without sounding either off-hand or pretentious. She wasn't sure herself why she'd chosen it; she'd practised it over the months since leaving Japan, and it sounded full and good in its solo form, but the same went for other pieces, and this was one she had never been convinced she had done justice to in the past.

She ceased to wonder about it, and forgot about the lights and the man behind them, and the gun at Sucre's waist and the people trapped and trussed on the *Nadia*, and simply played, submerging herself in the silky depths of the music's hope and sorrow.

When it was over, and the last notes died, finally giving themselves up to the air, to the flesh of her fingertips and to the ancient wood of the instrument, she kept her eyes closed for a time, still in her deep red cave of heartache and loss. There were strange patterns behind her eyelids, swimming and pulsing to the strong beat of her blood. The music seemed to have set them into a theme of movement of its own, and they were only now unravelling into their natural semi-chaos. She watched them.

Clap clap clap. The sudden sound of applause shook her. She opened her eyes quickly. A glimpse of white hands clapping in the light, before they pulled back. The figure moved to one side, towards Sucre, and he started clapping too, matching the other man. Sucre nodded vigorously, glancing from her to the man in the seat beside him.

Clap clap. Clap. The applause subsided, stopped.

Hisako sat blinking in the light.

Sucre leant towards the man. 'Beautiful,' Sucre said, straightening.

'Thank you.' She relaxed, let the bow tip touch the carpet. Would he want more?

Sucre bent again, then said, '*Señorita*, please turn round; face the other way.'

She stared. Then turned, awkwardly with the cello, shifting the seat, looked back at the door to the corridor outside.

Why? she thought. *Surely not to shoot me? Do I play for him, then obediently perform this last gesture which will make the killing of me easier for them?* Light flared behind her. She stiffened.

'OK,' Sucre said easily. 'Turn back now.'

She pivoted on the seat, taking the cello round in front of her. The red glowing end of a cigar glowed dimly behind the lights. A cloud of smoke drifted in front of the beams, further obscuring the view behind. She smelled sulphur.

'The *jefe* wants to know what you were thinking of when you play this piece,' Sucre said.

She thought, conscious of her frown and of looking away from the lights into the darkness, seeking her answer there. 'I thought of . . . leaving. Of leaving Japan. Of leaving . . .' she hesitated, then knew there was no point in pretending. 'I thought of leaving . . . thé people on the ship; the *Nadia*.' She had meant to say 'one person' or 'someone' on the ship, but something had deflected her even as she'd spoken, though she knew that Sucre already knew about Philippe. Even in these tiny, hopeless increments do we try to protect those we love, she thought, and looked up into the lights. 'I thought of leaving life; of this being my last chance to play.' She drew herself up straight in the seat. 'That's what I thought of.'

She heard the man behind the lights draw in his breath. Perhaps he nodded. Sucre drew up a seat and sat down by the other man. 'The *jefe* wants to know what you think of us.' It was as though one of the lights was talking.

'Of the *venceristas*?'

'*Sí*.'

She wondered what was the right thing to say. But they would know she'd try to say the right thing, so what was the point of it? She shrugged, looked down at the cello, fingered the strings. 'I don't know. I don't know everything that you stand for.'

After a pause; 'Freedom for the people of Panamá. Eventually, a greater Columbia. Cutting the puppet strings of the *yanquis*.'

'Well, that might be good,' she said, not looking up. Silence from the far end of the table. The coal of the cigar glowed brightly for a moment. 'I am not a politician,' she said. 'I am a musician. Anyway, this is not my fight. I'm sorry.' She looked up. 'We all just want to get out alive.'

The cigar coal dipped towards Sucre. She heard a deep voice, smoky, as though it had taken on some of the character of the pungent blue fumes it passed through on its way to her.

'But the *yanquis* forced you to open up your country, yes? 1854; the American Navy made you trade.' She sensed Sucre lean close to the other man again, heard the rumble of his voice once more. 'And then, less than a century later, they nuke you.' The cigar coal was out to one side; she could just see it, under the glare of the left-hand light, and she could imagine the seated figure, arm on an arm of the chair. 'Huh?' Sucre said.

'That has all happened,' she said. 'We . . . ' she struggled to find the words to describe a century and a half of the most radical change any country had ever undergone. 'We had strengths in our isolation, but it could not persist for ever. When we were . . . forced to change, we changed and found new strengths . . . or new expressions of the old ones. We tried too much; we tried to fit ourselves to the peoples outside; behave the way they did. We defeated China and Russia, and the world was amazed, and amazed too that we treated our prisoners so well . . . then we became . . . arrogant, perhaps, and thought we could take on America, and treat the . . . foreign devils as less than human. So we were treated the same way. It was wrong, but we were too. Since then we have flourished. We have sadnesses, but,' she sighed again, looking down at the strings, resting her fingers on them, imagining the chord she was producing, 'we can have few complaints.' The lights still blazed. The cigar was centred again, and bright.

'You think the people on the other ship support us?' Sucre said, after a pause.

'They want to live,' she said. 'Maybe some want you to succeed, maybe some don't. They all want to live. That is stronger.'

A noise that might have been a 'hmm'. Smoke billowed like a sail into the twin cones of light and flowed across the table in a slowly fluid tumble.

'Will you play in America?' Sucre said.

'After Europe, I said I would think about it. I may.' She wondered how much the man behind the lights was taking in. She wasn't choosing her words to make them easy.

'You play for the *yanquis*?' Sucre said, sounding amused.

'I'd swear I wouldn't, if it would make any difference to you.'

Definite amusement from the far end of the table. The rumbling voice again. 'We don't ask that, *Señorita*,' Sucre said, laughing.

'What do you ask?'

Sucre waited for the low voice, then said, 'We ask that you should play another— '

The lights flickered and went out; some tone in the ship, never noticed because always there, altered, whined down. The lights came on dimly for a moment, then faded slowly, filaments passing through yellow to orange to red; the same colour as the cigar. They went out.

The emergency lights came on from the corners of the room, filling the mess with a flat neon glow.

She was looking at a man in olive fatigues; square shoulders, square face. For a second she thought he was bald, then saw he had blond hair, crew cut. His eyes were glittering blue. She saw Sucre stand quickly. There was noise from behind her, and the door opened. A voice behind her said, '*Jefe* . . . ' then trailed off.

Frozen, the scene seemed cardboard and drained of colour; almost monochromatic. Sucre moved uncertainly towards her. The man holding the cigar raised it to thin lips under a thin blond moustache; the red glow brought colour to his face.

The voice behind her made a throat-clearing noise. '*Jefe?*'

The *jefe* looked steadily at Hisako. The deep voice rumbled, 'Sucre; check out the engine room. If somebody's . . . made a mistake with that generator . . . I want to see him.'

Sucre nodded and left quickly. The man at the door must still have been there; she saw the *jefe* look above and behind her, raising his eyebrows fractionally and giving just the slightest inclination of his head. '*Sí,*' said the voice. The door closed, and she felt alone; alone with the *jefe*.

The blond man sighed, looked at the end of his cigar. He tapped a couple of centimetres of ash into an ashtray on the table directly in front of him.

'Havana,' he said, holding the cigar up for a moment. He studied the end again. 'You can tell the quality of the cigar . . . well, by the leaf . . . but also by how much ash it'll support.' He rolled the cigar round in his fingers for a few seconds. 'Rolled between the thighs of *señoritas*.' He smiled at her, and smoked.

He reached down to his waist, pulled out an automatic pistol and laid it gently on the table beside the ashtray. He looked at her. 'Don't be alarmed, ma'am.' He put one hand on the gun, running his fingers over the barrel and stock, looking at it. His hands were broad, large-fingered, yet he touched the gun with a sort of delicacy. 'Colt nineteen-eleven A-one,' he said, his voice filling the room, bassy and full. She imagined cigar tar in his lungs; vocal cords scarred by smoke. The cello seemed to feel his voice, responding.

The large hands stroked the pistol again. 'Still a damn fine gun, after all these years. This is a seventy-three model.' He raised his eyes to her. 'Not as old as your cello though, I guess.'

She swallowed. 'No. Not by . . . two and a half centuries.'

'Yeah?' He seemed amused, leant back in the chair. 'That much, huh?' He sat, nodding. The cigar smoke made a ragged rising line in the air.

She wanted to ask if she was dead now, if seeing him was her sentence, and the light her executioner, but she could not. She bit her lips, looked down at the cello strings again. She tried to finger a silent chord, but her hand was shaking too much.

'You played real good, Miss Onoda.' The deep voice shook her, a sympathetic frequency to her trembling hands.

'Thank you,' she whispered.

'Ma'am,' he said quietly. She didn't look up, but had the feeling he'd leant closer. 'I don't want you to worry. It wasn't my intention you should see me, but now you have, all it means is you can't go back to the others until our job here is finished.'

His elbows were on the table, between the lamps, straddling the ashtray and gun. His eyes disappeared behind a veil of smoke. 'I don't want you to worry none, see?'

'Oh,' she said, looking straight at him. 'Fine. I won't.'

He gave a throaty laugh. 'Damn, Sucre said you were cool, Miss Onoda. I see what the man meant now.' He laughed again. The seat creaked as he sat back in it. 'I'd just love to know what you thought was going on here, you know that? Strikes me you might have all sorts of ideas.'

'None worth repeating.' The trembling in her hands was subsiding. She could finger a chord.

'No; I'd really like to know.'

She shrugged. One chord to another; the change made just so.

'What if I said nothing you say to me makes any difference?' The voice seemed to rise a little, as though stretching. 'My job is to out-think people, ma'am, and I seriously suspect I out-thought you some time ago, so why not— ' she heard the indrawn breath, could see the cigar glow reflected '—just tell me what you think?' The hand waved the cigar around, never far from the lying gun. 'Can't be worse than what I already think you think.'

All the people who'd gone meekly; all the people who'd gone weakly. Now I am dead, she thought. Well, it had to happen.

She looked into the blue eyes, put the bow down to one side, let the cello down to the carpet on the other and put her hands together on her lap. She said, 'You are American.'

No reaction. The man like a still photograph, caught in the light.

'You are here because of the plane and the congressmen. I couldn't see why the *venceristas* wanted to shoot down the plane; it would be madness; the whole world would despise them. It would be an opportunity for the US fleet to retaliate, the Marines to come in. There would be no sense to it. But for you? . . . For the CIA? . . . It might be a worthwhile sacrifice.'

It was said. The words seemed to dry her mouth as they were spoken, but they came out, blossomed like flowers in the cold, smoky air of the room. 'You had us all fooled,' she added, still trying to save the others. 'Nobody imagined you'd shoot down your own plane. Steve Orrick was fooled; the young man your men grenaded to death.'

'Oh yeah; shame about that.' The blond man looked concerned. 'Boy showed promise; he thought he was doing the right thing for America. Can't blame him for that.' The *jefe* shrugged, his shoulders moving like a great wave gathering, falling. 'There are always casualties. That's the way it is.'

'And the people on the plane?'

The man looked at her for a long time, then nodded slowly. 'Well,' he said, putting the hand holding the cigar slowly through his cropped hair, massaging his scalp, 'there's a long and honourable tradition of shooting down commercial airliners, Miss Onoda. The Israelis did it back in . . . oh, early seventies, I believe; Egyptian plane, over Sinai. KAL 007 was chalked up to the Russians, and we downed an Airbus over the Persian Gulf, back in eighty-eight. An Italian plane probably took a NATO missile in an exercise, by mistake, back in the seventies too . . . not to mention terrorist bombs.' He shrugged. 'These things have to happen sometimes.'

Hisako looked down again. 'I saw a banner once, on television,' she said, 'from England, many years ago, outside an American missile base. The banner said "Take the toys from the boys".'

He laughed. 'That the way you see it, Miss Onoda? The men to blame? That simple?'

She shrugged. 'Just a thought.'

He laughed again. 'Hell, I hope we're here a while yet, Miss Onoda; I want to talk to you.' He stroked the gun, tapped the cigar on the edge of the ashtray, but did not dislodge the grey cone. 'I hope you'll play for me again, too.'

She thought for a moment, then bent down and took up the bow from where it lay on the carpet, and – holding an end in each hand (and thinking, *This is stupid; why am I doing this?*) – she snapped it in two. The wood gave, like a rifle shot. The horsehair held the pieces together.

She threw the broken bow down the table towards him. It skidded to a halt between the darkened lights, clunking against the ashtray and the gun, where his hand was already hovering.

He looked at the shattered wood for a moment, then took it slowly in the hand that had gone for the Colt, lifting the dark, splintered bow up, one end dangling by the length of horsehair. 'Hmm,' he said.

The door behind her opened. One of the others came in, hurrying to the far end of the table, only glancing at her, then leaning to speak to the blond man. She caught enough; *aeroplano* and *mañana*.

He stood, taking up the Colt.

She watched the gun. *I don't know,* she told herself calmly. *How do you prepare? How does anybody ever prepare? When it actually happens, you can never find out. Ask an ancestor.*

The blond man – tall, close to two metres – whispered something to the soldier who'd given him the message. The background noise in the room altered, increased, humming. The lights flickered on, off, then on again, flooding the room with brilliance, outlining the two men. She was waiting to see what else the whisper was about; too late to take advantage of any surprise caused by the lights. Always too late.

The other man nodded, reached into a pocket. He came round behind her while the *jefe* smiled down, smoking his cigar. He took the cello case from where it leant against one bulkhead.

The soldier behind her took her wrists, put something small and hard round them, and pulled it tight.

The blond man took her cello and gently placed it in the case. 'Take Miss Onoda back to her ship, will you?' he said.

The soldier pulled her to her feet. The *jefe* nodded his crew-cut head. 'Dandridge,' he told her. 'Earl Dandridge.' He handed the closed cello case to the soldier. 'Nice meeting you, Miss Onoda. Safe journey back.'

It was at the airport she killed a man.

(After the fiasco with the American tour, and after a few tearful days with her mother, unable to go out, unwilling to see any of her old friends, she went back to Tokyo, took out her savings and went on holiday, travelling by train and bus and ferry through the country, staying in *ryokans* whenever she could. The land steadied her with its masses and textures and simple scale; the distance from one place to the next. The quiet, relaxed formality of the old, traditional inns slowly soothed her.)

The body fell to the muddy, trampled grass, eyes still startled, while the feet pounded and the cries rang and the sound of a jet landing shattered the air above them. His legs kicked once.

(She took the *Shinkansen* to Kyoto, watching the sea and the land whizz by as the bullet train sang down the steel rails, heading south and west. In that old city she was a tourist, walking quietly through the network of streets, visiting temples and shrines. In the hills, at Nanzenji temple, she sat watching the waterfall she'd discovered by following the red brick aqueduct through the grounds. At Kiyomizu, she looked down from its wooden veranda, down the gulf of space beyond the cliff and the wooden rails, for so long that a temple guide came up to ask her if she was all right. She was embarrassed, and left quickly. She went to Kinkakuji, as much to see the setting of Mishima's *Golden Pavilion* as to see the temple for its own sake. Ryoanji was too crowded and noisy for her; she left the famous gravel garden unseen. Todaiji intimidated her just by its size; she turned away outside it, feeling weak and foolish. Instead, she bought a postcard of the bronze Buddha inside, and sent it to her mother.)

She stabbed at his throat with her fingers, instantly furious, beyond all reason or normality, the pressure of all her frustration hammering her bones and flesh into his neck. He dropped the baton. His eyes went white.

(At Toba she watched the pearl divers. They still dived for pearls sometimes, though mostly it was for sea plants now; cultured pearls were cheaper and easier to harvest. She sat on the rocks for half a day, watching the dark-suited ladies swim out with their wooden buckets, then sound, disappearing for minutes at a time. When they surfaced, it was with a strange whistling noise she could never quite place on the conventional musical scale, no matter how many times she listened to it.)

He struggled, body armour making him hard and insect-like behind his gas mask. The orange smoke folded round them. The wet rag round her mouth kept the smoke out better than the tear gas. Ten metres in front of them, over the heads of the students, batons rose and fell like winnowing poles. A surge in the screaming, pressing crowd pushed them over; they staggered, each sinking to their knees. The ground was damp through her needlecords. The riot policeman put his hand out, down to the ground. She thought it was to steady himself, but he had found the baton. He swung it at her; her crash helmet took the blow, sending her down to the wet grass; one of her hands was trampled on, filling her with pain. The baton swung down at her again and she dodged; it struck the ground. The pain in her buzzing head and the burning, impaled hand took her, choked her, filled her. She steadied herself, and saw through her tears and the curling orange smoke the policeman's exposed throat as he brought the baton up again.

(So Hiroshima. The girder skullcap and empty eye windows of the ruined trade hall. She went through the museum, she read the English captions, and could not believe the cenotaph was so incompetent. The flensed stone and bleached concrete of the wrecked trade hall was much more eloquent.

She stood on the banks of the river with her back to the Peace Park, watching her shadow lengthen across the grey-brown waters while the sky turned red, and felt the tears roll down her cheeks.

Too much, turn away.

* * *

126

In the train again, she passed through Kitakyushu, where the second bomb would have been dropped if the visibility had been better that day. The cluttered hills of Nagasaki took it instead. The monument there – a giant human statue, epicentric – she found more fitting; what had happened to the two cities – both crowded, busy places again – was beyond abstraction.)

The line pressed forward; they chanted and yelled, voices muffled by the damp cloths many had over their mouths and noses to keep out the worst of the tear gas. She had forgotten to bring a pair of goggles, and the crash helmet had no visor. Her arms were held on either side; linked with the students. She felt good; frightened but purposeful, acting with the others, part of a team, greater than herself. They heard screams from ahead. Batons like a fence rose into the air in front of them. They stormed onwards, the line breaking and giving way; people tripped in front, something whacked her crash helmet as she stumbled over a pile of people and caught a glimpse of police riot gear, visors glinting in the remnant sunlight. Her arms were wrenched from those of the youths on either side, and the orange smoke wrapped itself around her like thick fog. The riot policeman came rocketing backwards through the orange haze, crashing into her. His right glove was off, and she saw the leather thong attaching him to his baton slip from his wrist as they both tried to regain their balance. He grabbed for the falling baton as he turned, then punched her in the face. She heard something click, and tasted blood. She rocked back, ducked to the right, expecting another blow but unable to see, then lunged forward, grappling with the man.

(She ate satsumas on the ferry ride across from Kagoshima City to Sakurajima, to see the volcano. Dust fell on the city that evening, and she realised – as her hair filled with the fine, gritty stuff, and her eyes smarted – that it was true; people in Kagoshima really did carry umbrellas all the time. She'd always thought it was a joke.

At Ibusuki she watched the sand bathers lie on the beach, smiling and chattering to each other while the hot black sand was piled over them. They lay like darkly swaddled infants near the waves, progeny of some strange human-turtle god, long-laboured on the black sands.)

Orange smoke and the sting of tear gas. The orange smoke

was theirs, the tear gas belonged to the riot police. The air was a choking thick mixture and the sun shone through the braids of dark smoke twisting through the sky from piles of burning tyres on the perimeter of the demonstration. High cloud completed the set of filters. Marshals wearing bright waistcoats and specially marked crash helmets shouted at them from megaphones, voices drowned by the sporadic screams of the planes. Between them and the airport perimeter fence, the riot police lines were advancing, dark waves over the long grass and reeds, like the wind made solid. Heavy water cannons lumbered over to one side, where the ground was solid enough to support the trucks. The signal came to advance, and the students cheered, strode forward, arms linked, chanting, their flags and banners and placards catching in the wind. The shadows of planes flickered over them.

(At Beppu Spa, on the side of the hill, in the great gaudy steamy aircraft hangar of the jungle bath-house, surrounded by blue water, trees, ferns, a standing golden Buddha, thousands of coloured globes like *gaijin* Christmas decorations and arching girders overhead, with the vague smell of sulphur coming and going in her nose, she bathed. She came back on the Sea of Japan coast; through Hagi and Tottori, and Tsuraga and Kanazawa. She went to see Crow Castle, sitting blackly on its compressed rock base. She worked up the courage, and visited the Suzuki school, near by in Matsumoto, talking to the teachers and watching the little children play the instruments. It depressed her; how much better she might have been if she'd started really early, and with this fascinating method. She was years behind, as well as years ahead of, these children.

She held off returning to Tokyo, but stayed near by; returning to the Fuji Five Lakes as her money slowly ran out, then to Izu Peninsula, then across by ferry to Chiba. Finally, fretting, she realised she was only circling, in a holding pattern of her own, and so came back to the capital. She passed Narita on the way. There were demonstrations over the plans to expand the airport.

When she got back to the city the orchestra was still on tour. There were several messages and letters asking, then telling her to contact the orchestra's business manager, who'd stayed in Tokyo. Instead she went out, and found some of her old student friends in a bar near Akasaka Mitsuke station. They were demonstrating

128

against the airport extension on Sunday. She asked if she could come along.)

I will pay for this, she thought, as the policeman's eyes closed and the orange mist rolled around her. I will pay for this.

Her hands ached. She sniffed the blood back into her nose.

Something was flapping on top of her, and she fought her way out from under a fallen banner. People streamed past her again, heading back. The tear gas was thicker; like a million tiny needles being worked into the nose and eyes and tingling in the mouth and throat. Her eyes flooded. The banner covering the policeman fluttered in the orange wind. She turned and ran, driven back with the rest.

Hisako sat midships in the Gemini, the cello case lying at her feet. The outboard puttered, idling. She could feel the small eyes of the soldier in the stern watching her as she stared out across the lake to the folded green hills on the western shore.

Sucre appeared at the top of the steps, and clattered down them. He got into the inflatable, grinning broadly. He reached forward and slapped her hard across the cheek, rattling her teeth and almost knocking her out of the boat, then sat back in the bows, laughing, and told the soldier at the outboard to head back to the *Nadia*.

Her head pounded, her ears rang. She tasted blood. The boat bucked and slapped across the glittering surface of the lake. She felt sick, and still felt so when they got to the ship. Sucre supported her by one elbow as she stepped shakily from the Gemini to the *Nadia*'s pontoon. Her wrists felt numb where the restrainer bit into them. Sucre said something to the other soldier, then punched her in the belly, winding her. She collapsed to her knees on the wooden planking. Sucre gripped her from behind while the other man put a large piece of black masking tape across her mouth.

Then, dazed and bruised and terrified she would vomit and drown, she was pushed and pulled up the companionway to the deck. She caught a last glimpse of the cello case, lying in the bottom of the Gemini.

Sucre and the other man met a third soldier at the door to the *Nadia*'s saloon. Sucre opened it. She saw Philippe and the others.

129

He looked relieved. She closed her eyes, shook her head.

They took her into the room, then Sucre crossed to Mrs Bleveans, took her by the elbow, and with her in tow collected Marie Boulard. He made them stand at the bar, and put restrainers on them as well.

Nobody talked in the room. Sucre had the two women kneel in front of the semi-circle of low stools, facing the bar like worshippers. Down at the far end of the room, the Koreans, the North Africans and the remaining crewmen had been collected into three giant circles; they too were kneeling, facing outwards, their wrists apparently strapped to those of the men on each side of them. One of the fake *venceristas* was completing tying up the Koreans, who formed the largest of the three groups. The men looked out into the room with frightened eyes. Sucre had a word with the man behind the bar with the heavy machine-gun, then went down the room to the third of the circles, patting the shoulder of the soldier who'd just finished tying the men up. She was watching now, eyes bright with pain and terror, her bowels feeling loose, her stomach churning behind the bruise. She saw Sucre pretend to inspect the bonds of the men making up the far circle. She saw him take the grenade even though nobody else seemed to. She saw him wander away from the group, towards the second one. The soldier behind her tightened his grip on the restrainer.

One of the men in the first circle must have felt it. He shouted something in Korean, screamed, tried desperately to get up, almost dragging part of the circle with him while the others looked round bewildered. Sucre skipped to the second circle and dropped the grenade into the middle of it, repeated the action at the last circle of men, then ran for the door. The saloon filled with screams. Sucre ducked behind a couch with the soldier who'd tied up the men. The soldier holding Hisako stepped back so that he was shielded by the door; the man behind the bar disappeared behind it.

The noise was more muffled than it had been earlier, when Orrick had attacked. She watched. Her eyes closed for the instant of the detonation, but she saw the circle of men rise up, saw the red cloud burst from one part, on the far side. The second circle of men had almost managed to stand; some had been hit by shrapnel from the first blast, but somehow they were almost on their feet. She

130

saw Lekkas then, yelling at the others and trying to kick behind him, where the grenade had to be. The ringing blast of the first grenade was just giving way to the screams and moans of the injured in the first group when the second detonated, throwing men across the room, flaying legs, smacking blood and flesh off the ceiling. Something whined past her left ear. The men in the third group were almost on their feet; the grenade blasted their legs out from under them.

The machine-gun opened up; Sucre and the soldier who'd tied the men up scrambled to the side of the room and started firing too. The man holding her shoved her forward and started firing with a small Uzi, making a cracking, drilling noise by her head.

Philippe, Broekman, Endo and Bleveans were struggling to their feet. Marie Boulard and Mrs Bleveans knelt, shivering as though the noise itself shook them. Mrs Bleveans was trying to look back, to where her husband was. Hisako couldn't see Mandamus. The saloon was filling with smoke like a thick sea fog.

Sucre saw the officers standing, and turned his fire on them. She saw Broekman whipped back as though pulled by a hawser fastened to his back, and Philippe hit in the belly, doubling up: she closed her eyes.

She opened them again when she heard Mrs Bleveans scream, over the noise of the firing. The woman crashed through the barrier of stools towards her husband, who lay on his side on the floor, shirt covered with blood. His wife fell towards him, over him. Sucre kept on firing; Mrs Bleveans's blouse kicked out in four or five places. Marie Boulard had risen at the same time, and threw herself at Sucre; the soldier holding Hisako flicked the Uzi to one side, bringing the woman down in a cloud of smoke and noise.

They finished all the men off. Mr Mandamus was, miraculously, uninjured, and protested to the last, before being silenced with a single shot from Sucre's pistol. The soldiers decided both the other women were indeed dead. They threw Hisako to the floor and tore the *yukata* off.

They were going to rape her there, but instead dragged her by the feet, out, across the corridor and into the ship's television lounge, because the air in the saloon was so thick with choking, acrid smoke.

FORCE MAJEURE

force majeure (fors mahzher') *n.* Irresistible compulsion or coercion, unforeseeable course of events excusing from fulfilment of contract. [F, = superior strength]

9: Aguaceros

Her fingers ached whenever she touched the cello.

After the demonstration they regrouped before dispersing, to see who had been arrested or injured. One of the students volunteered to go with the group of people who would follow the police buses back into the city and find out what had happened to those who were missing. The rest of them returned by cars and hired minibuses.

She found it easy to be quiet; her shock passed unnoticed. Everybody else was high on the exhilaration of the demonstration and the fact they'd survived with nothing worse than red eyes and sniffly noses. They chattered, relived and retold their experiences. Nobody seemed to have heard about the dead policeman.

They went back to the same bar she'd met them in earlier that week. She went to the toilets and threw up.

The television showed the news; the clash outside the airport was the lead story, with the murdered riot policeman providing the headline. The students were divided; some had bruises from the batons, or knew people who'd had arms broken by the riot police, at the University, the airport or in the streets on Vietnam demos, and muttered that the man probably deserved it, or that another policeman might have done it, settling some old score in the heat of the battle . . . while the rest went as quiet as Hisako.

She left as soon as she could, coughing and complaining of a headache. In the flat she sat in darkness, staring at the patterns of light the city cast on to the ceiling and walls through the window blinds. She was still staring at the white and orange barred wedges of light when they gradually faded under the pervasive grey of a new day.

135

She didn't know what to do; to confess, to run away, to pretend nothing had happened . . . .

She didn't know what had made her do it. Anger and pain, perhaps, but so what? There must have been hundreds of people there who'd been more angry, and been hurt worse than she. They hadn't killed anybody.

What was in her that could do such a thing? She wasn't normally violent; she'd been accused of attacking the music sometimes, of being too aggressive with the bow and her fingers, but (as she put her hands into her armpits, staring at the grey day dawning) that wasn't *murder*.

She still could hardly believe she'd done it, but the memory was there, livid and raw, like the taste and sting of the gas. And the memory resided not just in her brain, behind her eyes, but in her bones; in her fingers. She could feel again the crumpling and cracking as they lanced into the man's neck; they hurt again as she thought of her bones and his, buckling, compressing.

She hugged herself tighter and put her head down on to her knees, sobbing into the jeans and forcing her arms into her sides as though trying to crush her hands.

It was impossible to sleep the next night too, so she walked through the city until dawn, through the Soapland sleaze and past the quiet parks and down the side streets where the pachinko parlours sounded like a million tiny nails being rattled in a drum and the *karaoke* bars echoed with drunk businessmen singing badly, down the streets where the plaster European models stood in bright windows, hung with million-yen dresses, and electronics companies displayed the latest crop of gadgets like glittering jewellery, and through suburbs, where the small houses sat crammed and dark and the only sound was the distant city grumble and faraway trains screeching through points.

That day she slept, fitfully, always waking with the feeling of shock, convinced that some incredibly violent noise had just stopped echoing, that a titanic explosion had caused her to wake and the air had barely finished ringing with the aftershock. Once a small earthquake did wake her, but it was only enough to rattle the flat a little; nothing remarkable. She'd never been bothered by quakes before, but now she lay awake, worrying that it was just a prelude to a big one; a shock that would bring all Tokyo down, crushing her in her flat, squashing her under tons of rubble, suffocating her on the bed like a pinned insect, grinding her bones, destroying her while she tried to scream.

She got up, took to the streets again.

And when she did try to play the cello, her fingers ached. The left hand, the one that had been stepped on, hurt a little, but the right, which had to hold the bow, filled her with agony. It was as though all the bones had been recently broken, and the act of trying to move the bow across the strings fractured them once more. She kept dropping the bow. Eventually she gave up. She walked, she sat in the flat, she ate next to nothing, she tried to sleep but couldn't, then fell suddenly asleep and had to claw her way out of dreams of cruelty and pain, and she waited for the police to come. They never did.

Later, she found it difficult to work out quite how she ended up in hospital. The orchestra came back, and the two girls she shared the flat with, but she hardly noticed. She had settled into a routine by that time, and the girls hardly impinged upon that. She knew without looking at a clock roughly when to try to sleep, when to go out walking, when to try and play the cello and have her fingers ache (sometimes she only thought about playing the cello, and her fingers ached anyway), when to eat a little from cold tin cans, when to sit and wait, drained, for sleep to take her, knowing that dreams and fear would wake her while sheer exhaustion tried to keep her under.

The girls tried to talk to her (she remembered them showing her photographs of the tour; bright, very colourful, but she had the impression all the smiles were somehow pasted crudely on and she couldn't work out why they were showing her these sad, obviously faked and painful photographs), and later one of the orchestra managers came as well, but he left, and another man came, who was very calm and quiet and professional and she trusted him and tried to talk to him, and the next day two young men who *really did* have white coats came and took her away without any trouble at all. Her two flatmates were there, and seemed to think she should take the cello with her, but she refused, wouldn't let them do it, made a scene and left the immediate source of her pain behind.

The hospital was in the hills near Uenohara. During the day,

137

if it wasn't cloudy or foggy, you could see Fuji. In the evening, Tokyo blazed on the plain to the east. She spent the first week crying, unable to talk, her every expression a currency of tears, because she was sure this was costing so much money and she had spent all her savings running away and her mother would go into debt and bankruptcy paying for it all, until she managed to voice her anxiety to somebody from the orchestra who'd come to visit her, and they told her the orchestra's medical insurance was paying, not her mother. She cried even more.

Her mother came to visit on the second week. She tried to explain to her that there was something she'd done, some terrible thing she was sure, and she couldn't remember what it was, but it was terrible, terrible, and nobody would ever forgive her if they knew; her mother buried her face in her hands. Hisako went to her and hugged her, which was very wrong, far too open and obvious, but she did it with a sort of glee that hurt, as though to take her own mother in her arms in a public veranda overlooking the wooded hills near Uenohara with other people near by and quite possibly looking on was some sort of secretive attack, and she really hated her mother and this was a way of getting back at her, subjecting her.

She tried to go for walks, tempted by the lights of the city on the plain and the mountain hovering like an immense black and white tent over the hills to the south. But they kept catching her, finding her, and she kept encountering locked doors and high fences too finely meshed to climb, and had to wait there, banging on the door or the fence with her palm or fist until her hands ached just enough or started to bleed, and they came to take her away.

She slept sitting up, propped by *gaijin* pillows, afraid to lie down in case the roof collapsed. The ward ceiling was too broad and big and she didn't think there were enough pillars or walls to support it properly; one good tremor and the lot would come down, smashing into her bed, flattening her there and grinding up her bones and crushing her neck with ferro-concrete beams and suffocating her over the years while the orchestra went bankrupt and her mother turned to prostitution and she lay not alive and not dead with a necklace of reinforced concrete slowly choking her, a burden upon all of them, hated but indulged.

Mr Kawamitsu came to see her. This confused her, because he was from another time, when she was young and still innocent and had no blood on her hands and no real dreams in her head, and she couldn't understand how he'd got here from there; had they built the rail tunnel already? They ought to tell her about these things.

She was disturbed that day, anyway. They'd been watching television the evening before and the nurse had been out of the room for a while, during a programme about Vietnam which showed terrible, terrible things; things of suffering and flame and blackened flesh and the orange flash and white pulse in the green green jungle; a bruise in the forest while the sticky orange (sticks tumbling lazily from the pretty plane) fire and the white (explosion cloud and tiny trailing threads, medusa) phosphorus gnawed their way through the olive skin to the white bone, while the Rome ploughs ripped and the Hercules sprayed Agent Orange (ha, gasp pant, and she saw the word-picture for tree mutate before her eyes, and thought in English it would go trees ree re e . . .) and only the screams of some of the patients brought the nurse back Adjusting His Clothing (ho, she noticed), and turned the set on to a game show instead and everybody seemed to forget what they had seen.

Except her. She remembered, and dreamed that night, up-propped, muttering, plagued, asweat, and as she replayed and remembered and relived, she laughed with each flicked frame of pain and grief, because it had all already happened and *demonstrating* wasn't going to do any good now, and because it made her feel good, which made her feel bad, but still she felt good in the end.

The dawn was bright and clear and blue that morning. Mr Kawamitsu brought a cello.

He put her hands upon it, showed her how to hold the device. The sunlight leant shafts of gold against the walls of the room, and Fuji was invisible beyond the hills and inside the clouds. She stroked the instrument, remembering. It wasn't hers, but she remembered not just playing a cello, she somehow remembered this cello, even though she knew she'd never seen or held it before. It smelled good, felt good, sounded deep and rich and sensuous. It played her rather than the other way round, so her fingers didn't hurt. She was sure she'd talked to Mr Kawamitsu, but didn't remember what she'd said.

He left, taking the beautiful cello with him. The pillows were uncomfortable that night, and the ceiling looked a bit more secure. She swept the pillows from the bed and slept with her head on her arm, soundly until the morning light.

She dreamed that her four fingers were strings, and her thumb was a bow. In the dream, the strings stretched and snapped, bursting and unravelling and disappearing in a cloud of mist. The bow scraped against the neck of the instrument and snapped, flailing; tendon still attached, bone broken. It ought to have hurt but it didn't, and she felt as though she'd been untied, let loose. She studied her fingers the next morning. They looked fine; nothing wrong with them. She made a tent of them and tapped the tips against each other, checking out the rainy weather and wondering what was for breakfast.

They put it down to her fear, and the idea that she'd been so ashamed at letting everybody else down she'd gone crazy. She felt demeaned by such a judgement, but accepted it as lenient compared to what she deserved for what had really driven her.

The cello belonged to a businessman in Sapporo who'd bought the instrument as an investment, and because he thought it looked a pretty colour. Mr Kawamitsu knew him. He'd persuaded the man that the Stradivari should be used rather than stored. Mr Kawamitsu always meant that Hisako should have the chance to play it, and perhaps own it one day. Bringing it to her now was all he could think of that might help. It did, but she told Mr Kawamitsu to take it back to Sapporo with him. When she could afford to, she'd buy it.

He went. Her mother stayed; she left. Her mother slept in the same room with her for the first two weeks after she moved back to Tokyo, back into the same flat with the other two girls (she couldn't believe it, they wanted her to be there. She wondered if maybe they were crazy too). Then her mother went back to Hokkaido, and she went to see the orchestra manager.

She could stay, as a guest soloist. She wouldn't be expected to tour abroad, she couldn't expect to be a fully paid-up member of the orchestra – no more subsidised stays in exclusive mental hospitals from now on – but she could play; play with the orchestra when it was in its Tokyo base, or anywhere else in Japan. It was more than she'd hoped for, much more than she deserved. She accepted, wondering as she did so what the down side would be; how life would get back at her for such apparent clemency.

She stayed and played. She found herself in another quartet, even more in demand than the first, and she was asked to do recordings. She was introduced to a man called Mr Moriya, who was professionally appalled to discover how much she was being paid, especially for recordings, and helped her make more.

Life went on; she visited, or was visited by, her mother; she took the occasional lover, in or out of the orchestra, watched her savings mount up, and wondered what she was really doing with her life, and why. Her hands hardly ever ached, and even if she did wake up sometimes, in the early morning, with her hands crumpled and cramped and compressed into tearfully painful fists, nails digging into her palms, or caught between her arms and her chest, stuffed into her armpits, while she dreamed of fingers crushed in car doors (great too-thick car doors, with lots of handles and levers and patches of obscurely important writing on them) and even if she did wake panting and sweating now and again, it was still nothing; normal and fair and better than she deserved.

Came a day when she could afford the down payment on the fabulous Strad. She travelled to Sapporo to meet it and Mr Kawamitsu, and Mr Kubota, the owner. There; it was in her hands.

It was like meeting a husband picked out by your parents, yet who you'd already – secretly – known and loved.

She took the cello away to a *ryokan* just outside Wajima for two weeks. She had a double room in an outhouse across the courtyard from the main inn. She played there. It was a sort of honeymoon.

The cello was ancient, made sometime between 1729 and 1734. It had belonged to a San Marinan composer at the Hapsburg court, had narrowly escaped being used as firewood by Napoleon's army as it swept through Piedmont in 1796, travelled to America with an Italian virtuoso to celebrate fifty years of American independence, had its spike shot off in the Boxer Rebellion in Beijing, survived an entire string quartet during the Second World War because it was put on the wrong DC3, flying to Algiers, not Cairo (the Dakota flying to Cairo with the string quartet crashed below sea level, in the Qattâra Depression, while the puzzled pilot tried to work out what had gone wrong with his altimeter), and spent thirty years in a bank vault in Venice before being sold at auction by Sotheby's of London, to Mr Kubota.

Mr Kubota brought the cello back from England on a JAL 747, strapped into the seat between him and his wife; he was watching from his first-class window as the plane came into land at Narita, and saw what looked like a medieval battle going on underneath; two armies; banners, smoke and fumes and lumbering cannon. He remembered pointing it out to his wife.

It was that day, that demonstration, she'd discovered, when – stuttering, incredulous, hardly daring to believe fate could dispense such undeserved balm – she'd asked him. But it was true.

She'd hugged Mr Kubota, startling him and Mr Kawamitsu.

Hisako Onoda saw the cello obliterated by AK47 and Uzi fire, ripped to splinters against the stem of the *Nadia* in the hazy sunlight of late afternoon.

Strings tugged, snapped, flailed. Wood burst and sprang, turned to dust and splinters under the hail of fire. Bullets sang and sparked against the metal of the bows behind the instrument as it disintegrated and collapsed in a cloud of dark and pale-brown fragments, strings waving like anemone limbs, like a drowning man's fingers. Blood was in her mouth and bruises puffed round her eyes and cigarette burns burned on her breasts and the seed of a boatful of men ran down her thighs and she kept seeing Philippe crumple under the first bullet that hit, but it was the cello; the needless, pointless (apart from to hurt) destruction of the cello that finally killed her. Old wood. New metal. Guess which won? No surprise there. Killed, she was free.

She heard the scream of the engines in the rasp of the guns. The sky was filled with thunder and fire, and she felt something die.

Now she couldn't be who or what she had been. She hadn't asked for this, hadn't wanted it, but it was here. Not her fault. There was no forbearance, no vengeance, just chance. But it had

142

happened, all the same, and she did not feel she had simply to succumb; acceptance was not nearly enough and far too much. This took the scab off. Truth always hurts, she told herself; hurt sometimes truths. They made her watch, as the afternoon wore out and the clouds sailed and the wind moved as it always had and the water sparkled just so and the Kalashnikovs and Uzis barked and rapped and the cello dissolved under their fire.

She suspected she'd disappointed them; they'd ripped the masking tape off her mouth so they could hear her scream when they shot the instrument, but she'd kept quiet.

They took her away. But it wasn't the same person they led off, and something that was her lay there in the string-tangled debris of the wrecked instrument, turned to less than sawdust by the impact.

She was a toy, a mascot; they fucked her and made themselves whole, together. But toys could corrupt, she thought (as they took her away from the sunlight, back to her cage and captivity and torture), and mascots might bite back.

They showed her their other toys, too, on the bridge; the SAM launcher (they played at readying it to fire and pointing it at her, once poked it between her legs, joking about whether she was hot enough down there to attract the missile), the plastique charges they'd sink at least one of the ships with, once they'd downed the plane, the *vencerista* literature and equipment they'd leave behind with a couple of their uniforms, so that when the National Guard did come to investigate, there'd be no doubt who'd shot down the Americans and massacred the people on the ships.

The radio operators were dead too. She'd seen the bodies in the *Nadia*'s radio cabin as they'd dragged her along to the bridge, past the scars and gouge marks of the fire fight Orrick had started. The ship's radio was officially out of action; the Americans were jamming every frequency in sight to combat *vencerista* radio signals, fearing a large-scale attack, they said. The soldiers let her listen to one of the infrequent news broadcasts. Radio Panama was playing martial music, apart from the news programmes, which were meant to be hourly but weren't. The jamming came right up against the station's frequency on both sides, producing a background of whistles and rumbles and a sound somewhere between a heavy machine-gun and a helicopter.

When they'd got to the bridge, they'd tied her to the *Nadia*'s small wheel, forcing her to stand awkwardly, unable to rest her legs, her arms strapped to the wood and brass of the wheel. Her head was down, and sheltered behind her greasy, unwashed hair. She looked down at the bruised, burned body revealed by the ripped *yukata*, and listened to the sounds of a world losing its head.

Panama City was under martial law. The President of Columbia had been shot dead and five groups had claimed responsibility. More US carrier groups were arriving off the Pacific Coast of Central America and in the Caribbean. Cuba said it was preparing to be invaded. The Kremlin was threatening a new blockade of Berlin. America and Russia had both called for an emergency session of the UN. The US peace mission was on again; the plane would leave Dulles the following morning. A thousand rioters were dead in Hong Kong, and the Azanian Army had found a giant glass crater in the sands three hundred kilometres east of Otjiwarongo, which they claimed was the site of Johannesburg's unsubtle cruise-missile warning shot. The news ended with American baseball scores, then the martial music resumed.

Hisako laughed until they hit her so hard she blacked out for a moment. She still giggled, even as the plastic restrainers bit into her wrists and the weight of her body tore at her arm sockets; she watched the blood fall like little bombs from her mouth to the cushioned deck of the bridge, and felt herself snigger. The music they were playing now was a Sousa march; it reminded her of a group of lecturers she'd known in the Todai English department who held a small party each week for staff and students. They'd invite visiting English speakers along; businessmen, scientists, politicians, and sometimes somebody from the American or British Embassy. A Brit diplomat appeared with a video tape one time, and some of them watched it. Not everybody found the programme funny or even comprehensible, but she loved it, wanted more. A sub-group formed to watch the latest tape, flown in from London in the diplomatic bag each week. She became addicted to the programme. The music – this music – had meant

144

that and that only to her for almost a quarter of a century.

So Radio Panama played the Sousa march which had become the theme to *Monty Python's Flying Circus*, and she could only laugh, no matter how hard they hit her. The world was absurd, she decided, and the pain and cruelty and stupidity were all just side effects of that basic grotesqueness, not the intended results after all. The realisation came as a relief.

When Dandridge called through on their unjammed walkie-talkies, they put another piece of masking tape over her mouth. She had to swallow her blood. Dandridge said something about coming over to the *Nadia*, and they untied her from the wheel and after some discussion in Spanish took her down into the bowels of the ship through the engine room and locked her in the engineering workshop with the light off.

She slept.

Somebody had stabbed her. She had just woken up and she'd been stabbed; the knife hung from her belly, dripping blood. She tried to pull it out but couldn't. The room was dark, echoingly big. There was a line of red light at floor level, all around her. It flickered slightly.

She got up out of the dirty bed, tangled in the grease and grimy sweat of the sheets. She kicked them away and stumbled on the metal floor, holding the knife carefully so that it wouldn't move around too much and hurt her even more. There wasn't as much blood as she'd expected, and she wondered if there would only be a gush when she got somebody to pull it out. She wanted to cry, but found that she couldn't.

She came to the wall of the room and felt under the rim of the metal, between floor and wall, looking for a place to lift. She moved round, feeling under the wall with one hand, holding the knife in the other. Eventually she came to a set of steps leading up out of the room to a very dim red outside where long, booming noises shook the air and the ground. The steps, made of compacted sand, were edged with wooden slats held in by little tuft-headed posts.

She came up out of the bunker into the gory glow of late evening; strips of close-packed cloud lay overhead, alternating with streaks of red, like blood staining black sheets. The thunder of the guns sounded in the distance, and the earth trembled. Down in the trench she found the men, lying exhausted against the sides of crumbling earth and rotten wood. The mud was up to their knees and their eyes were closed. Red light hung like oil on their rifles. They were bandaged; every one wore a filthy grey bandage; on head or arm, or over one eye or both, or over their chest, over their uniform, or round one leg. She wondered why they didn't see her, and stopped and looked into the face of one whose eyes were open. Red light reflected in the darkness of his pupils. He sniffed and wiped his nose. She tried to talk to the soldier, but no noise came from her mouth, and the man ignored her. She started to worry that she wouldn't find anybody to take the knife out.

At the end of the trench were men who looked like their boots. Their eyes were threaded, up and down their leathery faces. Their mouths were stuck open, like the top of a shoe, tongues flapping spastically as they tried to talk to her. Their arms were like thick laces, and couldn't pull the knife out of her. One raised his foot out of the mud and she saw that the top of his boot melded naturally and easily into a naked human foot, without a break. She puzzled over this, sure she'd seen it before, but then the boot soldier put the foot under the mud again and a whistle sounded. The boot soldiers picked up their guns with all the rest and put rickety wooden ladders against the sides of the trenches. She walked up out of the trench, back to where a line of blasted tree stumps lay on the brow of a small hill, like teeth.

The village on the far side of the hill was wrecked; every building damaged. Roofs had collapsed, walls fallen, doors and windows been blown out, and huge holes filled the road and streets. She saw people in the town square, facing in towards the centre, where a red light shone.

She walked down the broad, crater-pitted streets, passing people who stood looking to the central square. She used sign language to ask for help, but they all ignored her.

It took a long time to walk through the suburbs; the crowd of silent, raggedly dressed people became gradually thicker until she had to push her way through them, which was difficult while she still held the knife. She could hear a roaring noise in the distance.

The people looked exhausted and hollow-eyed, and some of them collapsed as she pushed past.

The roaring noise sounded thick and heavy, like a great waterfall slowed down. The people fell around her, crumpling to the ground as soon as she touched them, no matter how careful she tried to be. She wanted to say sorry. She could see the silhouette of the giant fountain ahead against the crimson sky now. The people were thick about her; she pushed between them and they fell, knocking into their neighbours so that they fell, too, and hit the people near them, who also fell and took others down with them. The wave of collapsing people spread out like ripples in a pond, knocking everybody to the ground until only she was left standing and the fountain was there, huge, in front of her, with the lake beyond.

The fountain was tiered, shaped like a wedding cake. It gushed blood; blood roaring and falling and steaming through the cold evening air. She fell to her knees when she saw it, half-suffocated by the smell of it, mouth blocked. A cataract of blood flowed away from it to the inland sea beyond the city. She got up, stepped over the fallen people, stumbled down the steps by the side of the violet rapids until she stood on the shore of the lake, red waves lapping at her feet.

She pulled the knife out and threw it into the lake. No blood rushed out of the wound, but the knife splashed when it hit, and some of the blood splattered her face and feet, and some hit the place where the knife had been embedded, and a single strand dribbled down to the lake at her feet, and the strand thickened, and pulsed, and the blood flowed into her not out of her, falling up out of the lake, as if a tap had been turned on.

She tried to stop it, beating it down with her fists, but the blood burned her, breaking her fingers; she fell back, but the blood rushed out of the lake into her, the stream thick as an arm, filling her, bloating her, choking her, sealing her mouth. She lifted her ruined hands to the dark clouds and tried to scream, and the sky flashed once, above her; the lake shivered. The sky went dark once more. At last her lips tore open, and she screamed, with all her strength, and the sky lit up all over, as though the clouds were catching fire. The lake spasmed, whipping the strand that joined it to her, almost breaking its thin grip. She drew air in through her ruined lips, to scream with all the power of the lake itself, while the sky trembled above her, glittering and sparking on the brink of release, poised and ready to catch and blast.

She woke up on the floor. The place was dark, the deck hard and cold. Breathing sounded loud and ragged in the harsh steel container of the room, but it was only her own, coursing through her nostrils. The tape over her mouth still clamped her lips. Her breath quieted slowly while she sat, trying to ease the ache in her shoulders.

It was late. She didn't know how long she'd slept, but she knew it had been some hours; early morning by now, if not later.

She'd been secured against a metal bench, her hands attached to its leg by the plastic strap of the restrainer. As soon as she awoke she hurt; her backside had been spread in the same position for so long she felt welded to the deck, her shoulders ached, her wrists and hands felt numb, and the places on her breasts where they'd touched her with their cigarettes burned as though the glowing red coals were still there, sizzling through her flesh. Between her legs wasn't as bad as she'd expected. Sucre had been small and the rest had added their own lubrication with each violation. The pain didn't matter so much; it was the feeling of being used, of mattering so little as another human being, and so much as a warm, slippery container, to be taken and crowed over; look what I've done; I did this even though she didn't want to.

The ship hummed around her. She couldn't see a thing. The light in the corridor outside, between the engine room itself and the *Nadia*'s steering-gear compartment, must be turned off as well. She tried to remember how the room had looked when they brought her in, but couldn't. Too complicated, for one thing; full of machinery, lathes and drills and benches with vices and tools. It ought to be an ideal place to escape from, but she didn't know how to begin.

She felt what she could, starting with her fingers.

And stopped.

The rear flange of the L-shaped leg supporting the bench, which the restrainer was looped around, was ragged. It rasped against her fingers, hurting. Blood welled on her fingers, making them slick then sticky. She explored the jagged edge. She pulled forward and moved her wrists quickly up and down, then stopped and felt the inner surface of the restrainer where it had been rubbing against the metal. The material felt roughened. She put it back where it had been and sawed up and down as hard and fast as she could.

She could hear it, and after a while she could smell it too, and that seemed like a good sign.

She was almost free when she heard steps, and the light outside in the corridor went on. She stopped for a second, then resumed her sawing, frantic with the effort. Footsteps clanged against metal, stopped at the door. She threw her hands up and down, drawing her spine back to the metal edge of the bench with the effort of forcing the restrainer against the leg.

The door swung open just as the restrainer snapped.

10: Average Adjuster

Light swamped in. She scuttled to the left, behind another
bench. But too late; she knew it was too late. There was too
much light and she must have been seen.

She expected the soldier to shout out, but he didn't. There
was a noise like a chuckle, and the sound of a hand moving over
metal. Something clinked on the far wall. The soldier spoke to
her in Spanish but she couldn't make out the words. She peeped
over the top of the bench. The opened white loop of the plastic
restrainer lay by the leg of the bench she'd been attached to; it
ought to be obvious, but the man hadn't reacted yet. He slapped
the metal bulkhead at the side of the door, cursing. Looking for
the light, but still it didn't come on.

She realised then that her eyes had adjusted over the hours,
and his were still tuned to the wash of luminescence in the
corridor outside and in the rest of the ship. She was looking
for a weapon, but couldn't see anything on the surface of the
bench she was hiding behind, or anywhere near by. A wrench;
a big screwdriver or a length of angle iron; there ought to be
hundreds of things she could use but she couldn't see any of them.
She looked round in desperation as the soldier said something else
and came further into the workshop. She peeped over the top of
the bench again, hoping she'd missed something on its surface.
The man was smoking; she could see the red glowing tip of the
cigarette, being transferred from mouth to hand. '*Señorita* . . . '

Behind her she glimpsed something long and thin and glinting;
stacked rods of some sort. She reached back, grasped. The soldier
bumped into something, cursed in the semi-darkness.

It was like taking hold of a skeletal arm; two thin pipes,

cold as bone and close together; humerus and radius. She felt up to a knurled collar like a cold brass knuckle. That was when she realised what she was holding. The soldier made a sound like hand rubbing flesh through cloth and said again, '*Señorita?*' The red tip of the cigarette glowed brighter, waving around in the darkness in front of the man. Light from the corridor reflected from his rifle.

She felt the end of the brasswork, then the twin hoses. They led back a few coiled metres to the tanks. They were upright, but in the shadow of the door. She was still under the level of the bench. Her fingers crept up to the valves. She'd seen Broekman do this; even Philippe. She found the taps, whirled them round. The hiss of escaping gas sounded like a whole family of disturbed snakes. The soldier stopped, hesitated, then changed direction, came towards her. 'Hello . . . ?' he said. The glowing cigarette tip came closer, brandished like a sword.

When he was close enough, and the smell of the unignited gases was wafting back over her, making her dizzy, she threw herself forward, still holding the brass limbs of the oxyacetylene torch.

The gases flared on the tip of the cigarette, igniting with a whoosh and blowing flame towards the surprised soldier, flashing through the air in a vivid yellow ball. The man's hair caught; she saw his face, mouth opening, eyes closing as his brows sizzled and shrivelled and flamed blue. His burning hair lit up the beret stuffed underneath his left epaulette, the two grenades attached to his chest, the Kalashnikov strapped over his right shoulder and the belt with the oily black holster hanging over his left hip. He drew in a breath and screamed as his hair sputtered and crackled and lit up the whole workshop.

He lit the place well enough for her to see a massive wrench hanging on the wall not a metre away. She stepped smartly to it, unclipped and swung it in one movement. His scream had barely started and he had hardly moved – the cigarette he'd dropped hadn't even hit the deck – before the jaws of the wrench buried themselves in his skull, and he slammed into the metal deck as though he'd thrown himself there. His hair billowed yellow and blue for a moment, then sizzled out against his scalp, crisping it brown-black in places. The fumes stank, made her gag, and only then did she slowly pull the black tape from her mouth.

The last lick of flame, slowly consuming a set of curls over the soldier's left ear, was extinguished by the black ooze of blood welling from where the circular head of the wrench had hit.

She watched. Thought: *How do I feel?*

Cold, she decided. So cold. She kicked him over, pulled the assault rifle free and hoisted it, checking the safety was off. No noise from the open doorway. She waited for a few seconds then put the gun down and reached forward to take the man's uniform off. She hesitated before she touched him, then stood, hefted the wrench and smashed it into his forehead. Only after that did she strip him.

She whistled under her breath as she did it; Sousa.

She didn't mean to impersonate a soldier, she was just sick of the torn, soiled *yukata*. She wanted to be clothed again.

She tore some relatively clean strips off the *yukata*, wiped herself as clean as she could with a couple of them and tied one narrow strand round her head, keeping her hair back. The soldier wasn't too much bigger than her, so the uniform fitted. He'd been one of the ones who'd raped her; the one who'd bitten her ears. She fingered her earlobes; puffy and scabbed with blood.

She studied one of the grenades in the light spilling from the corridor. She even held the little shiny handle down, extracted the pin, inspected it, and then replaced it, letting the handle click back. She tried to recall how much time had passed between Sucre dropping a grenade into one of the groups of men, and the explosion. A bit more than five seconds, she decided.

The Kalashnikov was easier. She'd watched; safety, semi-automatic, automatic. The emplaced magazine was full and two more hung on his belt. The pistol was a Colt, just like Dandridge's; the safety was a simple switch, on and off. The soldier had a Bowie knife on the belt, so she gained that as well. A cigarette lighter and packet of Marlboros in one breast pocket. She threw the cigarettes away. She looked for a radio but he didn't have one.

She was at the door before she thought to go back and take his watch. The little Casio said 6:04.

She stared at it. It couldn't be that late. Next morning, already? She tilted the display. 6:04.

P, said the little letter to one side. P6:04.

152

Evening. The same day. She couldn't believe it. She was sure she'd slept for hours. She shook her head, stuffed the watch in a trouser pocket.

The corridor seemed very bright. The engine room was more brilliant still, and hummed noisily; it smelled of oil and electrics. Deserted.

She crept along the open grillework of the catwalk between the two main engines, towards the high girn of the donkey engine and the whining AC generator. The stairway to the main deck level left her feeling exposed and vulnerable, but nothing happened.

The evening air was still warm. In one corner of the sky, off to the west, a single dab of red hung thick and dim; above, over all the sky, a uniform darkness extended, starless and without moon. Thick cloud like a layer of something more than night. She decided the watch was right, and her senses had been wrong. She waited a moment, felt the eastern wind move across her face and hands, and watched the lid of cloud close over the red hole where the sun still shone, until darkness consumed the lake and the land.

The exterior of the ship was darker than she was used to; they'd turned the mast floodlights off, or hadn't ever thought to turn them on. She slunk along the side of the superstructure, past dark portholes, heading forwards. She didn't know what to do. She'd dressed herself as a soldier but she wasn't one. She'd left the real soldier lying there and they'd have to go looking for him soon, so maybe she ought to forget about dressing as a soldier and strip off again and get into the water and swim away; she was a strong swimmer and the coast wasn't far. . . .

She got to the forward edge of the superstructure. Light came from above. It wasn't the masthead floodlights; it seemed very bright in the darkness but it wasn't really, just the lights from the bridge. They weren't bothering to use the red night-lights which would keep their eyes adapted; maybe they didn't know about them. She looked at the deep shadows created by the hatches, and at the bows; the stem. Pale splinters. She went slowly forward, looking up. The bridge shone, end to end. She saw nobody. She walked backwards, then ducked into the shadow.

On hands and knees, she crawled up the slope of deck to the winches and lockers of the forecastle apron. She looked back at the bridge again; still nobody; it looked abandoned, until she saw a bloom of grey smoke climb into the air near midships, then another alongside. She waited for the smokers to appear, but they didn't. She edged forward to the closed-off V of the prow, and found herself stirring the splinters.

She was looking for the strings, but discovered the spike alone. The rest was matchwood. The pegs and strings must have been blown overboard. Whatever, she couldn't find them. She scuttled back into the shadows, the cello's spike jammed into the holster along with the Colt.

Back at the superstructure she could stand again, and did so, still trying to think what she was supposed to do. She took the spike out and felt foolish. She squatted down, gun between her knees, and looked out into the darkness beyond the bows. Insects curled above her, attracted by the lights of the bridge.

She saw Philippe fall, heard Mandamus shut up by a pistol shot, watched the cello blast out and fall, felt the soldiers push into her, smelled her own flesh burn as they pressed the cigarettes against her. She thought of the sky on fire, and looked up into the night, trying to imagine the stars beyond the cloud. The length of bridge-light was made busy by the circling insects.

She crept into the ship.

The saloon was dark and silent, and smelled of dried blood and expended smoke; the whole lower deck seemed deserted. The television lounge still smelled of semen. She sniffed the dark air, drawing the sharp, animal scent into her, stomach churning.

She took to the stairs and went up to the bridge.

Snoring came through the half-open door of the captain's cabin. She pushed the door further, waiting for a creak, or at least for the snoring to stop. No creak; the snoring continued.

She edged in, fingering the door a little wider behind her as she went, to give her more light. A suite, of course; another open door. She let her eyes adjust, then approached the bedroom. The cabin smelled of dampness and shampoo. There was a man lying on the bed, torso tangled with a single sheet, arms drawn up behind his head, face turned away into the corner of the bulkhead beneath and to the side of the porthole.

Sucre. His chest was smooth, almost hairless; nipples very dark

154

in the half-light. She crossed quietly to the bed and fumbled with the holster at her hip.

She kissed him, hair brushing the sides of his face, shadowing. He jerked awake, eyes white. She drew back a little so that he could see her; he relaxed fractionally, then the eyes balled wide and he started up, hands clutching together at the sheet beneath him before one went back up to his head, fumbling beneath the pillow.

But he was too late, and she was already pumping down with the heels of her hands, the tip of the old cello spike on his chest then bursting through as she put all her weight on it, forcing it between his ribs and into his heart.

He tried to beat her face but she dodged, and waggled the spike inside his chest with one hand while she leant forward and round and slipped the pistol out from under his pillow with the other. He gurgled once, like somebody rinsing his mouth, and darkness spread around his lips and the hole the spike had made in his chest; the moon-white sheets turned black where his blood touched.

The last noise he made as his chest subsided surprised her; then she realised it came not from his mouth but from the wound around the cello spike. She watched the dark bubbles for a moment.

She put the pistol – another Colt – into a pocket in the fatigue jacket. There was a walkie-talkie on the bedside table, so she stuffed that in a trouser pocket. She left the spike where it was. She was terrified of one of them coming back to life, so she pressed her thumb down on to Sucre's right eye while she held the Colt against one of his ears. She pressed hard but nothing happened. She drew her hand away with a shiver, suddenly afraid of the eye bursting and the fluid trickling down his cheek.

She decided Sucre was really dead. She took his Kalashnikov because it had a nightsight and dumped the other one. There was an Uzi on the table; she took that, a silencer for it and a few extra magazines. She was starting to get weighed down, and had to walk carefully as she left, trying not to clink.

The bridge smelled of tobacco, but there was nobody there. She felt cheated. She looked in all the cabins on that deck, even the one where Orrick had killed the first soldier, but there was nobody in any of them.

She went down to the next deck.

Nothing. She looked out through the blinds covering the windows on the forward lounge and saw somebody at the bows; the light from the bridge was just enough to make the man out. She scratched her head, went back out into the corridor and stood by the companionways leading up and down but heard nothing. She went back down to the main deck level and out on to the external deck under the overhang. She could still see the man. He seemed to be leaning at the very prow of the ship, his feet in the cello splinters, looking out into the night to where the dimmed lights of the distant *Nakodo* shimmered on the water.

She took the beret out of the epaulette, pushed the hair not held by the strip of *yukata* up underneath the beret, and walked quietly up the deck towards the man. She glanced up once at the bridge as she went, seeing nothing but emptiness and lights.

He didn't even hear her until she was less than five metres away. He turned, saw her, turned away again, gazing out over the water, and only then looked back, face puzzled.

She was on him while the expression of puzzlement was starting to turn into suspicion and he was reaching for his rifle. She already had hers; it cracked up and into his chin, throwing his head back and whacking it off the bulwark. He clattered to the deck like a broken doll.

He was not one of those who'd raped her and she didn't have the heart to kill him just like that, so she dragged him to the starboard anchor's chain locker, stripped him of weaponry, chucked him in, gently closed the hatch and dogged it. Carting all this hardware around was exhausting her, so she tipped all his armament and one of the Colts overboard. The splashes sounded very small and far away. She crept away again, back to the main body of the ship.

Then she found the others.

They were playing cards, below deck level, under an opened skylight set in the deck just in front of the leading edge of the superstructure. Smoke drifted out of the aperture; tobacco and hash. She took a peek over the lip and saw a table, cans of San

Miguel, a thick joint, and hands of cards and hands of men.

It had been a long time since she'd smoked any dope. She lay there, shoulder against the raised metal lip round the skylight, remembering, then quietly took a grenade out of its velcro fastening, clutched the handle, removed the pin, let go the handle, sub-vocalised 'wun-ih erephantu, two-ri erephantu, tri erephantu, fori erephantu, favi erephantu', and was still chuckling to herself as she reached up and dropped the grenade through the skylight.

She heard it hit, heard a few intakes of breath, but didn't hear it bounce before the deck beneath her slammed up, the skylight flipped back on a cloud of bright mist and smashed, and a noise like planets colliding boxed her ears like an angry school bully.

She lay waiting. Her ears were singing again, ringing with their own tired noise. She unholstered the Colt, heaved herself up, looked into the cabin beneath through the smoke, and couldn't see very much. She levered herself up further, stuck her head and gun, then her head and gun and upper torso in through the gap, took a look round, and decided they were all dead or very close to it. She let a little more of the smoke clear, listening as best she could, watching the bridge and the sides of the superstructure at main deck level.

Then she swung in through the skylight, on to the table. It had been blown almost in two; strips of brown laminate sticking up like obstreperous licks of hair. She had to swing her feet to make sure she landed close to the bulkhead so that what was left of the table would take her weight. She dropped down, through the stinging smoke. Her loosely booted feet grated on grenade shards and scattered playing cards. One of the men moved and groaned. She wanted to use the knife but somehow couldn't, so put the gun to his head and fired. She did the same with the other three, though only one other showed any signs of life. Blood was making the floor sticky, glueing the cards to the deck.

Incredibly, the joint was still alight and almost intact, burning a brown mark in a shrapnel-punctured plastic seat. She knocked the end of the tip off it where a little black bit of plastic hung, and took a toke. It still tasted bad so she ground it out under one heel. It sizzled.

She sauntered from the cabin, amazed nobody had come,

and only then started to think that perhaps they were all dead.

Still she didn't believe it, and searched the entire ship. She found their SAMs and their plastique charges, in the chartroom off the bridge, looked again at Sucre, swathed in black and white, spike like a cupid's arrow in his unmoving chest, found the bloodstains on the bed in the cabin she'd been in briefly with Orrick (but could not find the body of the man Orrick had killed), found the three dead radio operators and the dead radio equipment (she tried to make it work, but couldn't even get the jamming signal; empty fuse cradles mocked her), looked again into the TV lounge where they'd raped her, and braved the shadowy depths of the main saloon, where the bodies still lay heaped and spread and she couldn't bear to turn on the light for fear of seeing one of them. She felt for the heavy machine-gun, needing both hands, and lifted a metal box full of ammunition. She left the gun lying in the corridor outside, then retraced her steps to the engineering workshop where the first one to die had spread his blood through his head over half the deck under the gleaming, businesslike benches.

An hour after she'd freed herself she was back on the bridge after a tour of the bows, where the soldier she'd poleaxed was making a fuss in the chain locker. She'd turned the bridge lights to red on her first visit, and strode through the blood-coloured gloom to the winch/anchor console. She tapped one finger against her lips as she inspected the controls, then reached out and flicked a switch. The starboard anchor dropped to the lake and splashed. Its chain rattled massively after it, links whipping through the chain locker where the soldier was.

The rasp of falling chain drowned the man's scream, though it must have been short anyway. If she'd waited till dawn, she thought, she'd have seen him exit through the eye of the anchor port in a red spray, but she shivered at the thought of his blood spreading over the surface of the lake.

The anchor chain's thunder sounded through the ship, making the deck beneath her tremble. Unbraked, the chain kept on spilling out under its own weight. There was a boom as it stopped; she couldn't tell whether it parted or held. She rubbed one of her breasts absently, grimacing slightly when she touched one of the places where they'd burned her, and reflected that revenge could taste remarkably bland when you'd stopped feeling.

Hisako Onoda came to the conclusion there was almost certainly nobody left to kill on the *Nadia*. She decided to go and see Mr Dandridge, who deserved a visit like nobody else did.

It was all still hopeless, she knew, but this was better than doing nothing.

The crumpled black Gemini Orrick had knifed lay draped over one end of the pontoon. She looked at one of its bulky, silenced engines, worked out how to take it off, and dragged it over to where the *Nadia*'s own inflatable lay moored. She stuck the military engine's prop in the water, pushed the starter. The engine trembled, rumbled; even idling, the prop tried to push itself under the pontoon. She switched the outboard off, unbolted the Evinrude from the sternplate of the *Nadia*'s Gemini and let it slip into the black waters. She replaced it with the big military engine, working by the light from the ship above, and sweating with the effort, arms aching. The pontoon was on the near side of the ship to the other two vessels. She had the walkie-talkie switched on, and was vaguely surprised it had stayed silent; it seemed nobody had heard or seen anything on the other two ships. As she worked she waited for gunfire, or the radio to rattle off some incomprehensible Spanish at her, but – in that perverse sense – waited in vain.

It took her two trips to bring all the weaponry down to the boat. She topped up the outboard fuel tank with one of the jerry cans on the pontoon, then stowed that with the missile launchers and explosives in the bottom of the inflatable and restarted the engine.

She pushed the Gemini away from the pontoon. The inflatable purred off into the night, taking a curving course towards the bulky rectangular shape of the *Nakodo*.

Her mother kept a scrapbook. It glossed over the time she was in hospital. Sometimes when she was home she would look through the scrapbook when her mother wasn't there. The pages flipped through her fingers; the glued-in programmes with her name in them, the cuttings from papers mentioning her individually, a few cassette inserts, some magazine interviews and features, and as the pages slipped and sped and fell through her hands she thought that the times the heavy pages covered had themselves gone just as fast, just as suddenly and inevitably.

The years mounted up, like a sentence. She played, and her modest fame grew. She tried a few more times to board a plane, from single-engine Cesnas to 747s, but could not ever suffer the doors to be closed. She got as far as Okinawa for a couple of holidays, and went to Korea for the Olympics and a few concerts, but pressure of work stopped her from making sea journeys that lasted any longer. There was talk once, by a Greek ship owner impressed with her playing, of her string quartet playing on board a luxury cruise ship for anything up to a year; state rooms, good money, and a world cruise . . . but she visited one of the cruise ships in Yokohama and decided she didn't much like the people, the décor or the idea of being expected to play the safe, predictable music that seemed to be expected of her. So it came to nothing.

She grew to know Japan well; the places she didn't go to with the orchestra she visited alone, on her frequent vacations. Mr Moriya fretted that she wasn't maximising her potential, which she took to mean making all the money she could, but then she scarcely knew what to do with what she did have. She paid off the loan on the Stradivarius, bought a house in the hills above Kamakura, which cost a fortune, and had long since paid the loan on her mother's little apartment, but she didn't know what else to do. Driving didn't interest her; she always had a small Honda, but hated the crowded roads and was always relieved to get out of the machine. She felt awkward and conspicuous in very expensive clothes, and couldn't see the point of jewellery you worried about. She saved, for want of anything better to do, and thought vaguely about founding a school in her later years.

Mr Moriya decided she was right to go for quality rather than quantity, and renegotiated her contract with the orchestra. She started to ration public appearances, and only recorded when she absolutely had to. Western music critics who heard her made flattering comparisons; she thought about going to Europe but kept putting it off. She was looking forward to travelling on the Trans-Siberian Railway, but it seemed like something she should do only once each way (to reduce it to some sort of absurdist

160

commuter journey each year would seem like sacrilege), and was anyway nervous of actually playing in Europe. At first she had worried that nobody would want to listen to her, then, when it became clear they did, that she'd been built up too highly, and they'd be disappointed. Mr Moriya, to her surprise, didn't try to pressure her into going. He seemed content to let the offers mount up, the venues increase in size, and the proposed money inflate.

She fell into the music, whenever she played. It was real; colourful. Her life, for all the friends and holidays and for all the respect of other musicians and adulation of audiences, seemed, if not actually monochrome, then missing some vital component; as if one colour was missing, one gun in the set misfiring, so infecting the image with its absence.

One day she trudged through the woods north of Fuji, taking the old path she'd first travelled as little more than a child, struggling with her water-warped and salt-stained cello and case.

When she got to the bald summit of the hill, the little clearing where she'd watched Fuji dance in the flames she'd made, she discovered it had become a picnic area; half a dozen smiling, chattering families sat at stout wooden tables, unpacking boxes, spreading dishes, opening bottles, taking their rubbish to cheerfully bright plastic bins which said 'Thank you' when you fed them. Children's laughter filled the place, and smoke from a portable barbecue wavered like some incipient genie in front of the view of Fuji. Western pop music tinkled from a ghetto blaster hanging from a tree.

She turned and walked away, and never went there again.

She was halfway across the kilometre of dark water between the *Nadia* and the *Nakodo* when the radio came alive in her trouser pocket. The noise startled her, made her let go of the throttle, clutch at her thigh where the speech was coming from. She pulled the radio out.

'—hey, Sucre . . . ?' She let the Gemini's engine idle, looked round at the lights of the ships. 'Arturo, Arturo . . . *La Nadia*, 'allo? Yo, *venceristas en La Nadia . . . muchachos*?' It was Dandridge's voice, chuckling. '*Despertad vosotros!*'

She heard other voices in the background. More Spanish, too quick for her to follow. Eventually; 'Sucre; anybody. Hello. Hello? God damn it, you guys. Hello. Hello! Hello! Jesus— ' The radio went dead. She looked round to the lights of the *Nakodo*.

She switched the engine off. It was very quiet.

She remembered the nightscope on the AK47 she'd taken from Sucre's cabin, lifted the gun and sighted.

The view of the *Nakodo*'s hull was dim grey and grainy. There was no movement on the deck or in the bridge, though it was hard to tell in the bridge because the lights there were almost too bright for the nightsight. She dropped the sight, watched the pontoon and the steps down to it. Still nothing.

She kept watching, and kept checking the radio, thinking she had somehow turned it off. Then she heard something, behind her.

She swung, steadied the sight on the *Nadia*. She swept the ship, stem to stern, and found a Gemini, heading round from the rear of the ship, making for the pontoon. One man; that was all she could see.

She put the gun down, started the engine up again, and swung the inflatable back, towards the *Nadia*.

She kept checking with the rifle nightsight, in case whoever was in the Gemini approaching the ship showed any signs of having heard – or seen – her, but the inflatable just motored on, slowing, for the pontoon she'd left a few minutes earlier. She was a couple of hundred metres away from the *Nadia* when the other boat docked. One man got out. She saw him raise one arm to his face.

'Here,' said the radio. The man hefted a rifle, started up the steps towards the *Nadia*'s deck. She kept on motoring towards the ship. She was watching the single figure climb towards the top of the steps when he stopped. He looked down towards the pontoon. The view she had was made shaky by the progress of her own boat through the waves. She let go the throttle; the Gemini coasted forward, dropping and dying in the water. The man brought something up from his waist. 'Wait,' said the radio. 'The Gemini; the other one. Did anybody— ?' She saw him raise something else to his face; to his eyes; held like a pair of binoculars. He looked down, then out, scanning, looked straight towards her. 'Holy sh— , Arturo? Hello? Who is— '

She had to look to find the safety, flicked it and resighted. The rifle filled the world with sound; the sight flared with the gun's own flame. 'Holy sh— ' the radio said again.

She had the impression of bullets flying and falling. She brought the gun up, kicking against her shoulder.

Fire came back from the ship, halfway up the steps to the deck. She dropped the rifle, hearing distant, tinny echoes of firing coming back from behind her, reflected from the boxy hull of the *Nakodo*.

She found the heavy machine-gun, lifted it rattling from the bottom of the Gemini. She supported it as best she could, fired.

The gun kicked against her shoulder, almost throwing her over the stern of the boat. Lazy lines of tracer swung round, heading towards the *Nadia*, spiralling into the night sky. The Gemini was turning, forced round by the weight of flung metal arching away from her towards the distant ship. Return fire flickered from the ship's hull.

She cursed, dropped forward, hearing plashy pops of bullets striking the water somewhere in front of her. She steadied the big machine-gun on the bulbous prow of the Gemini, swinging the inverted V of its barrel-support into place on the taut rubber of the bows. In the ship's own glow she could make out enough of the steps and pontoon to see where to aim. Light glittered there. By the time the noise arrived she was firing.

The tracer helped. She swung the stuttered trail and raised it, until the trail ended where the firing had been coming from. The Gemini was starting to swing again. The belt of bullets clinked and clattered like a bottling plant beneath her; the cartridges were thrown out to one side, hissing as they hit the waters of the lake.

'Hey! Get – ah! Son of a *bitch*!' The radio came alive again with Dandridge's voice. She paused, and through the radio heard clinks and slaps that died away, and guessed those noises were her bullets hitting the hull of the ship. 'Get over here, you motherfuckers. Ah! Shit!' The sound of something thumping and clattering.

She fired again. The chain of bullets ripped its way up into the gun and finished. She spun round, grabbed the ammunition box, found the end of the cartridge belt and snapped the gun open, hauling the weight of articulated belt up, fumbling with the first round until it clicked into place and she could close the breech mechanism again. She fired once more, having to angle out over the starboard bow of the inflatable as it twisted in the water, swung by the recoil. She put the gun's stock down, felt for the AK47 and studied the nightsight. Against the *Nadia*'s hull, a figure limped and fell down the last few steps to the pontoon, threw itself behind the deflated corpse of the black Gemini.

'Hey! Hey!' said the radio. 'Come on! Who *is* that?'

'We coming, *jefe.*'

She took the radio up, clicked the button that fell beneath her thumb. 'Mr Dandridge?' she said. She leant forward, took up the machine-gun again, shifting it to the side of the Gemini, aiming at the pontoon, dimly seen against *Nadia*'s hull.

'Wha— shee-it! Ms Onoda?' Dandridge coughed, laughed. 'Our little yellow friend? That you out there with the heavy weaponry?'

She clicked the send button again. 'Hello,' she said.

'Jesus aitch, I do believe it is. You still alive?'

'No,' she said.

The Gemini was still drifting. She took up the AK47 again, scanning the grey view. The *Nakodo* still showed no sign of life. *Le Cercle* was hidden behind the stern of the *Nadia*. She listened for engines.

'Ha, Ms Onoda.' The radio cut out, came back. Dandridge wheezed, 'Dead and kicking, huh? Who the hell taught you to shoot like that?' She didn't reply. She checked the machine-gun again, put it down and went back to the stern of the boat, restarted the outboard. 'What've you been doing, lady? What you been up to? How come you got a radio?' She angled the inflatable parallel with the ship, sent it in the direction of the *Nadia*'s bows, away from the course a boat from either of the other two ships would take. Dandridge had come from *Le Cercle*, not the *Nakodo*. The AK47 sight still showed nothing happening on or near the *Nakodo*.

'Ms Onoda; talk to me. You're screwing things up here. I think I deserve a little explanation. Let's talk.'

'Did I hit you?' she asked, putting down the assault rifle to talk into the radio.

'Just a scratch, as we say in the trade,' Dandridge laughed. 'You don't cease to amaze me, ma'am. Hell, what you got against us?' He laughed again.

'You comfortable, Mr Dandridge?' she said.

'Hell, never felt better. How about you?'

'Same here.' She was within fifty metres of the *Nadia*'s port bow. She swung the Gemini round until it was pointing back towards the pontoon. She let the throttle go, killed the engine, and went forwards to shift the machine-gun to the inflatable's bows again.

'Great. Well, look, we seem to have a minor disagreement here, but I'm sure we can talk it out. I just want you to know I personally don't bear you any ill will, you know— ' she heard him grunt, imagined him shifting position on the pontoon. She took another look through the nightsight. No movement. '—but this is a real stupid way to negotiate, you know? I realise you have your own point of view and all, but I want to talk to you for a moment, and I hope you'll do me the honour of listening, right? There are aspects to what we're trying to do here that I don't think you fully appreciate. Now, you don't have to tell me that every, umm, aspect of these guys' behaviour has been everything you might expect under the Geneva Convention and all, but— '

She held one of the little metal legs of the machine-gun down on to the pliant rubber with her left hand, squeezed the trigger with the index finger of the right.

The gun tried to leap; it barked and rattled and hissed. Fire trailed out across the water, calm enough to reflect it in places, and raised white feathers of water around the pontoon. She heard Dandridge shout as she paused, adjusted. The gun pulsed against her shoulder again, tracer bowing and falling. She saw sparks, then a ball of flame as the jerrycans on the pontoon ignited.

She looked up. The little mushroom of fire rose rolling, doughnut-like, against the dark hull, gathering itself under and through like a woman hoisting her skirts. Beneath it, a neck of flame throbbed in and out, and fire spilled over the deck of the pontoon, spreading over the waters to either side. She put the gun down.

'Hot damn, Ms Onoda, good shooting!' Dandridge shouted

165

from the radio. 'Outstanding! Just when I was starting to feel cold. Well thank you, ma'am.'

She felt back into the pile of weaponry in the bottom of the Gemini, found what she was looking for and lifted it. She turned away from the distant light of the burning pontoon and used the cigarette lighter from her breast pocket to inspect the device.

'*Jefe*— '

'*Shut up*. Ma'am, you have me quite incredibly impressed. You should be on our side, and I mean that as a compliment, I really do. And that's what I want to talk to you about. See, there's things in all this I don't think you fully understand. We are talking about the geopolitical situation here. What I mean is, you actually *are* on our side, if you only knew it. I mean that. You're a mercantile nation; this is about what matters to you, too. Ah, hell, Ms Onoda, it's all about trade; yes, *trade*; trade and spheres of influence and . . . and *opportunities*; the possibility of influence and power . . . you still listening, Ms Onoda?'

'Keep talking,' she said absently, wishing she knew more about the Cyrillic alphabet.

'Good. We have to keep talking. That's very important. I think that's very important. Don't you think that's important, Ms Onoda?'

She lifted the weight to her shoulder, tried a couple of switches. The device whined but the sight stayed dark. She tried different sequences, found a trigger guard and pushed it up and forward. The whine altered its tone.

'Well, I'm sure you do. You're one sensible lady. I can tell that. Very sensible and very clever and very sensitive. I hope we can talk as equals, and that's just what I intend to do. See, the great have to stoop, sometimes, Ms Onoda. To stay great you have to stoop; no ways round that. You can try and distance yourself from the people who do the stooping; I mean distance yourself from the cutting edge, but it still remains your responsibility. You have to do bad things in a bad world, if you want to stay able to be good. Do you understand that? I mean there's all these people think goodness and rightness is somehow indivisible, but it isn't; can't be, in fact. It's a razor's edge, Ms Onoda; a real razor's edge. You have to balance, you have to keep working, you know. You try to stop, you ever think you got it all taped so well you can just let things drift, and you're dead. Not the next day, not the next year even, but soon; and it starts as soon as you let go. Romans found that; the Spanish and the English too. You got to remain *dynamic*, or you fall down; you sink into your own indulgence; you get decadent. Free society . . . free society like America's, that sort of stuff is bubbling away under the surface all the time; always people want to have a quiet life, be hippies, live in what they think is peace . . . and damn it, it might be, for a little while, but— '

She clicked a button. The sight came alive; grainier than the rifle's nightsight, but the boiling stem of fire on the pontoon showed bright, like a vivid tear in the night. Centring, the whine became a guttural coughing noise, a protesting, damaged clock stuttering in her ear. Red symbols lit up above the display. She squeezed the trigger.

There was a moment of hesitation, and she almost put the missile launcher down, preparing to look at it again.

But while she was still waiting, just starting to wonder what she'd done wrong this time and what she'd have to do to make the thing work, it happened.

The tube shook, hammered her shoulder, kicked against her neck and the side of her head. The noise was not a noise; it was the end of sound, an editing mark that cut her off from the world beyond her suddenly deadened ears.

Flame burst around her. It swept, narrowed, funnelled, while she was still trying to cope with the image of herself the backwash of light had thrown before her, over the grey plastic of the Gemini's bows and the rippled lake beyond.

The spark roared across the waters, dipping, swinging, spiralling.

It met the bloom of flame on the pontoon and burst.

The explosion seemed not to start; she thought she must have blinked, and missed the start. It was suddenly there; white, yellow; a jagged splayed froth of incandescence, already falling, collapsing, dimming through orange and red.

The noise came through the ringing in her ears, and was followed by its echo, once sharply, then more muffled versions, fading and disappearing.

'*Jefe!*' she heard through the radio. Then '*Allá!*'

167

The water jumped around the Gemini. The inflatable shuddered as she threw the SAM launcher away and saw the flickering light of gunfire over to her right. The Gemini shook again, and she heard a hissing noise. Sparks struck off the engine, and the dying, zinging noise of ricochets filled the air above as more white fountains leapt into the air in front of her. The Gemini bucked under her and the engine stopped suddenly. She had one hand on the side of the inflatable, and felt it go soft under her fingers. The flickering light went on; three or four ragged points of fire.

She threw herself backwards out of the boat, into the water.

11: Oneiric

The water was strange and cloying, insinuating through the fabric of the fatigues, slicking the material against her skin. She took a deep breath, sounded, struggling through the black water away from the Gemini. The bullets hitting the water made deep thrumming noises, starting loud and violent, quickly fading. The high whine of the other inflatable's outboard drilled through the water under the percussive bullet beats.

The boots were holding her back and dragging her down. She came up for air, twisting her head to look back at the inflatable; still dishearteningly close. She brought one foot then the other up, hauling the loose boots off. She hyperventilated as she watched; the other boat was hidden by the one she'd just jumped from, but the noise of the firing swarmed through the air above her. Water burst whitely around the Gemini. She tore the remaining grenade from her breast and unbuckled the belt as she turned, took a last deep breath and dived again, heading away. Grenade and belt sank from her fingers into the dark lake.

She swam under water until she thought her mouth was about to open of its own accord and the darkness in front of her eyes had turned to a dreamy, pulsing purple, then she came up, surfacing as quietly as she could. Still no sign of the other boat, but the firing was much louder, and the Gemini she'd been on was half-collapsed in the water, shaking and bouncing as shots tore into it; sparks flew from the outboard casing, and as she watched, fire burst from the inflatable; at the stern first as the outboard's fuel tank finally gave way, then along the length of the craft; the jerry can must have ruptured. She didn't know if the plastique would explode or not. She gulped air, sounded, and angled away, hearing and feeling a last few shots thump into the water. Then the firing stopped. The note of the outboard was deepening, slowing. She waited for the blast and shock of the explosion, but it didn't come then. Her lungs burned and she surfaced once again, carefully. She looked back.

The second inflatable was silhouetted against the end-to-end flames of her Gemini; three or four men. The outboard revved, and the Gemini curved away from the burning inflatable, heading in the direction she'd swum at first. She went under, just as the ammunition on the burning Gemini started to detonate. It made a series of frenzied, booming bursts of noise, all but obliterating the sound of the outboard.

She swam until she thought she was about to black out, heading almost at right angles to the direction she'd taken initially. The outboard, when she could hear it, sounded distant.

The next time she looked the ammunition in the burning boat had reached the finale; tracer erupted into the night sky like fireworks. There was no sign of the other Gemini. She took another deep breath. An explosion kicked her, and she thought the plastique had blown, but then another came, and another, and the outboard noise whined closer. She wriggled away, changing course, realising they were using grenades.

When she had to come up, she tried not to make any noise. The Gemini was twenty metres away, lit by flames. Four men. One with what looked like a set of stubby, large-lensed binoculars. Another threw something ahead and to port; something splashed into the water ten or fifteen metres away from her. She wanted to dive then, but didn't. She watched the man with the nightscope swing round towards her.

The grenade blew, pounding her, squeezing her. She heard herself gasp with the pain of it, though the noise was hidden in the roar of the water bursting and fluting out above the grenade. Just as the man scanning the waves came round to face her, she sounded, slipping under the surface. The outboard grumbled and spat, this close. Then it whined again, roared past her. Another grenade; close enough to hammer her ears but not as painful as the one before.

When she next surfaced they were a hundred metres away. The light from the burning Gemini was waning; she heard the

170

sound of the fire through the ringing that had re-established itself in her ears like an old friend.

After a few more grenades, the four men in the inflatable broke off and went to look at what was left of the *Nadia*'s pontoon.

They cruised up and down that part of the ship's hull, tiny voices calling, '*Jefe! Jefe! Señor Dandridge!*'

She swam a little closer, wanting to see for herself. The *Nadia*'s own lights and the dregs of the flames licking round the gutted Gemini shone upon the pontoon where Dandridge had been. A small fire burned there still, in the ripped fragments of the pontoon's wooden planks and empty oil drums. One of the men in the boat was scanning the water with the nightscope; another shone a torch. The *Nadia*'s dark hull rose behind them like a cliff, glistening in the dying orange light of the foundering Gemini.

They called Dandridge's name a few more times, then one of them pointed at the water and shouted. The outboard was silent, but the boat surged forward, white under the bow, then fell and slowed again. One of the men pulled something out of the water. They shone a torch on it. Whatever it was it wasn't very big, and none of them said anything. It splashed when they threw it back. The black Gemini creased white from the surface of the lake, curving round and taking them back to the pontoon; two of them picked their way across the wreckage and went up the steps. Hisako looked back at the burning Gemini. Lit by the flames on what was left of its own crumpled bows, it slipped stern-first into the waves.

She trod water, moving a little all the time, letting the waves break over her, ducking her head under the water now and again. Torchlight swung haphazardly about the black Gemini waiting at the ruined pontoon.

The men on the ship were gone some time.

Once she sat in a train beneath the bottom of the sea.

The line from Honshu to Hokkaido had long since been completed; the tunnel ran under the waters of the Tsugaru-kaikyō for thirty kilometres, beneath the autumn fogs and the winter storms, from one island to the other. She took the train rather than the ferry between late autumn and spring, and whenever the weather forecast was bad. One December day her train broke down, ten kilometres from land, under a raging sea.

People talked nervously. They'd been told over the intercom a relief engine was on its way; there was no danger. The guard came down the carriages, reassuring people personally. Conversations started between strangers. Children played in the aisle, but she still sat looking out of the window, into the stony darkness. It had been black while they were moving; it was black now they'd stopped. She found you could ignore the reflections as long as nobody moved. The Strad occupied the seat next to her.

She wasn't afraid; she thought some people were, just because they were no longer moving, because something had gone wrong and things might continue to go wrong and it all might end in disaster, but she didn't think anything like that would happen; what would happen would be a long boring wait, then the journey resumed, some of the conversations maintained, some allowed to end. Finally everybody's own arrival, along the line, or in Sapporo; some met with smiles and helping hands, some walking quickly away, heads down, breath steaming from their mouths and noses, scattering for taxis, cars, buses and subway trains.

Life was not exotic; even disasters were almost welcome, sometimes. She put her elbow on the table in front of her, her chin in her hand, and studied her own dark reflection in the glass.

She was glad of the breakdown. Things could work too smoothly.

This was like a time out; somehow, even when there was time to think, there was never time to think. All her life was taken care of, each month and week and day and hour ascribed a certain function, filled with duties and performances, or left precisely blank, for the part of her existence that was not encased by music; for friends and relaxation and holidays. Holidays. Most of the people she knew hardly had any, but she took days and weeks off all the time, and could not understand how everybody else got by with so little. She was meant to enjoy her work more than most, but she kept trying to escape from it.

Whatever; this interlude, stuck in a train in a tunnel, at night, beneath the sea bed, while the cold waves rolled and the spray filled the gale, seemed like a bonus, a siding. Now, unexpectedly, she could take a step back from her life, and think properly. She felt she needed to.

Sanae Naritomi wanted to marry her.

The water was warm; the fatigues trapped a layer at blood heat. She felt strong, and she knew she could tread water for hours; it was practically resting. The men on the ship came back to the rail; she could hear the shock and anger in their voices even over that distance, even without knowing the words. '*Muerto*,' she heard, over and again. She knew what that meant, could make that out all right. Muerto muerto muerto muerto muerto muerto muerto muerto.

The small fire on the pontoon guttered and went out. The men rejoined the Gemini, and took the inflatable back to *Le Cercle*; she followed.

It was a long swim.

They'd met at a reception; his reception, arranged by the orchestra in honour of his return to Japan after ten almost unbroken years in Europe, first studying, then composing and conducting, then zooming to sudden fame as the glamorous new orchestral star; of Paris, Europe, the world. The cover of *Newsweek*; invitations everywhere; documentaries on television; a film made about his tour through the Soviet Union with the Hallé, which had been surprisingly funny, pleased the critics enough to win prizes at Cannes, and made money on general release; dates with starlets and models; a series of TV commercials for expensive Parisian colognes. Plus a workload her conducting colleagues shook their heads over; young as he was, he'd burn out.

She'd seen the *Newsweek* cover. San, as the *gaijin* had decided to call him, even looked like a film star. Jet-black hair, long and ringleted, inherited from his Eurasian mother, wild around a bright, pale, hawkish face, rarely photographed without a smile, a grin, a smirk. When there was no smile on his face he just looked broodingly romantic. He was still only thirty but he looked much less. *Newsweek* had made much of the number of pop idols ripped from teenage girls' bedroom walls to be replaced by San, grinning down, at once rakish and shy, head

173

lowered, eyes half-hidden behind a tangled black fringe.

She'd been appalled. The performances she'd heard of his were good; full of fire and drama without being brash; innovative without being contemptuous of previous interpretations. He could conduct, certainly, but why all the rest? Such wilful self-promotion seemed vulgar, egotistical. She'd already decided not to go to the reception even before the invitation arrived. Most of the others in the orchestra were excited at the thought of meeting him – only a few of the older men didn't seem too impressed with the idea – but she wouldn't go to his court, she wouldn't pay homage to the boy wonder. Thirty, she thought; the child. She suddenly remembered when thirty had seemed ancient. She was thirty-six and had never felt old before.

Then she thought; she'd have gone anyway, if it was anybody else, and besides there was a music journalist, recently back from the States, she'd had her eye on for a while; this would be an ideal opportunity to get talking to him. She *would* go; she just wouldn't ask to be introduced to the *Newsweek* cover-boy. She went through about half her clothes before she decided on the right thing; not too dowdy, but not something that looked as though it was trying to catch the eye of the media star. A western-looking black suit, jacket cut high, like a male flamenco dancer's; slim skirt with a discreet slit, there more for mobility than excitement. White silk shirt and sheer black stockings; flat black shoes because the journalist wasn't tall.

She went late, in case they had some sort of formal receiving line set up at the start. The journalist had a bad cold and left before she had time to do more than exchange pleasantries and check he wasn't there with anybody else. She almost went then, but didn't.

She wandered a little, sampled the buffet, was talked to variously. She decided to go home and read a book as soon as the first bore even approached.

Mr Okamoto bowed to her as she turned away from the buffet table holding a little paper plate. Sanae Naritomi stood at his side, beaming at her, dressed, she thought, rather in the style of a Mississippi gambler. He stuck one long, white hand out to her as Okamoto said, 'Naritomi-*san* asked to be introduced to you . . .'

She shifted the plate from one hand to the other. He shook her hand, bowed as well. 'Thank you, Mr Okamoto. Ms Onoda; I've wanted to meet you for years. I have all your recordings.' He flashed white teeth, tossed his hair quite naturally and with a 'May I?' took a roll of salmon from her plate and popped it in his mouth. Okamoto had gone; she hadn't noticed. 'Delicious,' Naritomi said. 'Mmm. I hope we can work together; I'd count that a privilege.'

'Well,' she said, unsettled, putting the plate down behind her on the table, then taking it back up again in case he thought she was being rude and had only done it to stop him taking any more food. She felt warm. 'Well,' she said again, feeling foolish and tongue-tied, as he probably expected all women to be with him. 'I do play with the orchestra. As you're going to guest, we're bound to work together.'

'Ah,' he snapped his fingers, shook his head quickly. 'I mean more closely than that. I'd be honoured to accompany you sometime; and I have some pieces . . . probably not very good, probably not much better than my barely competent piano playing— ' She'd heard his barely competent piano playing; he could probably have had a career as a concert pianist if he hadn't chosen conducting. '—but I'd be just,' he shook his head, clapped his hands together softly. She wondered if the scent she could smell was the same cologne he advertised, '*delighted* if you'd play them. I've always loved the cello, and your playing especially. I'm serious; I really hope you'll do this for me. But hey,' he slapped one hand gently off his forehead, mocking the theatricality of the gesture with a grin. 'I shouldn't be coming on like this, should I? What happened to small talk first, huh? I should soften you up with more embarrassing praise and tell you how much I love being back in Japan, and yes it was a good flight and yes I do wear the stuff I advertise on television and no the *gaijin* don't really – but now I'm rambling, yes? I'm just nervous. These salmon things taste really good you know; do you mind if I . . . ?'

He stood smiling, eating.

She realised she was smiling too, even more broadly, and wondered how long she'd looked like that. She nodded, bit down on her lips a little to help control herself. 'I'm sure we can arrange something,' she said.

175

They talked. Eventually he was dragged away to meet the Sony top brass who were sponsoring some of the concerts. 'Don't try to escape without saying goodbye!' he called back to her. She nodded, throat dry, face hot, eyes wide, and looked for a cooling, calming drink.

He begged her to stay an extra half-hour, to the end, when she tried to leave. There was a party in his suite in the New Otani; he insisted, pleaded.

More talk at the party; then the last half-dozen of them went to a *gaijin* club in Roppongi in the small hours. San played lightning-fast backgammon with a one-armed Australian (yes, he had fished for shark; no, a car accident), exchanged jokes with a mountainous Yakuza gangster with tattooed eyelids, and then played piano in the bar; he borrowed a waitress's little leather bag and stuck it on his head to do an impression of Chico Marx, plinking the keyboard with one flicked, pistol-like finger.

At dawn, he took the hired Mercedes down to the docks at Yokohama; in the back seat, the other two survivors – an early-balding television producer and a glamorous, long-legged advertising exec – had fallen asleep during the drive, and sat slumped on the brown leather, his shining head on her padded, sequined shoulder.

San looked vaguely disappointed they'd given up the fight for fun. He shrugged. They got out. San breathed in the dawn, then stood looking at the sleeping couple in the back of the Merc with a great grin on his face. It was the smile people normally wore when gazing at tiny babies. 'Don't they look *sweet*?' he said, then turned and walked down to the edge of the dock, and stood looking out over the misty lengths of ships and warehouses to where the dim red sun rose above the masts, cranes and derricks of the port. Horns sounded, the air was cool, and the breeze smelled of the ocean.

He put his jacket over a bollard for her, and sat at her feet, legs dangling over the edge of the empty dock, looking down at the sluggish water, where half-waterlogged planks and wind-skittery grey lumps of polystyrene foam bobbed together on a film of oil.

He took out a silver cigarette case. She hadn't seen him smoke. Then she smelled the hash. 'Do you?' he asked, offering her the joint after a couple of tokes. She took it.

He said, 'I've kept you up.'

'That's OK.'

'Had fun?'

'Uh-huh.' She passed the joint back.

'Think we can get on?'

'I think we are.'

'Didn't want to like me at first, did you?' He looked up at her.

'No,' she agreed, surprised. 'But I didn't hold out for long. Does everybody give in so quickly?'

'Oh no,' he said. 'Some people never get to like me.'

There was silence for a moment; she heard the water lap, watched steam plume from the funnel of a freighter – half a mile away, and heading for the sea – and then heard its horn, echoing off the warehouses and hulls around them, announcing its farewell. He handed her back the spliff. 'Did you sleep with all those film stars?' she asked him.

He laughed. 'One or two.' He looked up at her. 'I'm a man of easy virtue, Hisako.'

'Easily led astray,' she nodded through the smoke, feeling dizzy.

'I'm afraid so,' he said, stretching his arms up behind his back, as though in a gesture of surrender, then reaching in and scratching the back of his neck vigorously.

'Yeah,' she said, studying the end of the joint, 'same here.'

He gave a sort of coughing laugh, looked at her. 'Really?'

'Really. Dangerous these days, but . . .' she gave him the joint back.

'Yes, of course, but . . .' he nodded, looked out to the departing ship in the distance. He took a deep breath. 'Umm . . .'

'Yes?'

'Do you think . . .'

'Yes?'

'I might be able to tempt . . .'

'Yes.'

'. . . you back to . . .' his voice slowed as he looked round at her.

'Yes.'

'. . . my hotel?' he grinned.

'Yes.'

*   *   *

177

She rounded the stern of the *Nadia*, struck out for *Le Cercle*. The water stayed warm, and the waves small. She swam steadily, trying to find a rhythm that suited her body and the water, and felt half-hypnotised. She thought she heard thunder a few times. The wind did stiffen eventually, and the water became more choppy. The *Nadia* fell slowly behind her. The ship leaving for the open sea that misty dawn at Yokohama, years ago, an ocean away, had been a general cargo freighter.

She wondered vaguely what the chances were it had been the *Nadia*.

Le Cercle's pontoon was brightly lit; the rest of the ship looked dark in comparison. There was a man on the pontoon, scanning the waters with a nightscope. She angled away, towards the tanker's bows. Lightning flashed beyond the hills to the north-west, and thunder rolled across the dark lake, vague and long after. Rain was starting to patter down around her as she swam under the dark-on-dark cliff of the ship's port bow.

Fairy tale, she told her reflection in the dark train window. Too good to be true. Brilliant and handsome and now only a few months later he wanted them to be true only to each other, and to be married, and to live together (he'd stay in Japan, never fly again, if she wanted; she told him not to be crazy, and worried that he might have been even half-serious), and have children if she wanted. He loved her, wanted her, was made whole by her.

Sometimes he made her feel half her age, sometimes twice it. He could make her feel like a teenager, impressed by another's antics one second, struck dumb by his devotion; ardour, indeed, the next. Other times he seemed so energetically enthusiastic and excited – and even innocent, even naïve – she felt like a grandmother, shaking her head over the wild excesses of youth, knowing it would come to no good, grumbling it would end in tears.

She'd said she'd go to see her mother, think it over, talk it over. He wanted to come too, but she wouldn't let him. He'd been subdued and sad at the station, and only brightened when he saw a flower seller and bought so many roses she could hardly carry them. She'd left all but one with the guard, too embarrassed to cart them through the train. The one she'd kept lay on the table in front of her, its dark image on the table reflected in the rock-backed window glass.

She rolled the rose around on the table, holding its stem and watching the velvet-soft petals flatten and spring back as they took the flower's weight on the table surface, then released it again. She wondered what to tell her mother. She'd kept the whole affair secret from her, as she always did. She didn't know if her mother had heard anything through the gossip pages or not; she didn't normally read them, and Hisako didn't think any of her mother's friends did either, but. . . . Well, it would either come as a surprise or not; there wasn't anything she could do about it now. What would her mother say? She felt a heaviness in her at the thought her mother would probably be delighted, and encourage her. She wondered what that heaviness meant.

She kept on rolling the rose to and fro, to and fro. How happy she might become, she thought. How happy and fulfilled and content. She put her thumb on a thorn and pressed, felt the pain and watched a tiny bright bead of red form on the pale surface. She had spent, she thought, so much time playing music with the feeling that this was to compensate, that she did it to add to life, to make restitution. She had lived quietly if not virtuously, and if she took time off, she always knew she'd play better at the end of it. She'd kept her head down; never tried too hard to enjoy herself beyond her own pleasure in the music, the occasional lover and a small group of friends. She wasn't supposed to make too much of life, wasn't supposed to glory in her own existence too fully, too vivaciously.

Because.

After a while she stopped rolling the flower to and fro on the table, and took the single red rose, and shut it in the cello case.

She still hadn't made up her mind when distant clanking noises, and a single rocking judder pulsing down the carriages announced the arrival of the relief engine. People clapped as the train moved. Life resumed, and she kept on thinking, round and round.

She didn't deserve it, but then how many people ever had just what they deserved happen to them? It would be hell; he'd philander, he was younger after all; it would pass, this sudden rush of enthusiasm. Or they'd grow together, and he would always love what would always be there in her, what he must love anyway because she wasn't half so attractive as all those film stars and models. No, it was too much; she'd make a fool of herself . . . but life was short, and *something* had to happen.

Her mother was at the station, bright and full of life, looking younger than Hisako could remember. She was excited, didn't mention the three-hour wait. *She must know*, Hisako thought wearily.

Mrs Onoda took her daughter's arm. She wanted Hisako to be the first to know. A new friend, a wonderful man; she was sorry she'd kept it quiet, but people talked and she had wanted to wait until it was official. She just knew Hisako would like him too. She was so happy! And, think; now you won't be a half-orphan any more!

Hisako smiled, said she was very happy for her.

Flushed the rose down the toilet that evening.

She found the buoy, climbed up on to it. The rain came down in big, unseen drops, cold and hard. She rested a few minutes, looking up at the inverted V the tanker's bows made above her. The shape was more imagined than seen; the lights above were few and dim. The rain came harder, raking her face. She sighed, looked down, then shrugged, stood on the slightly tipped, slick top surface of the buoy, and took hold of the hawser sweeping up to the ship. She gripped it; wet, but not oily. She wrapped her legs round it too, gripping it with her ankles. Tensing her legs, she reached up and pulled with her arms. No problem.

She went on up.

By the time she got to the top, the rain was crashing down like pebbles off the back of a dumper truck; thunder bellowed in the hills. She peeped through the hawse pipe, saw only dim grey-black deck and spattering rain. She stuck her head through, remembering the cameras. They were pointed sternwards, away from her. She crawled through, on to the deck, and found cover behind a winch housing. Rain clattered around her. She raised her head again, looking down the pipe-cluttered length of deck to the island of superstructure.

She wondered what to do now. Why was she doing this?

Because. Because she couldn't think of anything better to do.

She laughed quietly to herself, and shivered inside the clinging fatigues.

They had the red lights on in the bridge. She could see somebody moving there, in the dry, red warmth. Lightning lit the starboard side of the ship, throwing electric blue shadows over the white cliff of the superstructure.

Not a weapon to her name, she thought. Not a thing to wield. Even the knife had gone when she took the belt off.

She saw movement, and a uniform appeared in the rain-scattered distance, coming up from the steps to the pontoon, from the blazing fan of rain under the lights into the shadow of the lower deck. She watched the soldier as he was met by another tiny figure; they disappeared into the ship. Shortly afterwards the remaining lights went out all over the tanker, leaving only the red night-lights of the bridge burning.

She was surprised at first, thinking that if they were really afraid of some sort of attack they ought to floodlight the vessel . . . but then she remembered the nightscopes. Perhaps it made sense after all; at first sight, anyway.

She let her eyes adjust. She could see them on the bridge, far away. There were several, all watching through the nightscopes at first. She could see a place to hide under a nearby pipe cluster, so that if they turned on the lights again and used the television cameras, or came out looking, she could hide. There were two soldiers looking out after a while, then only one, sitting on a stool near midships in the bridge, sweeping from side to side and now and again getting up to look from each wing of the bridge.

The thunder crashed and the lightning flickered overhead, lighting up the ships and hills and islands. After one flash, and while the man with the nightscope was looking out to port, she jumped over the first breakwater.

She waited for the same conjunction before tackling the next breakwater, then wriggled along the rain-slicked deck to the shelter of the main trunk lines. Under the pipes she felt relatively safe, and had a clear run – or crawl – along half the deck to the midships valve-head cluster, where the pumps and switchgear were sited that accepted and discharged the cargo. Lightning flashed blue images of the pipe network above her across the deck, catching a million falling raindrops in an instant of falling. She started edging forward.

She scraped and slid and coasted along the wet deck, blinking the rain out of her eyes. She pulled with her hands and elbows, pushed with her feet. She tried to think about what she ought to do, but nothing suggested itself. She suspected she'd had her share of luck that night, and these rattled, jumpy soldiers were not going to fall as easily as those on the *Nadia*. That had been a happy hunting ground; this felt wrong.

Her crotch itched; she stopped and scratched. Raw, and despite it all she ought to have taken the time to have a proper bath. But there you were; she hadn't had the time, and—

Suddenly, without warning, she was sick.

There was little enough in her stomach, so it was mostly bile, but she watched what there was come out, and tried to do it as silently as possible, while feeling the deepest surprise. This was unexpected. She hadn't felt sick. She forced the last heave, spat, then rolled over under a welded collar between two lengths of pipe above her, where the rain was dripping so hard and fast it was an almost unbroken stream. She let the water splash into her mouth, rinsing and spitting and rinsing and spitting and then swallowing and swallowing.

Huh, she said to herself.

She got back on her front, and kept on crawling. The rain would soon rinse the sickness away; there'd be no sign for them to find. The lightning glare burst through the pipes above and threw black bars across her back.

She got to the valve cluster and paused, looked up at the bridge again, through the pounding lines of rain. She watched for a while. Just the one man. Then two more came from behind. They held what looked like a SAM launcher. One of them took the nightscope and stood scanning the deck; she had to duck now and again, but watched when she could. It looked as though one of them was showing the man on the bridge how to work the launcher; holding it up, sighting, letting the other man repeat the actions. She ducked at each flash of lightning. The lightning was closer now, the thunder louder.

She stayed ducked after one flash, thinking. She looked around her, checking the bow cameras but unable to see which way they were pointing through the driving rain. She shivered again in the cool wash of water glueing the fatigues to her skin, and ran her hand over the rough-painted surface of the valve-head controls. Her hand stopped, invisible.

She patted the metal hatch cover.

The catches came undone easily, and the hatch swung open. She waited.

Darkness for a long time, then a brilliant flash, leaving an after-image. It was difficult to decide whether the controls here were set out similarly to those on the bridge, which she thought she could just about remember.

She remembered something else, and decided she was sufficiently hidden from the bridge by the high, thick pipes of the valve cluster. She took out the cigarette lighter from the fatigues' breast pocket. It sputtered, clicking. She blew on it, shook it hard, then tried it again, using her other hand as an umbrella. The lighter hissed, made a series of clicking noises at the same time, then lit. The clicking noises stopped. Still sheltering it, she held the little yellow flame to the open white cavity of the pump controls. The flame lessened, shrank, and the hiss decreased. She shook the lighter but its light continued to fade, running out. Never mind; she'd seen all she wanted.

She snapped the lighter off. Peeped at the bridge. No sign of concern; just the one man, scanning. The rain sang on the metal deck and pipes around her. She waited. The lightning preceded the thunder by ten seconds, then by five, then one or two. She put her hands on the switches.

Lightning flared and thunder bellowed all around the ship; probably hit it, she guessed. She turned the switches. The echoes of the thunder were still dying away as the pumps beneath her feet started up, making the deck thrum. Red lights appeared in front of her eyes.

She heard hisses and gurgles, then, over the noise of the rain, the rumble of the thick oil pouring out through the pipes and into the lake.

She wondered how long it would take them to realise. She watched the bridge for a few seconds. Nothing. Same man, same actions. Quite undisturbed. She felt the deck tremble as the pumps pulled the oil from the tanks and threw it into the lake. She watched the man on the red length of the bridge for a while longer, her eyes screwed up, trying to drill her sight through the waves of rain. Nothing; *nada*. Hadn't even seen the damn stuff spewing out from the sides of the ship. Hadn't noticed the lights on the cargo-handling board on the bridge. She looked at the lighter in her hand, thought about trying to set fire to the torrent of oil pouring from the pumps over the side of the boat and into the lake, then looked up, mouth opening, into the night, and with a last hurried look at the lighter, put it away, squatted on her haunches, and thought. She nodded once to herself, then spent a long time looking through the rain, through a small space between two pipes she reckoned would screen her from the nightscope and the lightning, watching the man on the bridge. She started to worry about the lightning.

After a while she got dizzy with tiredness. The storm was departing; the rain had settled to a steady downpour; the lightning had become less dramatic and urgent, the thunder less immediate and crackly.

She felt the deck resound beneath her, and lay down in the pouring rain, only half-sheltered by the thick pipes above.

She curled up, and slept.

Hisako Onoda dreamed of a lake full of blood and a sky full of fire. She watched from the depths of space and saw a great lever strike the world; it rang false and shattered, disintegrating into all the separate states and creeds, beliefs and prejudices that had riven it over the years, blowing like seeds from a flower.

She kept waking up, thinking she'd heard steps, or voices. Or maybe she only thought she kept waking up, she thought later.

Blood and fire, the dreams were always there waiting for her when she drifted off again.

When she did awake, properly, finally, the rain was gone, the first light of dawn was trying to burrow under the dark lid of the sky, the deck still trembled beneath her, the air smelled thick and the lake was full of blood.

12: The Heart of the Universe

Her father died three months before she was born; she had never been held by him. They told her she was lucky, all the same; she might have been born deformed. It was years after the *Pikadon*, and maybe he'd have died of cancer anyway. That was the way it worked, by statistics. It came down to probabilities, a cellular image of the jeopardising indeterminacies that lay beneath the physical world, and were its absolute – but absolutely uncertain – foundations. So maybe the bomb did kill him, eventually, or maybe it didn't.

They'd opened him up, hoping to deal with the tumour in his belly, but when they saw what was inside him, they just closed the incision again. He stayed in hospital, went home for a while to be with his pregnant wife, but after a few weeks the pain got so bad they took him back into the hospital once more.

He'd been with his unit in Kaita, a town a few kilometres from the city suburbs, when the *Pikadon* came. They'd seen the lone bomber from the barracks; tiny in the sky. One of the men claimed he'd seen the bomb itself, a dot falling. They heard the sirens from the city, went back to cleaning their rifles.

Then another sun lit the parade ground and the barrack buildings. They shielded their eyes, felt the heat, and watched dumbly while the light faded slowly and the vast cloud rose soundlessly into the sky, like the leg of a giant boot that had stamped upon the city. The noise came much later, like continuous heavy thunder.

On the way to the city, to help, they met the burned people, and once passed a group of soldiers; young men like themselves, but looking like black men, stumbling along in a crocodile line down the dusty road, each man with one hand on the shoulder of the man in front, following the leader. The soldier at the head of the strange, silent column had one eye left; the others were all blind. They weren't Negroes. They were Japanese. They'd been closer, and watched the bomb all the way, until it exploded in the air above the city, and that was the last thing they were ever to see; the light had melted their eyes. The fluids were still wet on their charcoal-black cheeks.

Through the increasing damage and the smoking wreckage, to the stripped centre, where the buildings had almost all gone, wiped from the ground-plan of the city as though by an immense scrubbing brush.

On the walls, he saw the shadows that had been people.

His unit stayed in Hiroshima, in the ruins and dust, for a few days. They did what they could. Ten years later, a quarter of the men who'd been there with him were dead. Eleven years later, so was he.

His widow went into labour just down the corridor from where he'd died. Hisako got tangled in her own cord, stuck and struggling, and had to be removed by Caesarean section; pulled from her mother's womb by the same surgeon who'd discovered the metastasising shadow of death in her father a season earlier.

Sanae was the first lover she'd ever told about it all. She told him the night she told him she would not marry him, and she cried as she told him, thinking about her father and the man she'd killed, and about something else she hadn't told Sanae about. He looked hurt and meek and pleading, like a beaten kid, like a whipped dog. She couldn't bear to look at him, so said what she had to say to the cup of coffee before her. They sat in a little *kissaten* in Roppongi, and he wanted to touch her, to hold her hand, to take her in his arms, but she wouldn't let him, couldn't risk him doing that and her dissolving, giving in. So she shrugged him off, took her hand away, shook her head. He sat, slumped and dejected on the stool, while she told him, but could not explain. It just didn't feel right. She wasn't ready. She'd hold him back. He mustn't distract himself from his career. She – here she had to swallow hard, fighting the tears again, biting her lip hard, squinting hot and angry into the brown dregs in the little white cup – she didn't want to have children.

It was the truth, but it was the hardest thing she could have said, just then.

Sanae left, eventually, in distress and despair, unable to understand. Her tears collected in the bottom of the coffee cup, turning the thick brown dregs watery again.

She had put off returning from Sapporo and meeting him and telling him until the day before he left for Los Angeles for a month to do some studio work.

She had the abortion while he was away, and the world went on.

Hisako Onoda woke to shouts and general consternation, and felt annoyed that her sleep had been disturbed. The deck was hard, the morning was cold and she yawned awake, aching and shivering and feeling like shit, itching and pained and with the hangover-like feeling that there was something very terrible she'd have to remember soon, and face.

The air stank of oil. Mist clung to the hills, hovered in discreet little clouds over the islands. Elsewhere there was mist, too; over the broad waters of the lake.

Not near by though, save on the ship itself. Near by the lake was thick and brown and perfectly, deathly, calm. Wisps of vapour were still rising from the broad, pipe-cluttered deck of the tanker, just parting enough now to reveal the gush of oil from the valve cluster, spreading in a dirty brown arc as it fell to the lake. The ship sat under a stem of mist in a cauldron of clarity, surrounded by cloud. She sat up, at once thrilled and appalled.

The oil stretched as far as the nearest islands, as far as the *Nakodo*, almost as far as she could see; the unsullied lake was just a blue sparkle beneath the mist in the distance. A disc, she thought; a great grubby brown coin of thick, glistening, stinking oil floating on the waters of the lake like a vast wet bruise.

She looked to the bridge. Harder to see now the sun was up. Vague movements behind the tipped glass; two soldiers leaning out of the open windows on the starboard wing of the bridge, gesturing and shouting.

She checked the bow camera again, but it was pointed away from her. The pump controls were still set as she'd left them, and hadn't been shut off from the bridge. She inspected them, yawning and stretching. No, there wasn't anything she could do to make it any worse; she'd done all she could. She checked the lighter, but it was spent; no hiss of gas, and even the tiny clicks sounded tired now. She put it back in her breast pocket.

She looked to the sky. Too much mist and low cloud to tell what the day would be like. Maybe cloudy, maybe clear; it could go both ways. She realised that she'd heard a weather forecast, on the radio, just the day before.

A day. Felt like a week, a year; forever.

Whatever; she couldn't remember the forecast. Wait and see. She shivered again. How stupid germs were. She was probably going to die in the next few hours, one way or the other, and here she was maybe getting a cold. What was the point?

The condemned man ate a hearty breakfast. Feast before *seppuku*.

She stretched again, putting her arms out, fists by shoulders, then brought her hands to the back of her neck, scratching vigorously.

You bastards, she thought. I remember Sanae and I remember Philippe, but the last act I'll take with me is yours; squalid thrusting being egged on and waiting, sneers of victory, trying to judge the level of anguish and noise they wanted to cause so not too hysterical but not too placid; a final acting, a faking when in all her life she'd *never* faked, and had counted that strength, made it a point of honour, and they'd sullied everything; a retrospective act, casting a shadow all the way back to . . . to . . . hell, this was a terrible thing, that poor Swede; she'd forgotten his name; Werner? Benny? She thought you were meant never to forget the name of your first . . .

Sanae was energetic and wild, like a storm over her, beneath her, around her, all gestures and noise; still childlike in that adult act, so self-absorbed, distracted and distracting, almost funny.

Philippe dived, skin on skin in skin, sweeping and plunging and such sweet encirclement, concentric with his homed immersion; quietly, almost sadly studious in his abandoned absorption.

But if her life passed in front of her it would end with a gang-bang, and the applause would be the crackle of breaking bones and the spatter of spilled blood, signature of her revenge.

188

Well, worse things happen at sea, she thought, and laughed out loud, before shushing herself.

She was feeling almost happy, resigned but oddly fulfilled, and at peace at last, when she thought of the dreams, and the lake of blood.

In the past, she'd always coped, she'd put up with it, with them. Dreams were dreams and took their cue from what had happened, accessories after the act. She'd dismissed those she'd been having recently as she'd dismissed those she'd always had. But now they spoke of a lake of blood, and it occurred to her that the brown slick of oil, the great dumped flat platelet she'd spread over the waters, was a kind of blood. Blood of the planet, blood of the human world. The oil-blood greased the world machine; the blood-oil carried energy to the workings of the states and systems. It welled and was pulled out, bled to the surface, was transfused and transported. It was the messenger of soil and progress; the refined lesson of its own development.

Now, a leech, she'd let it. She was making the dream.

She hadn't meant to pretend to such authority.

Hisako sat down heavily on her haunches, staring out at the brown horizon of oil. Well, she thought, too late now. She looked up at the sky. She heard the shouts of the soldiers over the thunder of the pumps, then stood again and peeped through the clutter of pipes, watching the superstructure.

There was movement behind the glass of the bridge.

Suddenly she heard clicks and buzzes to her left, and leapt away from the pump-control housing, heart hammering, dizzy with dread, waiting for the shots.

There was nobody there. The controls clicked again, and the pumps whined down to silence; the deck stilled. She was tempted to switch the pumps back on again, see who could overrule who with the controls. But then they might guess she was there. She left the controls alone and went back to watching through the square tangle of pipework.

After a few minutes, three men appeared at the top of the steps which led down to the pontoon. Even from a distance the soldiers looked nervous and harried; one was still pulling on his fatigue trousers. They all held bags and rucksacks, were weighed down with guns and missile launchers. They looked as if they were arguing; two disappeared down the steps to the pontoon. The third seemed to be shouting back into the ship. He dropped his rifle, jumped, picked the gun up quickly again, looking round as though he expected to be attacked at any moment. He shouted through the doorway again, then he too ran for the steps.

The fourth man followed a minute later, even more heavily laden than the rest. He looked up the deck, towards the bows, and for a moment she was convinced he was looking straight at her. He stayed in that position, and her mouth went dry. She wanted to duck but didn't; the soldier was too far away, and the gap she was looking through too small for him to be able to see her clearly; at most she must be a slightly odd pale dot in the midst of the pipework. He couldn't be sure the dot was a face. Only moving would settle the issue for him, so she stayed still. If he had binoculars, she'd just have to try and duck down as he brought them up to his eyes. He moved, turning to the gunwale and shouting down, then going quickly to the steps, disappearing down them. She let her breath out.

She wondered if they'd use the outboard. A military engine was probably safe to use on the oil, in theory, but she wasn't sure she'd like to trust her life to it. She crawled under and through the pipework, towards the port rail. When she was there she raised her head enough to glance over. No sign of the Gemini. She was puzzled, then afraid, and glanced back at the top of the steps where they came through the gunwale, fifty metres away. Shouts came from that direction, but beneath, where the pontoon was. She edged closer to the rail, craned her head out.

She found them; the ship had risen so much that the steps, which for months had ended virtually at water level, now hung four or five metres above the pontoon, which was itself near the end of its travel on the ropes attaching it to the ship; it was canted at an angle of thirty degrees or more, the hull-side edge pointing up towards the dangling steps. The soldiers were at the bottom of those steps, lowering a wire ladder to the pontoon.

She edged back from the rail, crawled to the centre-line pipework and got up on the far side. She kept ducked-down and ran sternwards, towards the superstructure. Her naked feet slapped quietly; the metal covering the half-empty tanks beneath her soles felt cool, and still wet from the morning mists.

The soldiers were on the port side; she entered the super-structure from starboard. Comparative silence. *Le Cercle*'s donkey engine was still running, creating that hardly audible, subtly soothing whine she'd grown used to in the nights aboard. She crept to the nearest companionway, listening, glancing all around.

The galley's gleaming surfaces were cluttered with opened tins and unwashed plates. Lekkas, she thought, would have had a fit.

She took the biggest kitchen knife she could find, and felt a little more comfortable.

The deck above was quiet too, and the one above that. She glanced into a couple of cabins, but couldn't see any guns. She'd hoped they might have left a few behind.

She approached the bridge deck slowly and carefully, then stole along it. The bridge was silent, a little messy, and smelled of cigarette smoke. From the port wing of the bridge she looked down to the lake surface.

There they were; rowing slowly away through the sticky brown mass of the oil, a man at each of the two stubby oars. The other two were shouting; encouragement, perhaps. They hadn't got very far. Two of them – one rowing – must have fallen in; they were brown with the clinging oil. She spared a few seconds for the view, surveying her handiwork; acres, hectares – a square kilometre perhaps, it was hard to tell with the islands and the other two ships blocking the view – of filthy brown, dead flat, glistening oil.

The boys at the nature reserve on Barro Colorado would probably have wrung her neck for this.

She took the flare gun from the chart room, loaded and cocked it, stuffed a few more rounds in her pockets and went to the radio room. No fuses, no power. The bridge radios were out too. She quickly searched the cabins, no guns or grenades. Another check on the progress the men were making through the sludge of oil; hardly out of the shadow of the ship.

She went outside to check the starboard lifeboat, feeling a sneer on her face as she thought of the fools taking to the Gemini.

Each of the tanker's lifeboats could hold the entire crew; they were big, bright orange, and fully enclosed. They were designed to survive high temperatures, and would work – and keep their occupants cool enough – on a sea on fire with spilled oil, if it came to it.

She came out on to the sunlit deck, beneath the starboard lifeboat.

It had been wrecked.

They must have machine-gunned it.

She looked at the ragged gap in the lifeboat's bows, at the bullet holes scattered around the main breach, and the shards of orange hull material lying on the deck. She ran back, into the ship and across the bridge, ducked down – the Gemini was still less than fifty metres away through the oil – and saw what was left of the port lifeboat. Smashed; a grenade, she guessed.

Hisako went back across the bridge, out on to the starboard lifeboat deck again and climbed up into the wrecked boat through its bow hatch. She held the kitchen knife in her teeth, and couldn't help but laugh at herself. Inside the lifeboat, she found the grey plastic flare container, twisted the thick red plastic top off, and rummaged through the big smoke-canisters and the hand-held flares until she found what she was looking for. She took two, just to be sure.

She stuffed the pistol from the chart room under one arm, walked back to the bridge, reading the instructions on the parachute flares.

Through the bridge, through the door on to the port lifeboat deck. The Gemini had been rowed another ten metres away. She tore the cap off the base of the flare, and hinged the trigger mechanism out, like a heavy-duty ring-pull. She stood behind a life-raft dispenser, a sloped rack of three bright, white plastic inflatable containers. She stripped the sticky tape off the red top of the flare casing and removed the plastic cap. Looking over the top of the life-rafts, she could just see the Gemini and the four men in it, still rowing carefully through the brown sludge, oars cloyed and dripping. They hadn't seen her. She put the kitchen knife down on the deck.

'Hey!' she screamed, standing on tip-toes. 'Hey, punks! Make my day! Don't push me! That ain't nice, you laughin'!'

They looked; the oars dipped, paused. Two looked straight at

her, the pair in the stern of the inflatable turned, stared back.
Hisako waved the readied flare. 'Uncle *Saaam!*'

One of the rowers reached back, started to stand, bringing his gun up; she heard shouting as she ducked, grabbing the flare pistol as it fell from her armpit, holding the parachute flare in the other hand. She peeked round the life-raft cluster. The Gemini was rocking, one of the men in the stern had stood up; he was grappling with the soldier holding the gun.

She put the flare pistol on the deck, stood, stuck her finger through the ring-pull. The soldiers were shouting. She pointed the flare into the sky and pulled the ring.

A moment's hesitation; enough, in cartoon-land, for her to look puzzled, turn the flare round and stare into the business end of the tube.

She waited.

The canister leapt back against her hands; detonating. Echoes rang off the metal walls behind her. The flare rocketed into the misty blue sky, spiralling and arching with a firework hiss.

She ducked, but still looked.

The men in the Gemini were in tableau; stood and sitting, clean and oil-soaked, all four staring up as the flare rose above and beyond them, rasping into the air. She threw the spent, smoking container away, rattling on the deck.

The rocket slowed, wavered. It had just started to drop when it puffed, sent a tiny little white cloud to the top of its arc, and suddenly blazed; incandescently brilliant and swinging like a pendulum beneath a miniature parachute.

Screams, when they realised.

She dropped to the deck, looked over the little metal flange beneath the deck rails.

One of the soldiers started rowing desperately, yelling at the others. The one holding the gun shook the man from the stern off, leaving him teetering. The gun fired. She spread herself on the deck, heard shouting and screaming through the percussive clatter of the machine-gun. In a few seconds, the superstructure above her sang to the noise of the bullets hitting. The deck rattled to one side; a window in the bridge shattered. The firing stopped. She popped up for a look. Two rowing now, though the Gemini was still going in a circle. One soldier was stabbing at the outboard, trying to start it, the fourth . . . the fourth was overboard, in the lake, astern and to the side of the inflatable; a brown shape screaming and thrashing inside the thick brown mass of oil. The parachute flare dropped gently, spiralling slowly down towards the oil, a white hole in the sky.

The soldier at the stern stood up and screamed at the outboard, slapping at it. He crouched, started tugging at the back-up toggle which should start it even if the electric starter didn't. Pulled and pulled. The man in the lake was only a couple of metres behind the black Gemini, reaching for it, trying to swim through the oily sludge. The other two were rowing mightily, glancing behind them into the sky as they did so, shouting incoherently. The flare swung, describing lazy bright circles in the air as it fell.

Then one of the rowers shouted something – while the man at the outboard tugged and pulled at the engine's lanyard – and took up a gun. He stood and fired at her; she ducked again, flattening, heard and felt shots slap and burst into the life-raft casings, sending curved white shards of plastic raining about her, bouncing over the deck, pattering on to her back like heavy snowflakes, making her flinch despite the relative weakness of each impact.

The firing went on, changing in tone, and the sounds around her ceased. She risked another look.

The man was firing at the flare.

The other oarsman tried to stop him, as the man at the outboard pulled again, snapped the lanyard and fell over backwards into the other two and the man in the lake splashed heavily towards the stationary inflatable.

The three men fell in a heap into the bows, gun still firing, then cutting off.

The flare had been hit.

The holed parachute sank through the air, ripped and fluttering. The white blaze of the magnesium charge plummeted to the brown surface of the lake.

They stopped, again. Frozen by the impending heat, like a photograph; three crumpled in the boat, in the act of scrabbling back up again; the one in the oil on the water like a dirty brown sculpture, one arm raised. All looking at the flare.

The flare sank, diving; met the oil and disappeared. The

tattered remnants of the parachute flopped into the greasy surface as the oil ignited.

She stood and watched.

The fire spread at a fast walk, blossoming outwards from the point of its birth in an ever-widening circle like a slow ripple on that thick brown tide. The flames were yellow and orange and red, the smoke dense and black.

One soldier went back to the outboard, stabbing at it again. The man in the lake did what looked like butterfly strokes towards the stern of the boat. One just looked at the spreading field of flame, the fourth one took up an oar again, screamed at the man still standing and looking, and with one foot kicked guns and missile launchers out of the bottom of the Gemini, sending them bouncing over the side, sliding into the brown surface without a splash.

She ran a hand through her hair, thinking how greasy it had become.

The boiling mass of yellow rolling flame expanded, smoke cutting off the view of the nearest island. The thick black billows rolled as high as the tanker's bridge, then its masts. The man in the lake reached, found one conical end of the inflatable's double stern; slipped off.

They were probably still yelling and shouting, but the noise of the blaze was starting to take over; roaring. Gradually, gradually increasing in volume.

The smoke was way above.

She took up the flare pistol, leant over the side, and fired directly down, the pistol jumping in her hand.

The flare burst upon the water to the stern of the canted pontoon, bursting fire around the impact point.

The smoke was starting to blank out the horizon, while the fire ate up the distance between it and the black Gemini. The man in the water reached between the stern hulls of the craft, grabbing at the outboard engine just as it fired. He was flicked round, oil splashing brown metres into the air; if he made a noise, she didn't hear it.

The outboard died; the man in the water floated broken behind the boat while the soldier at the Gemini's stern stabbed again at the engine casing and the other two rowed, trying to angle the boat away from the flames. But the fire was sweeping quickly round and past them, closing in on their bows, and the secondary wave-front was heading out towards the Gemini from the ship itself, sending billows of acrid, stinging black smoke up in front of her, blanking out the view.

She walked towards the stern of the lifeboat deck, to see.

When the fire was almost on them, one of the rowers took a pistol from his belt and put it in his mouth; his head jerked back and he flopped over the bows of the inflatable just as the flames got there.

The smoke swam up in front of her, hiding them. It was hot and windy now, even up where she was, and fire was almost all she could see.

She went back along the deck, ducking through the black clouds of smoke to the bridge.

Philippe's cabin; nothing.

The store where they usually left the gear; nothing.

Sweating, running and clattering down companionways in a daze, she burst into the engine room, through it to the engineering workshop.

Am I praying? she thought, *No, I'm not,* she decided.

The workshop.

There.

She hefted the gear. Full tank.

By the time she got out on to the starboard deck, the fire was closing round under the stern of *Le Cercle*, swinging in like a bright wave of cavalry wheeling for the final attack. She buckled in, checked her valves and gauges.

Glanced down. It was a long drop.

She looked up at what there was of the still unsullied sky, waited for her life to pass before her and decided that could wait, then climbed up and over the rail.

She hung there for a moment, gazing down at the flat shadow surface of the oil-carpeted lake. She put the mask over her eyes and nose, and held it there.

Ah, what the hell, she thought, and let go.

She dropped, crouched, foetal. She heard the wind whistle, increasing. The impact slammed her, made her think she'd somehow dropped off the wrong side and hit something solid;

196

the pontoon; a boat; rock. The mouthpiece burst from her as her breath flew out. She was suddenly nowhere, struggling and bereft and windless, flailing for the metal and the rubber, surrounded by coolness and pressure going *tic tic tic*.

She righted, flapped round, found the mouthpiece and rammed it in, sucked and spat, sucked again and found air; opened her eyes. The mask was still there, but the view was black.

Well, what else?

Tic tic tic. She sank, gathering herself.

Light from one side, slowly spreading. She drew on the air in the mouthpiece, then realised this was not her first breath. She calmed, swallowed a little water, tasting oil but finding clean sweet air after it. She was still sinking, so swam up a little, found a level, and stroked out, wishing for flippers.

The light spread over her. She kept her level by the clicking noises in her skull, unable to see the surface apart from the dimly burning orange light above, and without a torch to inspect the depth gauge. The current of air from the cylinders on her back was strong and sure, and the water coursed past, slower than with flippers but there . . . and the fire above covered the surface of the lake.

She waited for whatever had been wrong with the gear when Philippe had last used it to reassert itself, to stop and choke her – ha ha; not just a faulty needle after all; take that – but it didn't happen. The fire glowed overhead and she swam beneath it. She even rolled over at one point, and saw the burning oil above, and could have laughed.

Near to the edge – where the ordinary light of day filtered down like a great gauzy curved curtain sheltering some vast and unseen stage – Hisako Onoda looked back, and saw the blind spot, the black hole; the eye of the storm at the heart of the universe.

The fire was complete; it had covered all there was within its scope to cover (the water pulsed around her, and she guessed a tank on *Le Cercle* had blown, or some of the armaments still left on the husk of the soldiers' Gemini had exploded), and when the encircling arms of the blaze had joined, and the whole brown coin of oil was alight, there was no airspace left in or near its centre to feed any fire there, and all there was was the oxygen at the limit of the slick, round the circumference . . . so of course only the fringes burned; only the edge of the great circle could combust into the clear, isthmian air of Panama; a kilometre-wide ring of fire, enfolding and enclosing a dark and lifeless heart.

Hisako Onoda watched for a moment, then turned away, and swam on towards the distant falls of light, beneath a burning sky.